P9-CBS-634

The DEVIL HIMSELF

Also by Eric Dezenhall

Spinning Dixie

Damage Control:
Why Everything You Know About
Crisis Management Is Wrong

Turnpike Flameout

Shakedown Beach

Jackie Disaster

Money Wanders

Nail 'Em!:
Confronting High-Profile Attacks on
Celebrities and Businesses

The DEVIL HIMSELF

Eric Dezenhall

Thomas Dunne Books
St. Martin's Press New York

This is a work of fiction. All of the characters, organizations, and events portrayed in this novel are either products of the author's imagination or are used fictitiously.

THOMAS DUNNE BOOKS.
An imprint of St. Martin's Press.

www.thomasdunnebooks.com
www.stmartins.com

Design by Meryl Sussman Levavi

Library of Congress Cataloging-in-Publication Data

Dezenhall, Eric.
The devil himself : a novel / Eric Dezenhall. — 1st ed.
p. cm.
ISBN 978-0-312-66882-2
1. Lansky, Meyer, 1902—Fiction. 2. Luciano, Lucky, 1897–1962—Fiction. 3. United States. Office of Naval Intelligence—Fiction. 4. Mafia—New York (State)—New York—Fiction. 5. World War, 1939–1945—New York (State)—New York—Fiction. 6. World War, 1939–1945—Military intelligence—United States—Fiction. I. Title.
PS3604.E94D48 2011
813'.6—dc22

2011006353

First Edition: July 2011

10 9 8 7 6 5 4 3 2 1

For my in-laws, William (1920–2009)
and Lorraine Marsh,
and
for William O. McWorkman (1918–2006)
of the Twelfth Armored Division,
a Liberator of Dachau and
its satellite annihilation camps, 1945

Author's Note

The Devil Himself is a historical novel based upon a fascinating, real, and terrifying chapter in twentieth-century American history. You will find both factual details and creative liberties taken by a storyteller, including the selective changing of some of the names of people who were key players in these events.

While a few historians have written about Operation Underworld, a top-secret campaign by Naval Intelligence to secure the port of New York during World War II with the help of racketeers, and Operation Husky, the Allied invasion of Sicily, a lot of folklore surrounds these events. What is irrefutable is that after thirty-five years of denials that the U.S. Navy, under the direction of Lieutenant Commander Charles Radcliffe Haffenden, collaborated with gangland figures, a government report quietly confirmed its recruitment of Meyer Lansky and Charles "Lucky" Luciano for a sweeping counterespionage operation.

Time and serendipity reveal unexpected treasures. Toward the end of his life, Meyer Lansky, who once said, "Keep your business in your hat," wanted to make public his work with Naval Intelligence. Among other things, he kept handwritten notes that were discovered by my friend Cynthia Duncan, granddaughter of Thelma (Teddy) and Meyer Lansky, upon Teddy's death in 1997.

As this book came into focus, I thought of Hemingway's preface to *A Moveable Feast,* in which he wrote: "If the reader prefers, this book may be regarded as fiction. But there is always the chance that such a book of fiction may throw some light on what has been written as fact."

—E.B.D.
Washington, D.C., 2010

If a Chief of Police makes a deal with the leading gangsters and the deal results in no more hold-ups, that Chief of Police will be called a great man—but if the gangsters do not live up to their word the Chief of Police will go to jail.

—Franklin Delano Roosevelt

Prologue
Fever Dreams of February 9, 1942
Pier 88 on the Hudson River, Manhattan

After I lost Havana to Castro—and most of my worth—in '59 during the Cuban revolution, I spent a month in an oxygen tent back home in a Miami Beach hospital with a heart attack. I had a fever so high from the inflammation around my lungs, my wife, Teddy, brought in a rabbi because they didn't think I was going to make it. I have a fuzzy memory of doctors and nurses scraping around me saying, "Mr. Lansky, are you breathing better now?" I don't remember if I answered them or not, what with all the medicine.

You hear crazy stories about when a person comes back from what these *meshuga* psychics call a "near-death experience," how they see a white light and their loved ones calling them home. That's not what happened to me. I wasn't being escorted into heaven by some *goyish* saint; I was dreaming over and over that I was a welding foreman during World War II under contract from the navy, standing under a million sparks.

As my oxygen tent wheezed in and out, I was lost inside my own head, working on the biggest cruise ship in the world, the French liner *Normandie,* which was docked at Pier 88 in Manhattan. The job: convert the *Normandie* into a transport vessel to deliver American troops into the arms of that paper-hanging

Nazi psychopath with the black toothbrush under his nose. By next month. Christ, I thought, standing smack in the middle of the Grand Salon. The Dodgers could have banged out a doubleheader in this space.

Now, to be clear, I was never really a foreman on the *Normandie,* but the ship played a big role in my life during the terrible years of the war, and I came to know more about it, I suppose, than just about anybody else. Also, I had done a lot of mechanical work on the fleet of cars I used to run booze during Prohibition, so I knew a thing or two about this kind of labor.

As I looked through the sparks across the Grand Salon, I kept thinking: It could have been any of them, or it could have been none of them. Fifteen hundred men—sailors, contractors, welders, God knew who else—grinding into each other on a ship that was even bigger than the *Titanic* had been. We all know how that story ended.

Nobody knew what the hell he was doing. That was the one thing that all these Jack Armstrongs could agree on.

Only the government could cook up a scheme like this, I thought: Today's task was a real valentine. I had to direct a couple hundred men to remove the decorative stanchions in the Grand Salon on the *Normandie*'s promenade level.

The enormous room looked like a war zone: Wobbly scaffolding was propped up along all four walls and against the four stanchions, which looked like giant lipstick tubes. Just as flashy, too. Heavily lacquered with high-performance chemicals and fire-engine red like a baboon's ass. Or maybe some kind of flower. The French were big on flowers, weren't they? And the murals on the walls they were going to have to scrape down must have been worth some real gelt.

The wooden floor was a minefield of red linoleum rolls. The Grand Salon was, after all, going to become the troops' recreation center with pool tables, weights, boxing equipment, and basketball hoops. Wedged against the scaffolding were massive heaps of kapok-filled life preservers packed in burlap. More than fourteen hundred cartons in all, just delivered from the Brooklyn Navy Yard.

Knox, the navy secretary, assured President Roosevelt that he could turn the conversion around fast. *By next month.* That's what it said on the paper on my clipboard. America gets caught with our knickers down at Pearl Harbor, and the navy brass tries to make up for it by kissing Roosevelt's ass with this fairy-tale schedule.

I thought of a joke I once heard: Cohen is shipwrecked alone on a deserted island for twenty years. Eventually, a great navy destroyer finds him. The imposing captain comes ashore and sees that during his long desertion, Cohen has built two magnificent buildings and asks him what they are. Cohen points to the first one and lovingly announces, "This is my synagogue where I go every day to pray to my glorious God." Then the captain points to the other building and asks, "What's that one over there?" Cohen frowns and angrily says, "That one? *That* is a synagogue I wouldn't go in if my life depended on it!"

The folly of it all. A synagogue built for the purpose of not worshipping in it. And, now, in its infinite wisdom, the government was going to change the name of this ship from *Normandie* to the USS *Lafayette.* I remembered reading about the French big shot Lafayette in grade school. Friend of George Washington's. The United States snagged the *Normandie* when France fell to Hitler in 1940. Everybody's a ganef.

Sure, I thought, that's what this gunmetal whale needed, a new name. It was like asking a guy that just got hit by a train if he wanted some chicken soup on the grounds that it couldn't hurt.

The first order of business was getting my welders to burn through the lacquered stanchions so they could dismantle them.

Of the hundreds of men around me, I recognized the faces of maybe three. Skulking around one of the kapok heaps, I noticed a small, boyish sailor with short blond hair and a baby's skin, fingering a blowtorch. I wanted to yell at the kid to stop loafing and get his ass over here to take his assignment. Just as I was about to talk, the boy turned his head, showing an awful blaze of acne. The sailor's two faces *had* a comic-book contrast, like one of those *Dick Tracy* freaks. Repulsed, my vocal chords froze up, and I turned my attention to a less revolting target, a fresh-faced civilian welder standing a few feet away.

"You!" I shouted, feeling a little guilty about attacking the attackable. My voice echoed through the great hall.

The civilian pointed to himself and meekly said, "Me?"

"No, Winston Churchill, he's standing right behind you, *schmuck*," I said.

The young civilian turned around only to find out that the British prime minister was not there. Go figure. When I came into New York harbor from Eastern Europe as a small boy, never did I imagine there would be ten *schlemiels* for every scholar between those soaring skyscrapers that stole my imagination.

God help us, I thought, as other men began to gather.

"Do you geniuses think these stanchions are gonna dismantle themselves? Now fire up your torches and start slicing through 'em. And watch those flames with all this rubbish lying around!"

The men climbed the scaffolding and began blasting the stanchions with blue-tipped flames. Within minutes, the air was riddled with a chemical scent.

Sparks flew in a frantic motion, shooting from the scaffolding and landing on things that shouldn't have been there—the remaining wood floor, carpeting, and the mountains of life-preservers beneath bone-dry burlap.

The wild movement of the sparks, as they mixed with the frigid air blowing in off the promenade deck, made me think of fireflies that had gone insane. I would never have supervised my men so loosely under these conditions, but the order had come down that this was all about speed. It wouldn't take a pyromaniac wizard to light up this ship and roast her like the man-made glutton she was. It took balls to go out to sea in one of these. How the hell did they float? Too damned big, screw what they say about physics.

The Grand Salon had grown beastly hot, and somebody opened wide one of the great sliding doors that led to the promenade deck. Suddenly, a hissing sound came from somewhere very, well, wrong. It was as if the devil himself had blown the kapok mountain range a kiss that sent flames tearing across the burlap, and blasting the *Normandie* onto the top of Hitler's trophy case. The room exploded. All I could feel was searing heat as the holocaust began.

In my corner vision, I made out the ravaged side of the young, blond sailor from before. Turning his face to his more pleasant side, the sailor nodded at me, then slid, with his back against the huge sliding doors, out to the promenade deck and into the canyons of Manhattan.

On the other side of the world that same week, the Third Reich found a new use for a powerful pesticide called Zyklon B. The Nazis had been using the gas to destroy rats and other vermin, but when facing the Americans on the battlefield became a reality, Hitler demanded greater efficiency from his internal functions. Nazi engineers then set in motion a new industrial procedure where throngs of concentration camp "workers," mostly my people from Eastern Europe, were forced to strip completely, then were corralled into huge underground "bathing centers" with fake showerheads. Once they were inside, Zyklon B pellets would be released into the chambers, suffocating everybody in minutes. When this phase was done, the chambers were ventilated, and the bodies were taken on stretchers to a crematorium that could process more than a thousand a day. As Roosevelt was being snookered about how the *Lafayette* was coming along right on schedule, a man called Eichmann was being read the riot act for the disappointing consumption rate at the crematoriums. Meantime, Senator Nye from one of those Dakotas was saying the Jews were a bigger threat to America than Hitler.

As I recovered from my fever in the oxygen tent and needed less medication, sometimes I still saw sparks and two-faced men. I saw the acne-scarred sailor himself dropping the Zyklon B pellets down a pipe into the killing chambers. In some versions of the dream, the sailor was a Nazi brownshirt, a giant ripping apart children by their limbs as they ran through the woods. I told myself I was crazy to think that the two-faced sailor from my dream had started the fire on the *Normandie*.

One morning, a nice young nurse came into my hospital room and said, "Mr. Lansky, you're getting stronger, so we're going to take you to a nicer room." So I told this poor girl that I should have done more to protest the safety conditions on the great ship, as if it were my fault. How could such a thing happen in the Port of New York—not only the busiest ocean-liner hub in America, but the main entry point for the nation's immigrants, imported fuel and raw materials, not to mention its primary on-ramp to the heartland's highways and railroads? I told the poor girl that there's so much compromise in life that sometimes you don't have it in you—you just dig in and be who you are even if you know it's not good for you. The nurse must have thought I was nuts, or maybe she was used to people on strange medications talking such nonsense.

Whether my racing thoughts settled on the sparks or on the two-faced men that peppered my life, what I kept coming back to was that it could have been any of them, or it could have been none of them.

I.

The Whole Megillah

He not busy being born is busy dying.

—Bob Dylan,
"It's Alright, Ma (I'm Only Bleeding)"

The Intern: Jonah Eastman, 1982

WHEN YOU GROW UP WITH THESE GUYS, YOU KNOW THEY'RE NOTHing special. Everybody on the outside, the vast consumer public, though, assigns all these mystical skills to them. My favorite is that they killed President Kennedy. You know, the mob. Mafia. Whatever.

If you actually knew them, you'd know there was no way. A crime like that was way above their pay grade. All the mob ever was, was a loose affiliation of crooks that only wanted to steal as much as they could steal for as long as they could without ending up in the clink or on a slab. Assassinate the president of the United States—whose brother was the famously vindictive attorney general—and keep it quiet for twentysome years? Come on, the only people on the grassy knoll that day in Dallas were the wackadoos who needed their world ordered in such a way as to ascribe all forms of inexplicable mendacity to a shadowy group that couldn't step forward to defend itself. (Mafia: "Help, I'm being defamed!")

There's another banal reality: If the mob killed President Kennedy, the guy who pulled the trigger would be in a strip joint that night going up to strippers: "Yo, Bambi, Tiffany, you hear the news?" The strippers would say, "Oh, it's so awful they killed the president." The triggerman would fiddle with his collar, sniff that wiseguy smirk: "Awful, huh? You wanna know what really went down?" Then, impressed, the two whores would go in the back room and get to work on Vinnie Bag-a-Donuts, or whoever he was, then tell everybody they banged the guy who iced the president. The moron would be in custody before sunrise.

Look, it wasn't like these *gavones* had the choice between Yale Law School and breaking kneecaps, and chose breaking kneecaps. Different skill set, and sometimes the cliché of squandered talent collapses under the weight of no talent at all.

These guys were in my life before I could walk. I'm Jonah Eastman, and my grandfather is Mickey Price, the Atlantic City mob boss known as the Wizard of Odds. Gambling is his thing. Well, after booze was his thing. When Prohibition ended, he shut down his stills in the New Jersey Pine Barrens and focused on gambling. His investments extended from the back alleys of Philadelphia and Newark out to the "carpet joints" of Saratoga, and to the "class" strongholds of Las Vegas and Havana. Most of those places are all gone, at least as far as Mickey's involvement is concerned. When New Jersey okayed casino gambling, Mickey opened up his own boardwalk place in 1978 in Atlantic City, the Golden Prospect Hotel and Casino. He isn't the owner of record, of course. Official filings listed him as the bell captain. *Heh.* Mickey and my grandmother Deedee raised me after my parents died, and they're still there. As am I when I'm not at Dartmouth or working on an internship like the one I've got now in the White House.

My whole life I've been running from my primordial borscht, not because of the cinematic suffering of my "inner child," but because what I come from is so damned small-time. I would love to have a little inside knowledge that my grandfather's friends took down a president, but the reality is an endless procession of desperate little ganefs—and most of them are very small—trying to stay one step ahead of cops in suits from Sy Syms.

Maybe everybody goes though this at some point: that awful feeling that what you come from is staggeringly unspecial, that desire to be from someplace exotic, to descend from someone really cool. I remember a dream I had the summer before I went to college in 1980. In my dream, my grandfather was Jonas Salk, a somewhat more respected Jew than Mickey. My last name even was Salk. *Jonah Salk*. Clever. So I'd get to school, and people would ask, "Are you related to the guy who cured polio?" "Yeah," I'd say, and wouldn't have to do anything else. That would be it: *Yeah*. Kiss my ass. Skate through life.

Dreams of trading on the polio cure quickly gave way to the crucible of having to make it in this world by myself in spite of who Mickey Price was and is, and who I am and am not. I'm doing okay. I'm starting my junior year at Dartmouth after the New Year in a few weeks, right after I wrap up this internship I've got working for Tom Simmons, President Reagan's "image-maker-in-chief," as the press calls him.

I love my job, which consists mainly of helping to develop media strategy for the president. This isn't entirely true since I'm regarded as just another smart kid, not anybody with real influence. Still, I get to escort the press in and out of the Oval Office, direct reporters to the right spokesperson, and get to see President Reagan almost every day. I don't think he knows my name, but he recognizes me, I think, and he's got a way of tilting his head in the kind of deference that says, "Appreciate all you're doin', kid." Or maybe he's just a politician.

One day a few months ago, I made a comment about a Remington sculpture the president had in his office. His eyes brightened, and he said, "You know about horses." I answered, "Yes, I cared for horses when I worked at the Atlantic City

Race Track," which was true. He offered to let me ride with him on one of his Wednesday outings, which I did twice. It was a thrill, believe me, and it made Tom Simmons take note of me over the other political Smurfs.

Simmons was a tennis nut. Sometimes he'd grab my friend and immediate supervisor, Doug Elmets, and me to play on the White House court. Doug and I always kept our tennis gear in our offices just in case.

During one of these doubles games—the fourth guy was somebody from the national security adviser's office—Doug started ribbing me about being Mickey Price's grandson. Fascinated, Simmons peppered me with questions about my background, the symbiosis between the Kosher and Cosa Nostras, which I answered without trying to make it seem too sexy. It's strange the way my roots come back up at me like the taste of corned beef and coleslaw when *it* wants to, not when I want it to.

I never thought I'd have to discuss Mickey with Tom Simmons again, but the prospect hit me at the gonad level when one afternoon after Thanksgiving, Simmons's assistant said he wanted to meet with me alone, something that had never before happened.

Simmons had been with President Reagan since his days as governor of California. He still referred to Reagan as "Governor." More than any other person in Reagan's orbit, with the possible exception of the president's wife, Nancy, Simmons was the guardian of Reagan's reputation.

I showed up to Simmons's office, which was the one next to the Oval Office, located in the southern section of the West Wing, a few minutes early.

A small, balding man, bespectacled and bemused, Simmons gestured to the burnt-orange sofa in his office and took a seat in a striped chair facing me. He looked me over, his eyes blue and searing like stolen sapphires.

"Doug tells me you're doing good work," Simmons said.

"Thank you, I hope I am."

"We've had good luck with Dartmouth students. They've got that newspaper there, what, the *Review*?" This was the conservative, unauthorized paper that was causing a national sensation. I had never written for them, which was something that came up during my interview to get this job. I sensed that the interviewer didn't peg me as a "true" conservative. I wondered if my less-than-reactionary pedigree was the subject of our visit. But if I were getting axed, the task wouldn't fall to somebody as high up as Simmons.

"I've never written anything for them."

"Oh, I know," Simmons said. "Probably better to do more listening than pontificating at your age."

"It's a lot of fun to read, I'll tell you that much. Those guys are never boring."

"If they were boring, Jonah, they wouldn't have everybody in the Ivy League crapping their pants."

Something about the reference to people crapping their pants relaxed me a little. I find second-grade humor hilarious, especially when I'm a few yards away from the man who can end civilization if he spills his coffee on the wrong telephone.

"You're probably wondering why I wanted to speak with you," Simmons said.

"I was a little nervous, to be honest."

"Nothing to be nervous about, Jonah. Are you interested in national security issues?"

"Of course. I'm not an expert, but I follow defense."

"What about terrorism?"

"Scares the hell—sorry—scares the heck out of me."

"Me, too. The president, too," Simmons said. "Ever since the Iranian revolution, it's a whole new environment. This year alone, we had a colonel, Charles Ray, assassinated in Paris by a group tied to the Palestinian Liberation Organization. You may remember last March when we announced a Libyan plot to blow up an American recreational center in Sudan."

"Sure."

"And last July, David Dodge, the president of the American University in Beirut, was kidnapped by Hezbollah. Then we had an American Express office blow up in Athens to protest U.S. support for Israel's foray into Lebanon."

"I don't remember that one."

Simmons continued, "A bomb went off last August at an American military barracks in Frankfurt. We found PLO propaganda at the bomb site. And we're not done with the Iranians and Libyans, Jonah. A leader of an Iranian Islamic sect here in the U.S. was found with his throat slit in Connecticut, we believe at the direct order of Ayatollah Khomeini. I could go on and on, but you get the point."

"I get the point. We're hearing footsteps."

I did, of course, get the point, but not what it had to do with me. I figured that maybe he wanted me to compile a book of news clippings or something. But somebody far lower down could have given me that task.

"Here's the thing, Jonah: The president is looking at options for dealing with these bastards. This is a different kind of battle, not a conventional war because terrorists, well, terrorists hide in different places, so you have to . . . ah . . . handle things sometimes—"

"Covertly."

Simmons was visibly uncomfortable. "In theory. And that's all we're talking about here, an academic theory. Do you follow me?"

"I think so, Mr. Simmons—"

"Tom."

"Tom . . . but I don't know how I can help."

"Jonah—and understand I'm not trying to make you uncomfortable, but—"

But. My life story: But. Only one thing followed But, and that was Mickey Price.

"But," Tom continued, "the most interesting precedent we've found for this kind of assertive action is what happened during World War Two when President Roosevelt reached out to a man I believe you know, a man named Meyer Lansky. You mentioned your grandfather when we were playing tennis a few weeks ago. By any chance, while you were growing up, did you meet Mr. Lansky, who was supposedly a partner of Mr. Price in Cuba?"

"Of course. My grandfather and he are good friends."

"What about you and Mr. Lansky?"

I felt my heart skip in my chest. Was I under investigation? Was the Secret Service about to kick the door down and shout, "Spread-eagle, reprobate!?"

"Uh, Tom, I'm not sure where this is going. Am I in trouble here?"

"No, no, absolutely not, Jonah," Tom said in a way that struck me as being earnest. "I was wondering if you knew Mr. Lansky well enough to speak with him about this."

"Well, it's not like I could just call him myself," I said. "He's like my grandfather; he's not big on the phone. Besides, what would I talk to him about?"

"Fair enough. Were you aware of Mr. Lansky's work with the navy in World War Two to help look out for Nazis on the New York waterfront?"

"Nazis on the New York waterfront? No." I laughed a little.

"The Nazis sank hundreds of U.S. ships off the coast of

New York. The navy thought the Germans had spies on the waterfront, but they couldn't access it because the mob controlled the docks. Roosevelt demanded the navy do what was necessary to secure the ports, so they reached out to Meyer Lansky and Lucky Luciano."

"You're serious?"

"I'm serious."

The parallels were coming into focus: FDR played rough with Nazis; Reagan was considering playing rough with Muslim terrorists.

"Since Vietnam, Jonah, Americans don't believe we have natural enemies. All conflicts are misunderstandings that can be medicated with a sober exchange of facts, or they're perils that we Americans brought upon ourselves by our boorish aggression toward gentler souls. So, Jonah, given what the president may have to do to defend our country, the million-dollar question: Will you speak with Mr. Lansky about his service? Think about it like a school report with Mr. Lansky as your primary source."

I shifted uneasily on the sofa and pushed down on the pillows on either side of me as if I was shoring up my balance, which I was.

"What do you hope he could tell you that wasn't in government files?"

"For one thing, we don't imagine Mr. Lansky told the government everything they needed to know when the war was over. Hell, they probably didn't want to know. But most of what we want aren't facts, but insights. The man has seen it all, Jonah, and no doubt he's . . . I don't know . . . proud, bitter, patriotic, angry. Whatever. His, you know, *story*."

Tom closed his eyes, hard, for about ten seconds. "Between us, okay, I have no problem blasting these terrorist pricks straight to Allah, but I'm not going to advise the president to go on some crazy-ass holy war if it's going to blow him up politically. Again, I'll ask you: Will you talk to Lansky?"

"You may end up with a *bubbameisah*—"

Tom laughed. "What's that?"

"It means a 'grandma story,' a wives' tale or a myth. Here's the thing, Tom . . . it's not a question of will I, it's a question of will *he*?"

"I get that. How would you try to make it happen?"

"I'd go to my grandfather. He'd have to reach out to Unc—Mr. Lansky."

"Were you about to say *uncle*?" Tom asked. Grinning like a kid that had just slipped a whoopee cushion on the teacher's chair. I knew I had made a mistake, but had nowhere to hide.

"I call him 'Uncle Meyer,' but that's a Jewish thing. We're not related."

"So?"

The cliché one always hears is "my life flashed before my eyes." Mine was flashing now; however, it was not my past kicking like a chorus line across my pupils. It was my future. Here I was, an orphan, raised by a mobster in Atlantic City; I had slugged my way into the Ivy League, and at this moment only a thick wall separated me from the president of the United States.

I was being given an assignment. At some point in his career, hadn't Tom Simmons been given a career-making challenge? I bet it didn't involve interviewing one of the most powerful gangland figures America had ever known. Still, I was lucky to be here, I wanted to stay here, and, even more, someday I wanted to be a man like Tom Simmons, or the guy on the other side of this wall.

I remember Mickey once telling me that I should never tell anyone with power what couldn't be done; always tell them what *could* be. Sure, I didn't like that my big break involved the very thing I wanted to obscure, but you can't expect a custom fit in an off-the-rack world.

"I'll need to go up to Atlantic City," I said. "Talk to Mickey. Maybe I can get one of the other interns to cover for me here."

"That won't be a problem," Tom said, standing up. "One more thing, Jonah: Don't discuss this with anyone but me. Don't write a memo with anybody's name on it. Don't update me on the telephone. And don't let anyone discuss the White House's interest in this on the phone."

I was still seated when Tom told me these things, which was awkward, his looking down on me as if I had lime-green bird shit in my hair. I had a question on the tip of my tongue: What the hell was I going to say to pitch Uncle Meyer on this? But I thought better of it. Figure it the hell out, President Eastman. Life is improvisation.

"Tom," I said walking toward the door. "It would really help if there is something in the government's files about the World War Two stuff. You don't approach men like Mickey Price or Meyer Lansky half-assed."

Tom nodded. "I'll get you something."

"Thanks."

"Now you go get *me* something."

"I will, Tom. And I won't discuss this with anybody here."

"Of course you won't, Jonah. Besides, who the hell would believe you?"

Hebrews and Romans

I TOOK THE TRAIN FROM UNION STATION IN WASHINGTON TO Thirtieth Street Station in Philadelphia. Mickey's man Fuzzy Marino picked me up and drove me down to Atlantic City, which took about an hour. Fuzzy was a battleship of a man who taught me to curse after my parents died, which was nice, not to mention a valuable lesson in fourth grade when I was being picked on in school. "Did anybody ever tell you that bullies were really cowards underneath?" he asked me when I came home all banged up.

"Yes, I've heard that," I answered timidly.

"Well, it's fucking bullshit," Fuzzy shot back. "Most bullies are violent badasses, and your first choice should be to avoid them. If you can't, Jonah, get in close and hang on like a rip-snorting little piss-terrier because, see, a bully is always doing math, conserving his ammo. If he thinks there's one chance in a hundred that people will think, 'Hey, that Jonah kid is hangin' on pretty good,' he'll move on to somebody who's less of a pain in the ass.'" The next day, I jumped my nemesis, Dave Foriello, who beat the crap out of me, but looked like a schnook trying to shake me off his pant leg. It never happened again.

I knew where I could find Mickey. He would be in his favorite room in the Golden Prospect. The room was called the

Eye in the Sky because it contained a bank of television sets attached to cameras on the ceiling of the casino that spied out gaming tables to catch cheats. Home was a modest two-bedroom penthouse suite upstairs, with furniture that had been fashionable when John Glenn orbited the planet.

The hotel lobby contained giant golden columns with faux marble cracks and other fake Colosseum ruins. I once tried to explain to Mickey that if he was trying to imitate ancient Rome, he might want to consider that they weren't *ruins* in Caesar's time. "What," Mickey responded, "you think these Rhodes Scholars bringing their paychecks in from South Philly know that? They're just happy Caesar invented the salad."

Fuzzy gave me a tyrannosaurus hug and punched the ever-changing code into a keypad, which released the steel bars that protected my grandfather from the Visigoths and lesser goyim.

Mickey was sitting at a small table facing the winking television monitors. Lord knows what he was able to see on those screens. The casino was a cauldron of whack-a-mole sins, and I loathed gambling because I couldn't fathom losing so much self-control that I'd shred my paycheck at one of these green felt tables.

Mickey looked good not just for his age, but for a man who had spent more than sixty years dodging rackets killers, the FBI, and, perhaps most frighteningly, my grandmother. Not to mention the loss of his only child, my mother.

Mickey was small, tan, with thinning white, cottony hair, and was about as threatening in demeanor as Geppetto. He had little formal education, but devoured the newspaper, especially the sections that dealt with business, politics, or foreign policy. He routinely interrogated me about my college classes. Whereas I was going to a good college with the hope of becoming successful, Mickey's primary interest was *learning*, something he assured me I would someday understand.

"Hey, there he is!" Mickey said.

I kissed him on the forehead.

"You want me to send down for a sandwich or something?" he asked. "The deli's got some nice new lean corned beef."

"No, I'm all right." I usually had a big appetite, but given the subject I was about to bring up, that drive had been scuttled.

"So, this is a big honor having you up here so soon after Thanksgiving," Mickey said, clearly wondering what my visit was all about.

"I was hoping for a motorcade."

"You've got to get elected to something first, big shot."

"Who needs the hassle? I was hoping for a birthright."

"Wrong family, smart-ass," Mickey said. "I wasn't happy when your parents gave you my last name for your middle name."

"I'm fine with it."

"Not around those Ivy League silver spoons."

"That's what you always wanted for me."

"I wanted the education for you, not the mentality. You need a certain kind of name and a certain kind of bank account to carry that off." He said all this without turning his head away from the TV monitors.

"Give me a little time, Pop."

"Don't wait too long, kiddo. It moves fast."

"I'm off to a good start. With the education, with this White House job. I even had a private meeting today with Tom Simmons."

Mickey hesitated and turned his head away from the televisions toward me. "You had a private meeting with Simmons? That's pretty fancy, kid."

"I'm an elegant guy."

"What did you talk about?"

"Who really assassinated Kennedy. Nothing big."

Mickey took a sip from his glass of ice water. "C'mon, you gonna traffic in all that CIA-conspiracy bullshit?"

"I take it you don't think the CIA did it, Pop?"

"You kidding? Kennedy was the best friend the CIA ever had. He had them running hit teams all over the world. Cuba. Wherever the hell Trujillo was from. They clipped Diem in Vietnam. Your uncle Meyer had a million-dollar bounty on Castro, and Bobby Kennedy and Jack didn't blink. Only after those nuts killed them did the Kennedy boys become bleeding hearts who were going to spread peace and tulips all over the world."

"So, you're an Oswald man?"

"I'm a man who thinks you're a little full of shit," Mickey said, chomping down on a piece of ice. "To what do I owe this sudden visit from such an important government official?"

Mickey knew I didn't like it here. I had never become less mortified living in a casino even though my friends thought it was cool. That said, the whiff of my grandmother's cooking, the cleansing purity of the sea air, and the taste of saltwater taffy were perverse contraindications that the Jersey shore would always be sanctuary. You don't always have to like who you are, but you always have to know who you are.

"Well, Pop, it's what I talked to Tom Simmons about."

"What was that?"

"Uncle Meyer."

"Meyer? Lansky? What, was he jock-sniffing all that gangster bullshit?"

"No—"

"They're not investigating him again, are they? Because they're not going to find anything. He's been out of commission for twenty years. Besides, he's dying."

"He's dying?" I said, suddenly losing some breathing capacity.

After years of oft-chronicled heart trouble and chain-smoking, he finally started coughing up blood at the age of eighty. Lung cancer.

"Deedee and I were with him in Miami Beach a few weeks ago. He was philosophical about it. A tough old bird, that one. More talkative than usual."

Mickey glanced at the television monitors. I looked over, too. I still didn't see anything of interest on the casino floor. Then again, I hadn't spent a lifetime looking out for thieves. Takes one to know one.

"Simmons wants me to interview him."

"About what?"

"You know all these terror attacks against Americans? President Reagan is thinking about how to respond. Simmons said something about Uncle Meyer hunting down Nazis in World War Two. Is that nuts?"

"Nuts? It's true. Meyer roped us all into this deal he had going with the navy in the big war to screw with the Nazis."

"Screw with the Nazis?"

"Hitler had submarines up and down the East Coast." Mickey pointed with his thumb over his shoulder toward the Atlantic. "They spotted one in New York harbor, I think. A group of Nazis even came ashore—"

"That's what Simmons said."

"They had bombs and everything. They were going after bridges, railroads, big companies. It coulda been a disaster, we coulda lost World War Two. But some of Meyer's guys put an end to that crew at least."

"I've never read anything about this."

"Of course not, schmucko. Do you think the government is

gonna give any of my friends credit for helping with the war effort?"

I chewed my own piece of ice. "Do you think Uncle Meyer would talk to me? He sounds pretty sick."

"He *is* pretty sick," Mickey said, sadness kidnapping his face. "I don't trust these government guys. What do you think Simmons really wants?"

"He said 'insight.'"

"Insight? What is he, a Gypsy or something?"

"No. He plays things close to the vest, but if I read him right, I think Reagan is thinking about taking a shot at these Muslim nut jobs—"

"About time."

"And he's trying to get a sense of whether it would be worth it."

Mickey narrowed his eyes at me. He wasn't angry, he was just running the arithmetic in his head, seeing what added up and what didn't.

I started to speak and he held up his finger, still processing. "Simmons is the public-relations wizard, right?"

"Right."

"So with him, it's about how everything looks, right?"

"Right."

"So Reagan's got a hard-on for some of these towel-headed pygmies, but Simmons wants to keep his boss happy and protect him, too." Mickey strummed his fingers on the Formica tabletop. "He probably knows Meyer's guys were effective—because they were. But these government cowards hushed the whole thing up for years like it never happened."

"So where's this all leading? do you think."

"I think a couple things, Jonah. One, Simmons may take a sniff to our world, you know, like Sinatra did. But maybe he wants to figure the up- and downsides of going heavy on these Arabs."

"But you don't think Uncle Meyer can help with that?"

"Christ, no. Our guys couldn't even *zotz* Castro. We're an overestimated bunch of street rats thanks to the movies."

"Is it possible that Simmons wants exactly what he said he wants, insight?"

"It's possible. My guess is that he's made up his mind one way or the other, and he hasn't told you which way. He just wants to go in to the big *macher* and tell him he did his homework. What better way to do it than with a kid like you, no offense, who's off-the-books."

"What do you mean, Pop, *off-the-books*?"

"If it comes out that they're studying some rough stuff, they can say, 'What, are you nuts? This kid just was talking to his uncle on some school project.' "

"So Simmons is using me."

"Everybody uses everybody, Jonah."

"But this is a big chance for me, Pop. I don't want to go in to a man like Simmons and tell him I can't do something that's valuable. I can't run from it."

Mickey bit into the side of his mouth. "I've been trying to keep you away from my guys your whole life. You know that. But, no, you can't run from it. You have to run *toward* it. Remember what I told you when you were a little boy in the ocean, how you run toward the wave, not away?"

"I remember it a million times."

"So that's what we do. We run toward."

"Does that mean Uncle Meyer would talk to me about this?"

Mickey made a washing motion with his hands. "The thing is, Jonah, when a man is facing . . . what he's facing . . . I suppose you want to make things right. You want to clear things up. You want your life to make sense somehow. Maybe that's why he was so talky when we were there. But you know how Meyer is. He has all these thoughts, but doesn't express so hot. With guys in our business, there's no interest paid on being a chatterbox, but, who knows, I guess this thing's different. And he always liked you."

"*Liked* me? The last time he saw me, I was sixteen."

"He likes winners, Jonah. Nice, educated young men."

"Really? Some of those guys look at me like I'm wearing pantyhose."

Mickey sniffed out a laugh. "What guys?"

"You know. Your guys."

"Get the hell outta here."

"Not all your guys. Irv doesn't look at me that way." Irv the Curve, Mickey's Kissinger. "More the Italians."

Mickey scrunched up his lips, as if he were processing my tribal observation. "Could be. The Hebrews send their boys to school. The Romans send theirs to the street."

I tugged at my fingers. "So how do we do this?"

"You're the college boy, you tell me."

"Am I supposed to pick up the phone and call Meyer Lansky and invite myself to Miami Beach?"

Mickey sighed. "Good point. Meyer doesn't do telephones."

"You guys must have been separated at birth."

"You don't get to our age in our business by not building a little caution into your routine. Here's what I'll do. I'll have Irv reach out to Jimmy Blue Eyes, Uncle Meyer's friend, and we'll see if we can arrange something."

"Thanks, Pop. Did I hear you right that you played some role in going after the Nazis?"

"You heard right, Jonah."

"So?"

"One thing at a time."

Master of the Good Name

I DON'T KNOW WHAT TRANSPIRED IN THE TWENTY-FOUR HOURS IN between my talk with Mickey and my arrival in Miami Beach. It was one of many "black box" experiences I had with my grandfather over the years, in which I knew what had set events in motion, and I knew how they ended up, but had no idea what the mechanics had been that brought us there. Perhaps that's why I liked politics, that insatiable need to understand *how* things happened—and to discreetly make them happen myself—as opposed to being waved off by old crooks who just said, "Fuggeddabowdit."

If historians operate under the principle of Best Verifiable Data, as opposed to perfectly provable facts, the best I could determine was this: Mickey's man, Irv the Curve, called Jimmy Blue Eyes (real name: Vincent Alo), a long-standing force in the Genovese Cosa Nostra family; Jimmy Blue Eyes talked to Uncle Meyer; Uncle Meyer was intrigued—or desperate—enough to speak with me about his World War II experiences; and I was on an Eastern Airlines flight from Philadelphia to Miami the next afternoon.

I was picked up at the airport by a besieged little man named Hymie Krumholtz, who had a face like dried glue, and taken to the Singapore Hotel, which was said to be secretly owned by Uncle Meyer. Everything in South Florida was said to be secretly owned by Uncle Meyer, the way everything in South Jersey and Philly was said to be secretly owned by Mickey. Presumably, the FBI was sufficiently aware of Uncle Meyer's illness that Mickey was unconcerned that my visit would be refracted through a sinister lens. That said, given the need to move quickly, Mickey had no choice but to zigzag the connection because he wasn't going risk a RICO pinch by initiating a direct telephone call from Mickey Price, the Wizard of Odds, to his fellow evil mastermind Jew Meyer Lansky, the "Chairman of the Board of the National Crime Syndicate," as one purple biographer wrote.

The last thing Mickey said to me before he kissed me goodbye was, "Don't let Meyer see a pad and paper. If things go all right, ask permission. And be straight with him about the White House thing."

◚

The Singapore was a sad little art deco hotel that had been a big deal in its heyday in the late 1950s and 1960s. Red diamonds dripped down the front of the building like tears, as if the seven-story structure knew that it was only a matter of time before a big tourism company pounded it into oblivion. The employees, aging New York transplants, in the red-carpeted lobby also reflected this demeanor, wearing expressions that seemed to say, "That's right, kid, this is it." Even the South Pacific theme and holiday decorations were anemic, the doddering bellhop wearing a flaccid Santa hat. *Ho ho ho. (Oy oy oy.)*

Given the big showplaces such as the Fontainebleau, the Diplomat, and the Eden Roc, the Singapore struck me as the kind of place a mobster might actually own. No matter what the true-crime writers say to pimp books, the mob didn't control big places anymore. Too much heat. This was Mickey's logic anyway, which was why the Golden Prospect was the smallest hotel-casino on the boardwalk. As if the FBI wouldn't notice, or skip it as if they were the Angel of Death at Passover.

For my purposes, the Singapore was fine. It was on the beach in the Bal Harbour area, some forty blocks north of Uncle Meyer's place in the Imperial House condominium. Hymie Krumholtz told me to be in the lobby of the Imperial House at 6:00 A.M. This is when Uncle Meyer walked his dog. His punctuality was legendary.

My wake-up call came at four forty-five the next morning. I had intended to take a short run on the beach, but decided instead to make some notes on the legal pad I'd bought in a drugstore in Atlantic City and memorize them. I jammed a pen in one sock and a few sheets of folded-up paper in the other. It was chilly before sunrise, so I wore a light blue V-neck sweater and a pair of khaki pants. College boy, but not gay college boy. I left my tennis sweater back in A.C.

In the early-morning darkness, I called for a taxi and got to the Imperial House at five forty-five. It was a huge concrete high-rise on the beach. The automatic glass door that controlled entry to the lobby did not open when I stood outside it. An elderly woman with a face like a Siamese cat—"Mrs. Katz," *heh*—looked me over from behind a counter. Was there ever a time or place when a man found her attractive? I wondered. I couldn't imagine that she had ever actually been born or grown into a schoolgirl that a boy had a crush on. Rather, I envisioned Mrs. Katz as a utility that had been added at the last minute by the condominium architect. The woman did not appear to have any interest in admitting me, so I pulled out my sawed-off shotgun and blasted my way in and pumped two rounds into her. Her teeth flew out the back of her head. Then I shot the two henchmen guarding the elevator.

All right, I deal with anxiety with grotesque humor. I did no such thing; I just offered up a sheepish wave to Mrs. Katz. And no henchmen were by the elevator. It was just the antagonistic voice of Mrs. Katz coming over the intercom. No one else was in the lobby.

"May I help you?" By which she meant to say, "Fuck off." Totally confrontational. Classic condo-fascist bullshit.

"Yes, I am meeting a tenant."

"Oh, really?"

No, this is shtick I do hoping I'll get discovered for my own variety show.

"Yes, I am here to meet my uncle."

Mrs. Katz with arms folded: "Who's your uncle?"

"My uncle Meyer."

Never in the history of civilization did a sliding door open so quickly. "Well, good morning, young man," she said as I stepped into the spacious marble lobby.

"Good morning," I said, rejoicing in her terror. "I'm Jonah Eastman."

"It's a delight to have you here, Jonah. Your uncle Meyer should be down shortly."

"Thank you." After a pregnant pause, I asked, "How does he seem to you?"

"Oh, fine, fine. Coming along."

Huge lie. Terror. Party line.

I heard a bell ding and saw in my periphery a green light above the elevator light up. The first live being that emerged was a tiny, panting shih tzu. The second live being, seemingly being led by this weightless creature, was an exhausted old man who resembled a wisp of smoke.

I prayed that my face didn't register shock when I saw my haggard primary source, who surrendered a brief half smile. I stepped toward Uncle Meyer and did my best to suppress my true reaction. It was foolish, because after a lifetime of dodging treachery, who did I think I was to snooker this old jackal?

"Don't worry, boychick, I know I don't look like Tyrone Power anymore," he said with a wink. I forgot how guttural his voice was. All Brooklyn, but much weaker than it had once been. Almost inaudible.

"That's all right, I don't look like Tyrone Power either," I said, taking his hand. After he shook my hand, weakly, he patted my shoulder, wincing slightly from this insignificant motion.

"You look pretty good," he said. "Filled out since I saw you. Like a nice college man."

Uncle Meyer and Mickey could have been brothers. Both men were remarkably small, about five three or four. They had tanned, creased faces, and prominent noses. The chief differences were the color of their eyes—Mickey's were green, Uncle Meyer's were dark brown, almost a sharklike black—and their hair. Mickey's hair was sparse and cottony white; Uncle Meyer's was thick and metallic gray, although it was still flecked with a surprising amount of black, even at his age.

He was wearing a black sweater over a white shirt, black pants, black loafers. Also like Mickey, his clothing was spotless. Uncle Meyer's clothes, despite their quality, floated around him. While he had never been heavy, he had clearly lost a good deal of weight, maybe thirty pounds, which was profound given his size.

I noticed that he had missed some spots shaving near his neck. Even though the cancer was in his lungs, I assumed that either coughing or his treatments had made his throat tender.

"Let's walk," Uncle Meyer said, gesturing toward Collins Avenue.

I knew I would have to take the lead at some point, but I thought it best to proceed slowly. A part of me was terrified that this shuffling old soul would expire on our walk.

I tried to evaluate him as we proceeded north without coming off like a drooling teenybopper, and what struck me about Meyer Lansky was his absurd inconspicuousness. Was it possible, I wondered, if the sheer banality of his existence served as a blank screen onto which people with deep investments in certain agendas—commercial, political, psychic—projected fantastic narratives? That no one could catch a bogeymen such as Uncle Meyer doing anything seriously wrong only served as proof of his cunning. In 1692 Salem, they called this "spectral evidence," the gut feeling that something spooky was going on with the accused, validating the deep need of the culture to *believe,* in the absence of data. America is, after all, a nation of symbols, not facts, which is why we cherish the voluptuous criminality of an Al Capone or Bugsy Siegel.

"This is Bruzzer, by the way," Uncle Meyer said, pointing to the little dog.

"He looks pretty tough."

"As you can see, he leads me around pretty good."

"I wouldn't tangle with him."

Uncle Meyer agreed with my assessment.

"How'd you like the Singapore?" he asked. Again he was hard to hear, and I was thankful it was so early and that cars weren't whishing along Collins yet.

"Oh, it was great," I said.

"Better twenty years ago. Some of the old Cuban musicians who were sick of schlepping all over the country decided just to play there in the Bali Hai Lounge. That way the patrons had the best talent, and the talent was happy they didn't have to run all over the place. Things were good. They're all gone though. Did you get to do anything?"

"I was hoping to go for a run on the beach this morning, but wanted to get my thoughts together for our talk. I found some interesting news at the library yesterday I wanted to go over."

"What interesting news?"

"The Nazi admiral Karl Dönitz, the man who ran Hitler's U-boat campaign, died recently."

"I didn't know that. Didn't know he got to old age," Uncle Meyer said.

Uncle Meyer stopped while Bruzzer did his business on a palm tree. "You said you were going to take a run. Why the hell do people run?"

I wasn't quite sure how to tackle this. "It's exercise for the heart, I guess."

He shrugged. "I don't think people would run for exercise if they had to run in real life." He looked up at me with those hard pitch eyes. I knew exactly what he was referring to. He had fled the country years ago to seek asylum under Israel's Law of Return. Israel tossed him out. Mickey had had a similar problem a few years later, and I ended up going to high school for a while in France.

We began walking again. "You sure you want to talk to an old man about ancient history and not be with your nice young friends?"

I didn't want to tell him that I preferred being with old people, so I said I was looking forward to hearing him out.

Uncle Meyer pulled Bruzzer back, and I sensed he was straining with the leash. "Would you like me to take him?" I asked.

He stopped. "Sure, why not."

As I took Bruzzer's leash, I felt a sense of relief in the old man's hands as he let go. Prudent segue.

"Uncle Meyer, I'm not sure how much you were told regarding what I wanted to speak with you about."

"A history report or something?"

"In a way. I've taken some time away from college to work in the White House. I work for a man who reports to President Reagan. They're very upset about the increase in Islamic terrorist activities against Americans and think they have to do more to deal with the problem."

"They sure as hell better, kid. Gadhafi, those guys, are animals. Arabs don't think like we do."

"No doubt. Anyway, my boss told me about your work with the navy during World War Two. Mickey told me a bit about it, too."

"What did they tell you, Jonah?"

"That there were Nazis in New York."

"There were."

"He said you helped catch them."

"I did. Your grandfather played his part, too."

"Did he really?" I said like a six-year-old.

"We couldn't have done it without him."

"Really? Why?"

"There was a lot of action in your home state, kid. The Nazis were all over the New Jersey coast. They used to steer by the lights of Atlantic City."

"I thought everybody was supposed to turn the lights off?"

"Who listens?" Uncle Meyer said. "They didn't turn the lights off in Atlantic City until your grandfather told them to, but we'll get to that."

"It strikes me as an amazing story. I can't believe I hadn't read about it." I was thrilled by the idea that my own grandfather, the much maligned criminal, had played a part in defending the country whose laws he had so brazenly flouted.

Uncle Meyer liberated a little *heh,* then coughed, hard and painfully, into a handkerchief. I halted Bruzzer and put my hand on Uncle Meyer's back. He held up his hand as if to tell me he would be all right, and I saw a spot of blood on the small cloth as he returned it to his pocket.

Once he caught his breath, he said, "The government bastards said it never happened. A few years ago, they said they made a report that the whole thing really *did* happen. Operation Underworld they called it. It never went public to my knowledge. But they don't give my boys and men like your grandfather credit for helping. Doesn't fit their little story that the war was won only by brave soldiers who died in battle. Our soldiers were very brave, sure, but there were other things. Things that need to be told."

I detected bitterness in his spent voice. Moisture was in his eyes, and I didn't know if it was tied to his coughing fit or his emotional state.

"I would like to help you tell it," I said. "Maybe we can get it the recognition it deserves, at least by important people."

"You would, would you? People will think you're nuts. You'll bollix your standing with these big shots you work for by talking to me."

"I don't think that's so. My boss already acknowledged your role. I sense he thought it was underappreciated, and I've openly told them I know you. They don't want it to go public that they're thinking about this kind of thing—"

"Or that you're talking to me, right?"

"That anybody's talking to anybody. But I don't want to make you feel uncomfortable. I know you're a very private person."

"So what happens, I tell you my story, then what?"

"I go back to the White House and tell them, maybe write something up."

"Something's been written up, or so I'm told. The government ran the operation, what do they think I can tell them now?"

I wasn't quite sure I knew how to answer this. My heart skipped in my chest. Screw it, Jonah, *you're in it.*

"Well, Uncle Meyer, whatever files the government has, my sense is that my boss doesn't trust them. I think he's trying to determine if your efforts were worthwhile from the perspective of someone who was critical to it. He said he didn't just want facts, he wanted insight, your opinion."

"My opinion, huh?"

"Yes, sir."

"Well, I've got plenty of opinions."

"I don't want you to do anything that makes you uncomfortable," I said. "I just want you to know how things work."

"Make *me* uncomfortable? It's not me I'm worried about. I don't want you to get in trouble."

"If I'm telling the truth, how could I get in trouble?"

"You're being a little naïve, Jonah. Some truths get people in terrible trouble. They sure as hell did in my little drama. Reagan better watch his ass if he tries what Roosevelt did. These are different times."

"Maybe I could make that part of what I report."

"Maybe," he said. "Let's turn back."

As we walked south, Uncle Meyer hooked his arm in mine, more out of his need for balance, I sensed, than affection. But you never knew what people in this state needed to hold on to. More cars were now on the road, and several of them slowed down, and their passengers appeared to be staring at us. Lookyloos. These folks knew exactly who he was. The sun was rising with greater authority now, which prompted my new confidant to put his sunglasses on.

When we were a few blocks away from the Imperial House, I said, "Uncle Meyer, I appreciate your willingness to speak with me."

"I didn't plan on it, you know."

"I know. I just know . . . you remind me of my grandfather, and Mickey's not too big on rehashing ancient history."

"Mickey's not dying."

And there we had it. "I've got only weeks left, I figure," he continued. "A month or two, tops. I'm okay with talking to you. See, kid, you got your feet in two worlds. You're off at that Ivy League school. An education like that is a wonderful gift—and you've got a foot in *our* world. Mickey and mine. The Bible says, 'He that keepeth his mouth keepeth his life.' Telling it to you is almost like keeping it to myself. Anyhow, it doesn't matter at this stage; I could confess to kidnapping the Lindbergh baby and it wouldn't matter. You may not now, but someday you might have some appreciation for men like us. Men who did what we had to do with the little we had. Two-nickel bums. And people are more likely to listen to you because you've got the education from a fine college. Your kids? Your kids won't know men like me even existed, or, if they do, we'll be like those dinosaur skeletons in a museum. You follow?"

"I think so. You know I'm not a professional writer or anything."

"I don't want a professional writer," he snapped. "I don't trust these guys who write stories. They've got the story written before it's written, see. They've got all the players lined up like in a movie. Like those Woodward and Bernstein guys, they've got to turn up a Nixon, or else there's no story. Whether there is one or isn't one, you follow? In any story a pro tells about the Second World War, what are the chances I'm gonna be the hero? Bubkes, that's the chances."

"I'm sure there are writers out there who are interested in history."

"Not where the name Meyer Lansky is concerned, Jonah. My son named his son Meyer Lansky. My grandson. Nobody should have to go through life with that name. There's a Hebrew term,

Baal Shem Tov. Master of the Good Name. It means your name is everything. These writers all want some prize. That's where their loyalty is. My name is just a means to that payout. They don't write who you are; they write who they need you to be to get that prize. They all run the same play. They come to some mark whose mother told him he would be a great man. He lives his life wondering why he never became that great man. They ambush him and tell him he *is* that man after all, and he takes the action. You know what happens next?"

"No, I don't."

"Bruzzer, should we tell Jonah what happens next? Yeah? What happens is the sucker goes home without his wallet. All because he tried to explain. These reporters say they'll give me a chance to tell my story. No, it's a chance for them to tell *their* story. They confuse what's good for me with what's good for them."

He was on a roll now, just as Mickey said he had been when he and Deedee had seen him.

"But you, Jonah, are not putting the arm on me. You're not promising me anything. I like that. I've spent the better part of a century being chased by terrible enemies—Cossacks, mob killers, Dewey and other scalp-hunting prosecutors, Communist revolutionaries, J. Edgar Hoover, newspapermen. People want to get you talking, defending, *explaining*. You can't explain a damned thing to a bullet coming at your head. The bullet doesn't want to learn, it wants to kill you."

"You think you'll get a fair shake from me?"

Uncle Meyer nodded. "What the hell do I have to lose?"

"I hope I can do it justice."

"You will," he said, as if it were an order, which it may have been. "Most of the things I will tell you I personally lived, but there were other things that happened back then that I heard from other people."

"What kind of people?"

"People like Walter Winchell and Commander Haffenden, who was the most important person in all of this."

"The reporter Walter Winchell?"

"He was much more than a reporter, Jonah. I've got a pen and a writing tablet from Woolworth's upstairs. Let's go."

Keeping It in Your Hat

THE LANSKYS' ONE-BEDROOM CONDOMINIUM WAS ON THE SECOND floor on the south side of the Imperial House. The furnishings were precisely what one might expect from an upper-middle-class retiree in South Florida. The carpet was deep, and the sofas and chairs were comfortable and immaculate. One thing this apartment was not was the luxurious lair of a billionaire criminal mastermind. It was the concrete cubby of a modest Jewish immigrant who had made a little gelt gambling a long time ago, and who stayed alive because he paid steady dividends to homicidal shareholders.

The clicking of footsteps grew louder against kitchen tile. Teddy Lansky, Uncle Meyer's second wife, emerged from the kitchen in a comfortable jumpsuit, an ensemble that subtracted a decade from her age. She was surely in her seventies though. Even smaller than her husband, Teddy had short blond hair and delicate features. She could have been my own Deedee's sister, and in the spiritual sense she was. I had no doubt that they had shared more than one stiff drink while discussing their spousal choices.

"There's my boy," Teddy said with a grandmotherly hug.

Women like Teddy Lansky were a treasure. I've always felt the biggest crime within Hitler's Holocaust was depriving civilization of millions of Jewish grandmothers. The thing about them was that even if you didn't know them well, they adopted you anyway—and there was nothing posed or false about it.

"Did you have breakfast?" Teddy asked.

"Uh," I began articulately.

"No, you didn't," she correctly concluded. "How many eggs? Two, three?"

"Two is fine."

"And I'll throw in some bacon and toast. Your friend there"—she gestured to her husband, who was shuffling to the terrace—"eats like a bird these days. You want coffee?"

"No thank you."

"Then I'll get you some orange juice." Then Teddy said something chilling: "He should have talked to you years ago, Jonah. It's all that baggage that ate away at him and gave him those bleeding ulcers, heart attacks, and, you know, what he's got now."

I followed Uncle Meyer out onto the balcony, which faced another mammoth building. While the Atlantic Ocean was visible to the left, this was not an oceanfront apartment. He sat on the chair closest to the sliding door. I sat on the other side of the table where a writing tablet from Woolworth's, a shabby Webster's dictionary (which struck me as being quaint), and a Paper Mate ballpoint pen awaited me. Bingo. Free to write.

Teddy brought out a cup of coffee for her husband and dropped an obscene amount of pills into his hand.

"Some of these are for my heart. Some are for my ulcer. And some are for the radiation they're shooting me with. We better get to work quick. My doctors tell me I might lose my voice altogether."

One by one, he swallowed the pills, then frowned at the indignity.

"Open up the tablet and see how I started writing in it," Uncle Meyer said. "As you see, I didn't get too far."

I flipped open the cardboard cover and saw that he had, indeed, begun to write. His handwriting was immaculate with its cautionary loops; however, as I paged through it, I saw he had been unable to keep a narrative going.

"See, Jonah, I spent a life keeping my business in my hat, so when it came time to write something down, I didn't do it so good."

"That's okay. I'll take notes and ask questions. I think I should try to render this in your voice as much as I can."

"My voice, huh?" he surrendered. "I'm not Wayne Newton and I'm not Hemingway."

"That's fine. Tell me what you saw, how you felt at the time, how you feel now, what the people you worked with did and said, did they seem nervous."

He gently massaged his throat and, for the first time, managed a genuine smile. His eyes may even have sparkled. This visit was clearly more than an accommodation to Mickey. He *wanted* to do this.

"My voice, huh," he said again.

The story that follows belongs to Meyer Lansky, with all of its biases, self-delusions, and selective memories. Most of it comes right from him, but I filled in the gaps with information from the government records Tom Simmons let me study, the kinds of declassified military goodies the White House can access with greater aplomb than a Dartmouth junior. Tom's remark about looking for "insight" was dead-on. The archives had the records, but Uncle Meyer had the whole megillah.

II.

Are You American?

The only thing that ever really frightened me during the war was the U-boat peril. . . . The U-boat attack was our worst evil. It would have been wise for the Germans to stake all upon it.

—Winston Churchill

The Volunteer

February 10, 1942

MEYER LANSKY NEVER SAW ANYTHING LIKE IT. THE JAPS HAD JUST done their dance on Pearl Harbor. Everybody thought they were going to come at America again. Them or the Nazis. It was a matter of time. Guys in Hell's Kitchen were saying what they would do to Japs or Nazis if they invaded Manhattan. Empty tough-guy talk.

It was afternoon, around three. Meyer had just had a late lunch, something he didn't do a lot. He stepped outside of Lindy's when he heard all the sirens. Black smoke was everywhere. The young fellow who drove him around sometimes, Lilo, said, "Mr. Lansky, the Japs are bombing New York or somethin'." People were running around. Meyer couldn't see or hear any airplanes, so he knew it wasn't a big attack. Still, all kinds of fire trucks and ambulances were screaming by.

A little later he heard the Nazis blew up a cruise ship, *Normandie,* which was docked on Pier 88 on the Hudson. It was the biggest cruise ship in the world. The navy was converting it into a transport ship for American troops, rigging it up with new engines to outrun Hitler's U-boats, which went fast. The *Normandie* was the most powerful steam turboelectric passenger ship ever built.

Meyer was interested in engines because he got his start as

an automobile mechanic. He had worked on the cars he ran during Prohibition. He loved doing it, too, and once thought he might make a career in machines or engineering, but, life goes how it goes.

Meyer got Lilo to drive him down to the pier so he could see the action. He didn't get as close to the *Normandie* as he wanted to, but Lilo got him pretty near. It was like Armageddon. Black smoke was blowing out of every porthole, every door, of the ship. He couldn't believe its size. It's one thing to read the figures. A thousand feet long. Eighty-three thousand tons.

They had two thousand sailors and civilians trying to douse it. Hundreds of sailors, their clothes drenched, poured out on stretchers. They had to be treated by medics. People were walking out in a daze, and the minute they came out, nurses threw dry blankets on them. Meyer saw a shivering sailor, so he took off his overcoat and gave it to him. He assured a cop on the scene that he'd help find food or other assistance as best he could. He felt useless and wasn't sure what he expected he'd be doing down here.

Mayor La Guardia was at the scene. He was directing priests to talk to people, which was all he could do. Who knew there were that many priests in New York? Early the next morning, the *Normandie* capsized. With all that mess, only one man died, an Italian from Brooklyn. Something blew up in the fire and threw him over a railing and onto another deck. Meyer made sure some of his associates from Brooklyn did what they could for the man's family.

The first news reports said some of the sailors had been working on a recreation center for the troops when a torch lit up some mattresses wrapped in burlap. Everybody thought it was bullshit. Something else—something bad—had caused the fire. The fire chief said the blaze was under control and contained to the three upper decks. A moron could see things getting worse.

Some of the sailors were saying that gasoline was flowing from the sprinklers, which accelerated the fire. Others said members of the German-American Bund group—organized Nazi sympathizers in the United States—had been seen on deck before the blaze ignited. Meyer had dealt with some of those Bund bastards years ago when they started up. We'll get to them.

The next day, Lilo drove Meyer down to the army recruiting office in Midtown Manhattan. Plenty of Jewish men in his line of work enlisted because they wanted to take a whack at Hitler given what he was doing to the Jews in Europe. Sickening reports told of Jews being rounded up like livestock and taken someplace on trains. But where? Doc Stacher, from New Jersey, joined the army. Moe Dalitz in Cleveland entered the army a private and came out a captain. Davie Berman of Minneapolis and Charlie Baron of Chicago were turned down by draft boards, so they went to Canada, enlisted under fake names, and fought for the British Empire. A handful of *shtarkers*, tough guys, fighting for old King George. The guys called Charlie Baron "Colonel" the rest of his life. He loved that.

A line stretched around the block. The men were mostly in their late teens and early twenties. A few of the kids didn't even look eighteen. About half of the men were wearing suits; most of them were cheap and didn't fit.

Meyer felt strange when he got in line. He was older than most of these fellows. Thirty-nine. He had on a suit by Maurice. In those days, he wore white-on-white shirts made by Sulka, ties by Countess Mara, and a Cavanaugh hat—pearl gray with a black band. Things were good in the money department. Meyer had a lot of gambling operations and had millions in untaxed cash going through his fingers. He would have given it all up for a plain green army uniform.

A smart-ass kid farther down the line looked Meyer over and said to his buddy, "Why is some accountant from Ernst and Ernst looking to get his ass shot off in Poland?"

Because I was born there, schmuck, Meyer said to himself. *And because there's a psychopath killing my people.*

Meyer pretended not to hear the remark. When he was younger, he might have taken a shot at the guy, but these days he had a rule against getting physical if the situation didn't matter. In a way, he didn't blame the kid. He knew he was going to be in line for a while, so he'd brought a book called *Security Analysis* by a man named Graham. The line moved along slowly, so Meyer read from the book. When he saw a section that was interesting to him, he waved to Lilo and asked him to find him a pencil to make notes. The men in the line took notice of this tough Italian kid working for Meyer and got quiet fast.

Doctors gave Meyer a physical, then they sat him down in the guest chair of a sergeant who was behind a cheap wooden desk. His nameplate said HERMAN.

Sergeant Herman studied Meyer's paperwork and looked back and forth between the paperwork and the little man sitting in his guest chair.

"Meyer Lansky," Herman said eventually. He pronounced the first name wrong. "Mayor."

"It's Meyer." *MY*ur.

"Meyer. Pardon me. It says here you are forty, Mr. Lansky?"

"I will be on July fourth."

"Share a birthday with Uncle Sam, huh?"

"Yes, sir."

"You were born in Grodno. Where is that?"

"Russia or Poland, depending on what day it is."

"Tough part of the world. You're a little old to enlist in the army, aren't you? You realize that the chances of combat are high?"

"Things got pretty violent in my neighborhood during Prohibition, Sergeant. I would like to serve my country."

"Why, Mr. Lansky?"

"Because I love America."

"But you look like a very prosperous man. Why give that all up to get your head blown off? You say you love America, but, out of curiosity, why?"

"I suppose, Sergeant, because it is beautiful. There is not a day that goes by when I don't remember our ship pulling into New York harbor. Some immigrants say they remember seeing the Statue of Liberty when they came in. To be honest, I didn't. I remember that my mother, my brother, and my sister and I were terribly seasick. I noticed the skyscrapers. How could anybody miss them? Liberty . . . she was, well, small. But those skyscrapers, how high they went. . . . Who knows why you fall in love, am I right? But I saw what happened to the *Normandie,* so close to the buildings. Some things have to be answered, if you know what I mean."

"I don't mean to discount your patriotism, Mr. Lansky, but the army isn't taking men your age for combat. There is, uh, also the matter of your height."

"There are things I can do besides combat, although that would be my preference. I am good with automobile engines and machinery. I also have business skills."

"I appreciate that, Mr. Lansky, but we can't take you at this time."

Meyer stared at Herman. "Do you ever make exceptions, Sergeant?"

"What kind of exceptions?"

Meyer, who could tell Herman liked his persistence, said, "I don't know, that little French guy had a good run across Europe a while back. Maybe we're due for another small general."

Herman laughed.

"What did you do before the war, Sergeant?" Meyer asked.

"I ran a landscaping business in Westchester County."

"What happened to the business?"

"My brother is running it. Why do you ask?"

"I have some business interests in Westchester. If you give me your brother's information, I can pass it along in the event we need your services."

"What kind of business are you in, Mr. Lansky?"

"Diversified investments, music. I have an interest in some hotels and entertainment places up your way."

"Entertainment? The only show place I know up my way is run by some old gangster. They gamble there, too, so I'm told."

"I'll look into it. Do you have a calling card for your business, Sergeant?"

Herman looked at Meyer for a few seconds, then started rooting around in his briefcase. He found a card and handed it to Meyer.

"Thank you, Sergeant. Call me if anything opens up. I'd like to take a shot at the Nazis, but if you need some help with the Japs, I'm not too particular."

The Pitch

Meyer had a jukebox business called Manhattan Simplex in partnership with "Jimmy Blue Eyes" Alo and Frank Costello. Things were good there, too. Best of all to Meyer, it was a legal enterprise, even though sometimes they had to do a little assertive salesmanship to ensure proper distribution. But who didn't resort to a little muscle from time to time? That Ludlow Massacre Rockefeller pulled wasn't exactly a soft sell. The problems that the racket boys had with the police during Prohibition were long over. During the war years, if you ran a gambling joint, as long as you greased the police and the politicians, things would be copacetic.

One day, later in February, Meyer was sitting at his desk, and the girl they had working there told him Moses Polakoff was on the phone. That was never good. Polakoff was a defense lawyer. He represented Charlie Luciano—some people called him Charlie Lucky—who was up in Dannemora Prison near the Canadian border, probably for the rest of his life. Polakoff, who also did work for Meyer, was an impressive man. He had been a big prosecutor and didn't look like what they called in those days a "rackets mouthpiece." Even though Polakoff was a Jew, he looked like a *shaygetz* who could be on the Supreme Court. Tall, white hair, the whole package. Polakoff wanted Meyer to come down to his office, which meant he didn't want anybody listening in on them. They didn't wiretap lawyers' offices in those days.

Meyer got a taxi and went down to see Polakoff right away. Meyer's stomach started acting up. He didn't know he was working on an ulcer, but he was. Never in a million years would he have guessed what Polakoff wanted to talk about.

Polakoff said he got a visit from a navy officer, which made Meyer feel better. He knew Polakoff had been in the navy in World War I, and that Meyer wasn't going to get nicked on some charge with the navy. All Meyer knew about the navy is that sailors wore white outfits and ran around on boats.

Polakoff said the navy man told him he was responsible for nailing down security at the New York docks since the mess with the *Normandie*. Hitler had spies on the docks, not to mention U-boats out in the Atlantic sinking American warships and killing many sailors. Some of these U-boats may even have gotten into New York harbor. The Nazis were getting their information about U.S. convoys from someplace, probably the docks.

"Nazi U-boats in New York harbor?" Meyer said. "Is this guy nuts, Moe?"

"He says it's real, Meyer."

Meyer thought, *What the hell does this have to do with me?* Polakoff knew that when the German-American Bund had isolationist rallies a few years back, Meyer had Bugsy Siegel and Lepke Buchalter send some muscle to bust them up, but Meyer hadn't heard a peep about that for years, probably because the ten-thousand-member Bund never returned.

"Meyer," Polakoff said, "the navy is getting hassled on the docks. They're just trying to do their job and the longshoremen won't cooperate."

Now it was starting to make sense. Some rough customers

were on the docks. Meyer never had much business in that part of town, but he knew the guys who did.

"How did they get to you, Moe?"

"Believe it or not, through Frank Hogan."

This gave Meyer heartburn. He always worried when business was good because things could turn. You never knew with all that money in play who would decide to come at you and how—Mafia, other gamblers muscling in, Feds, or local authorities. Frank Hogan was the prosecutor who put Charlie Luciano away. Personally. Meyer got no joy seeing Luciano go to jail. He was his friend and his partner. But Meyer didn't know where that ball would stop bouncing. On one hand, if they put Luciano on ice, then they might start going after some of his partners next—such as Meyer, Costello, and Siegel. On the other, maybe the government would be happy with the collar on Luciano and they'd move on to a new menace.

Luciano had been away for six, seven years by then, and just to be on the safe side, Meyer had encouraged Siegel to go out West. From the time they were kids, Siegel walked around with a bull's-eye on his forehead. You can tell who's going to be a target when they get a nickname, and Siegel's was Bugsy because a cop said, "If you drill a hole in that kid's head, bedbugs would crawl out." Siegel hated the nickname. First, Dewey, the big-shot prosecutor, went after Dutch Schultz. Then the lunatic Dutchman got himself dead after he put a hit out on Dewey. Then Dewey aimed at Luciano with Frank Hogan as his point man. Vice charges. Whores and all. All trumped up, but that's the game. Now Hogan was the top guy, the district attorney, and who knew what he wanted to be when he grew up?

"Hogan has a young guy who works for him, Murray Gurfein," Polakoff said. "He's the rackets chief prosecutor. The navy went to them and told them they're getting resistance on the docks."

"Resistance from what?" Meyer asked.

"Resisting helping look out for Nazi spies."

"Who did he talk to?"

"Socks Lanza and Cockeye Dunn," Polakoff said.

Meyer didn't say anything right away. He was thinking, *Kineahora.* Talk about rough customers. Cockeye Dunn would slit your throat if he got bored. He had worked for the Dutchman, rest in peace.

"Does the navy think the Nazis burned that ship?" Meyer asked.

Polakoff said the officer didn't know. But he *did* know that the Nazis were sinking ships in the Atlantic, close to American shores, regularly, and killing Americans. Even if the Germans didn't cause the *Normandie* fire, the effect was still the same.

"The navy is worried, Meyer, that some of these guys might be helping the Nazis in some way, maybe because the Italians have loyalties to Mussolini."

"Some of them *do,* Moe. Vito Genovese for one. If your navy man thinks I can reason with Vito, he's going to be disappointed."

"That's not it, Meyer. They think if Charlie Luciano gave his blessing that it was okay to help the navy look out for spies, then maybe, you know—"

"They don't think that our Hebrew landsmen are helping Hitler, do they?"

"I don't think the subtlety of Jewish boys having an aversion to being Hitler's foot soldiers is lost on them, Meyer."

"You think this navy man's on the level? If he's coming from Hogan, it could be some kind of new collar. Follow-up to Dutch and Charlie."

"That's not Hogan's style," Polakoff said. "I think it's a war, plain and simple. Extraordinary times, extraordinary measures."

Meyer understood. He had broken up those Bund guys good when he had the chance because of what they were saying about Jews. Didn't get a nickel for it. Didn't want anything other than the satisfaction of running those shitbirds out of New York, which he did. The Italians didn't lend a hand either. And now there were reports in the newsreels about Hitler corralling Jews and sending them somewhere.

"Does the navy think the German-American Bund is behind this?" Meyer asked.

"He didn't say. But there's no question that the Nazis are closer than they should be, and he doesn't want them getting any more help on those docks."

"What did you promise, Moe?"

"*Promise?* Nothing, Meyer. I did tell him I thought you'd be willing to hear him out, that once you did, you'd see if you could take it to Charlie."

"You were right. I'll talk to him. Just one thing to think about?"

"Yes, Meyer?"

"What's in it for Charlie?"

Discipline Problems

The navy's point man on the dock problem was Lieutenant Commander Charles Radcliffe Haffenden. Unfortunately, as Meyer learned from Moe Polakoff, Meyer was not the first man from the wrong side of the tracks to meet Haffenden. Meyer got the whole story soon enough.

Socks Lanza and Cockeye Dunn were late to Pier 88 where they were supposed to meet Commander Haffenden. Not a good sign. One of Haffenden's men said he should start with Socks and Cockeye because of their union juice. Talk about a lousy tip. Haffenden had heard stories about how union issues were dealt with, including one about a troublesome labor official who was recently beaten to death in front of thirteen witnesses at an arbitration hearing. True, no doubt.

Haffenden looked at the mammoth *Normandie,* on its side. A murdered planet. He felt two hard taps on his shoulder. What he saw when he turned around was not comforting.

One of the men was a vicious-looking Irishman with a left eye that was permanently twisted into a fuck-you squint. This man looked Haffenden up and down in his navy uniform as if it were a sissy costume. The squinty fellow wrote off every man other than himself as a queer. This was John "Cockeye" Dunn, the Hell's Kitchen stevedore boss who had done time in Sing Sing for armed robbery and, given his apprenticeship with Dutch Schultz, was known to have some murders under his belt. Try proving it.

The other character was a thick, bulky Italian with a squashed, flat face. Joseph "Socks" Lanza was officially the "business agent" of the fishermen's union. He got his nickname because he had perfected the negotiating skill of "socking" anybody who didn't see things his way. Unofficially, Socks was the Luciano skipper who ran the Fulton Fish Market. He was free pending an appeal for an extortion conviction. From the looks of Socks, Haffenden couldn't picture him running anything more than a red light. In a bib stained bloody from chopping fish, Socks was apelike, while Cockeye was more like an oversize mongoose that saw humanity as a pit of cobras. While the navy was in charge of the waterfront during wartime, one look at these two *ballagoolahs* made Haffenden think the navy wasn't in charge of anything besides laundering sailors' suits.

"You must be Dunn and Lanza," Haffenden said.

Socks grunted. Cockeye did nothing.

Haffenden extended his hand. Socks shook it, shooting a smirk Cockeye's way. When Haffenden reached out for Cockeye, he pretended not to notice, turning to the side to face a bunch of longshoremen who materialized out of the mist. Cockeye barked out a laugh, which made the longshoremen snicker in appreciation of their boss's disrespect. Haffenden felt a wave of despair pass through him. What was he going to do, go to his boss and explain, "The reason why America is now part of the Third Reich is because I couldn't find a way for the United States Navy to beat back a handful of Neanderthals"?

"Well, men, I'm Commander Haffenden, and my job is to get to the bottom of what happened to the *Normandie* and try to figure out how the Nazis are getting information about American shipping convoys, not to mention getting the fuel to roam around New York harbor. I was told that you were the ones to see, that you're in charge of the docks. I was hoping you could help out the navy."

Cockeye sniffed. Socks shrugged and said, "We ain't in charge of nothing."

"I heard differently," Haffenden said. "Any idea what happened here?" He pointed to the destroyed ship.

Socks shrugged again. "Yeah, ship caught fire."

"I realize that, Mr. Lanza, but do you have any idea how?"

"Yeah," Socks said. "Burned up."

Cockeye thought this was funny, and he glanced back at his crew, who, despite being out of earshot, heaved as if they had heard the joke.

"What have you heard, Mr. Dunn?" Haffenden asked.

"I don't hear too good," Cockeye answered.

"Why not?"

"Gun went off once in my ear. Don't hear too good."

Haffenden tried to hide his impatience. These guys wanted him to lose his cool, and he wasn't going to let that happen.

"So, neither of you heard anything?"

Socks nodded no. Cockeye didn't want to waste the energy nodding.

"All right, boys," Haffenden said, "let me put it to you this way. If somebody wanted to sabotage a ship at this pier, or if somebody wanted to pass information to the Nazis about the routes our ships were taking in the Atlantic, or if somebody wanted to get fuel to Nazi submarines, how would they do it? Hypothetically?"

"Hypo-what?" Cockeye asked.

"If somebody wanted to do something like the things I just said, something bad, how would they do it?" Haffenden asked again, clenching his jaw.

"We didn't do nothing bad," Socks said.

"Nobody is suggesting you did anything bad," Haffenden said. "The navy is just trying to find out what's happening to American ships and sailors."

"What are you looking at us for?" Socks said.

"You work on the docks, right?" Haffenden asked.

Socks shrugged. Cockeye's mind drifted.

"Well," Haffenden continued, "I want to know how the docks work, how somebody might have gotten on that ship to sabotage it, how German spies could get information."

"I'm not German," Socks said. "You German?" he asked Cockeye.

"No, not me."

"We ain't German," Socks said.

"Are you American?" Haffenden asked.

Both wiseguys flashed anger.

"Are you American? I asked." Haffenden said, his voice getting louder.

Socks nodded.

"You're not American, Mr. Dunn?"

"Who you sayin' ain't American?" Cockeye answered.

"I'm not saying anything, Mr. Dunn. I'm asking if you, Cockeye Dunn, are an American. You can't seem to answer that question—just two months after Pearl Harbor, I might add. What exactly don't you understand?"

"Born right down the street," Cockeye said, stepping closer to Haffenden.

Cockeye looked back over his shoulder again and saw something he hadn't before. Gathered just beyond his longshoremen buddies were a half dozen large men in plain clothes. They were cleaner cut than the longshoremen, and several of them were visibly armed. Government boys, probably navy. Cockeye's expression remained hard, but Haffenden detected a twinge of worry in Socks, his fat face suddenly looking more childlike than thuggish.

"That wasn't hard, was it, Mr. Dunn?" Haffenden said, registering that he had never, not for a moment, truly been alone on these docks. "Now, I have come here, very nicely, to ask for your help. I have no reason to believe that either of you are anything but fine, upstanding Americans. All I'm trying to do is learn how Americans may be vulnerable to attack from the Nazis. It's like asking a chef how he prepares an omelet, not because he poisoned the king, but because he knows how to cook and at what stage during the making of an omelet an assassin might slip in a little arsenic. Am I making myself clear?"

"We didn't poison nobody," Cockeye huffed.

Christ. "I know you didn't poison anybody, Mr. Dunn," Haffenden said, calculating whether Cockeye was an imbecile or just a wiseguy who opposed authority on general principle. "Do you understand we're at war, Mr. Dunn?"

"You don't think I know Pearl Harbor?" Cockeye shot back.

Haffenden gave up on Cockeye and turned to Socks.

"Do *you* understand we're at war, Mr. Lanza?"

Socks shrugged and muttered, "Hitler."

"Were you born in America like Mr. Dunn?"

"There," Socks answered, pointing with his thumb somewhere over his shoulder, maybe Jupiter.

"There in New York, Mr. Lanza, or there in Italy?"

"Here," Socks said, annoyed, or perhaps worried. "New York."

"Not Italy?" Haffenden pushed.

"No, here."

"The man said *here*!" Cockeye cut in. "New York."

Haffenden pressed, "What do you think of Hitler, Mr. Lanza?"

"Hitler?" Socks asked, as if there might be some confusion as to which Hitler Haffenden was referring to.

"Yes, Hitler," Haffenden said.

"Goddam Nazi. What are you getting at?" *Whattayougetnat?* Socks asked.

"What do you think of Mussolini?"

"He's with Hitler," Socks said.

"That's correct. But what do you think of him?"

"Mussolini? I think he's with Hitler."

"That is a point of fact, Mr. Lanza, but it doesn't tell me what you think of Mr. Mussolini." Haffenden knew that something big was happening here. Socks was worried, which was a step in the right direction. Still, this was tricky. Haffenden needed to rattle him enough to give him incentive to help, but not so much that he hunkered down in complete resistance. Cockeye was useless, stone-cold. Socks was a hard case, but men ranged on a scale of toughness from those who were bloodless like sharks to those who could be tough like bears, which had a connection to something other than their own killer instincts.

"I think what Americans think," Socks said, inching closer to Haffenden's sweet spot.

"And what do Americans think?"

"Win the war. Beat 'em."

"Do the longshoremen and the men in the fishing union want to win the war?" Haffenden asked.

At this point, Cockeye broke just a little. "Look, navy man, everybody with me wants to win the war, but they ain't gonna tell you nothing."

"Why not, Mr. Dunn? Somebody on your docks is telling Hitler where American ships are going and what cargo they're carrying."

"Why not?" Cockeye said. "I'll tell you why not. You come down here at night. Bring a flashlight. You'll see rats the size of dogs. My guys would rather be those rats than talk to a guy dressed like a waiter."

"Okay, gentlemen, thank you for your time today," Haffenden said.

Haffenden walked away without giving Socks and Cockeye any next steps. He didn't get what he wanted, but he got the next best thing—reconnaissance. The bad news was that these guys were uncooperative by nature. There was a reason they were called wiseguys. The men who worked for them would be even worse because they had no permission to be helpful.

The dockworkers were mostly Italian and Irish. An Irishman might take a bribe, but the Irish were loyal to America. They may not have thought a war with Germany was their headache, though. The Italians were another story because their relatives were the enemy. Yes, Haffenden knew, most Italian-Americans were honorable and patriotic. The problem was that it didn't take most Italians to make trouble. It took a couple. Or less.

For all of their hardness, Cockeye and Socks didn't like having their patriotism questioned. With Cockeye, Haffenden sensed it was about being a man. Patriots were manly. Enemies were rodents.

It was different with Socks, though. That give-and-take about where he was born, where his loyalties were—this gave Haffenden room to maneuver. Socks didn't find it hard to disparage Hitler, but he had stumbled at Mussolini, which showed he was afraid that attacking the fascist *mamzer* would be greeted poorly by the Italians. The Jews were another story. They had nobody else to be loyal to because they hadn't come from anyplace in particular for a couple thousand years. America was the Holy Land.

The trick would be the boys from the Boot.

Reframe the Snitch

MOSES POLAKOFF CALLED MEYER AND ASKED HIM TO MEET HIM AND the navy big shot, Haffenden, at Longchamps restaurant on West Fifty-eighth Street between Fifth and Sixth avenues for breakfast. This was convenient for Meyer because he had an appointment with a tutor nearby. He went to a retired professor from Columbia to study arithmetic and economics. When Meyer got to Longchamps, he saw Polakoff at a table with a great big Irish naval officer in his fifties.

Polakoff waved Meyer over. When Haffenden turned and stood, he had a surprised look in his eye. Meyer got that look a lot. People were always expecting a bigger man, scary-looking. Meyer looked like a lot of businessmen walking around Manhattan, and no matter what terrible things people said, he saw himself that way. He used to read about the great Jewish moneymen such as Jacob Schiff, Otto Kahn, and Felix Warburg. He wondered how he could emulate them. That's why he read so much and was careful about how he dressed. Perhaps the officer was looking at a harmless chap wondering how in God's name *he* could ever help fight the Third Reich. Meyer would have wondered the same thing.

Haffenden's height and weight were imposing, but he was

nice-looking in the way you want a navy man to be. Very much in charge, a force to take seriously.

"I'm Lieutenant Commander Charles Haffenden."

"Meyer Lansky."

Haffenden gripped Meyer's hand a little longer than one might consider routine.

"You look surprised," Meyer said.

Haffenden was caught off guard, and despite his size, he seemed to be the more nervous one. "I suppose I am."

"You were expecting a bigger man? Maybe one wearing loud pinstripes and alligator shoes? A tommy gun, five-o'clock shadow?"

"After what I've been finding on those docks, I guess I was thinking that."

"Where are you from originally, Commander?" Meyer asked.

"Queens."

"So you're used to running into men who can handle themselves."

"Yes, I suppose so."

"And you survived growing up in Queens pretty good," Meyer said.

"You survived New York yourself, Mr. Lansky."

"Meyer."

Haffenden nodded. "I was a big Irish kid, but not much of a fighter. I survived by getting out, Meyer. You survived by staying."

"There are different kinds of toughness, Commander. Given my size, I had one kind."

"That's true. I guess it comes down to what kind of men you're commanding."

"Still, I managed to earn very good marks in school as a boy," Meyer said, although he wasn't sure why. They sat down. "But I had some scrapes with the law as a kid."

"Any arrests?"

Meyer sensed Haffenden already knew the answer, but was trying to see if he'd be straight with him. "Yes. I was a lookout for craps games. I carried a crowbar and occasionally had to use it. I ran liquor during Prohibition, but had no legal trouble there."

Haffenden grinned like a schoolkid. "Even the police regarded Volstead as a bad law."

Polakoff flagged down a waiter. They ordered. Haffenden loaded up on ham and eggs. Polakoff and Meyer were lighter eaters.

"Did you see the newspaper this morning?" Haffenden asked. He held up an article about an investigation into possible German sabotage of the *Normandie.*

"Yes, I did. I was going to ask you what you thought about it."

"I think we could go door-to-door to every house in America and tell people that it wasn't sabotage and they'd say, 'The bastards are covering it up.' The public is in the market for sabotage, and that's what the papers will give them. 'Remember the Maine!' and all that."

"You don't think the Nazis were responsible?" Meyer asked.

"We're not sure."

"But it couldn't hurt if people thought it was the Nazis."

Haffenden winced—or at least Meyer thought he did—for a second, as if a dentist had just scraped a nerve. "That's part of it. Even though I don't know you very well, Meyer, circumstances being what they are, and how I need your help, I'd like to share a few things with you."

"I'm also in a business where silence is golden, Commander."

Haffenden said the United States had lost more than two hundred ships to Nazi U-boats in the past year. Meyer was shocked. He hadn't heard anything about this, and he read the papers every day. He understood what Haffenden was saying about the *Normandie*: When people got scared, they didn't see random events, they just saw evil men. They blamed it on some strange group that won't step out into the light. Still, Meyer respected Haffenden for telling him that he wasn't sure the Nazis had burned the *Normandie,* which he could have done to rile Meyer up to his position.

Converting the *Normandie* into a troop transport ship had been a stupid idea from the get-go, Haffenden explained. Given all of the U-boats in the Atlantic, a well-aimed torpedo could have killed thousands of troops in one shot. Some in the navy thought the ship's demise was a blessing in disguise.

The U-boat campaign against America's East Coast was code-named Operation Drumbeat, or "Paukenschlag" in German, and it was so successful that the U-boat captains openly communicated with radios and referred to this period as their "happy time." Real chutzpah. Hitler was using what they called wolf packs, multiple U-boats attacking one ship at a time.

The Germans had their system of killing American sailors down to a science. The U-boat's first shot would be aimed at the boiler system to blow up the ship's propulsion, leaving it dead in the water. Sailors close by would either burn to death or die from the impact. A boiler-room direct hit would often trigger a second explosion of steam when ice-cold seawater washed over hot boilers. This reaction would be visible to the U-boat in the form of a plume of seawater spraying hundreds of feet into the air. When the plume fell, it would flood the ship's deck, often drowning the sailors.

Once hit, the ship would lurch, throwing men up to twenty feet. The force of the blast often killed sailors by smashing their bodies against steel. A sailor who suffered this fate was considered lucky. Procedures required that watertight passages be sealed to prevent more flooding. Crews that found themselves on the wrong side of the hatches would drown.

"I didn't know the Nazis had all that firepower so close," Meyer said, as a plate of toast with smoked salmon was set down before him.

"Our defenses are a joke. We've got about twenty navy ships, many of them obsolete barges, and about one hundred ill-maintained airplanes, very few that can actually fly," Haffenden said. "It would be hard, don't you think, to chase Hitler's state-of-the-art fleet of attack submarines out of the Atlantic with a garbage barge and a couple of crop dusters? U.S. troops are training with tanks that fire flour bags that are supposed to mimic artillery. What, we're going to soufflé Hitler into surrendering?"

Polakoff looked as surprised as Meyer did.

"This is terrible, Commander," Meyer said. "How did we end up so bad off?"

"Roosevelt has had a tough time selling a war on Germany, Meyer. With Pearl Harbor, everybody's riled up about the Japs, but there's still not a lot of enthusiasm about going after Hitler even though we've declared war on each other. Until Pearl, Roosevelt was a lot more worried about the Nazis than the Japs, but sometimes events go where they want to, not where you want them to."

"And you need the *Normandie* to be the German Pearl Harbor."

"Um, well, Meyer, I don't see it quite that way."

That is exactly how he sees it.

"It's really about security, first and foremost," Haffenden added.

"But sometimes there are twin agendas, two sides."

"That's true."

"Don't get me wrong. I believe what you're telling me, but . . . there's part of me that wonders why you're telling *me* these things when the army practically threw me into the street when I tried to join up."

Meyer thought Haffenden's face reddened a little. "Because, Meyer, I may be the worst negotiator in the world, but I'm under the gun." Haffenden held up his hands as if he were surrendering. "Just like you have to gamble in your business to chalk up a win, I need to gamble, too. I knew by your reputation that you were a very different man than the ones I met on Pier Eighty-eight. Still, I don't know you, and real trust takes real time to establish. I know about men in your world and what you're capable of. I'm not thrilled that I have to be here, maybe any more than you're thrilled to be here with me. But if I told you nothing of value, you wouldn't feel valuable. I need you to feel valuable. If that means you go back and tell your friends what we talked about and laugh about what a jackass I am, then I lost my bet. But I'll tell you something: I'll go right down the line and do the same thing again until I find the right man. It's not just our fleet I'm worried about. The port of New York is like the digestive tract for all America; you choke it off, we all die. . . . Do you know that dreadnought, the *Arizona*?"

"The one that went down at Pearl Harbor?" Meyer asked.

"Yes. Would you like to know who personally ordered the construction of that ship, right here at the Brooklyn yards, and who christened it? A young assistant secretary of the navy named Franklin D. Roosevelt. Do you see where I'm going with this?"

Meyer looked at Polakoff, who had not heard this before either. So Meyer said to Haffenden, "You're telling me that not only do you have Hitler on your back, you have Roosevelt's thumbs in your borscht."

"I'm under tremendous pressure to produce results. In the end, a war criminal is just an officer who had the bad luck to lose when the world was watching. Roosevelt is wise to the kind of bastards we're up against. Back in his navy days, some socialist who was against the First World War tried to bomb his house, but the bomber ended up blowing his own head off."

Haffenden said he was put in charge of a special navy unit to deal with waterfront sabotage called B-3. Meyer thought what Haffenden said about war criminals was interesting. Then Haffenden told him about what had happened to the men who were "held responsible" for Pearl Harbor, and he wasn't referring to the Japanese. He was thinking about Kimmel, the admiral who had been in charge of the Pacific. And Chief of Naval Operations Stark. Stark had personally called Roosevelt with the news about Pearl Harbor. Demoted.

Held responsible. Meyer couldn't believe the use of that term. Weren't the enemies responsible? He was pretty good at spotting a con, and his gut told him this Haffenden fellow really had his tit in the wringer. That red in his face wasn't anger. He had some health problems, too.

Meyer was getting excited. He felt bad that the army wouldn't take him, but this thing seemed like a big opportunity for a whole lot of reasons.

"Commander, please help me out with something," Meyer said. "What do you think spies on the docks are actually doing?"

"The Germans are getting information about our convoys and fuel somehow," Haffenden said. "B-3, which is the secret unit I work for, is operating on a theory that some of the men who ran liquor during Prohibition might be running fuel—and maybe information—to the Nazis. We also believe based upon where the attacks are occurring and some of the disinformation we've put out that the U-boats are being directed by a Nazi agent in America that the Germans have code-named Brahms."

"Like the composer?" Meyer said.

"Right, presumably because he puts American ships to sleep, you know, like the lullaby."

"Yes, I understood that."

Haffenden continued, "We're especially worried about the Italians who . . . well, may be more loyal to Mussolini than the United States. What does a bootlegger do for a living when his stills dry up?"

"I've never heard such a thing," Meyer said. "Bootleggers running fuel—"

"Is this the kind of thing that would come to your attention?"

"I used to be in the liquor business, Commander, so I hear things from time to time about my old associates. Some have stayed in the liquor business. Others opened automobile dealerships. Running fuel to Nazis in the middle of the ocean? That's a dangerous enterprise, a long bet, which would yield bubkes of a payout."

"Bubkes?" Haffenden asked.

"It means 'beans' or 'nothing' in Yiddish. In other words, lousy odds for chump change. The Italians don't like to do a great deal of work for such an unreliable return, and the Jews? For one thing, you're talking about *Nazis.* For another, my people aren't counting on God to part the sea twice for them."

Haffenden roared. Meyer didn't mean it to be funny, but Haffenden's warm reaction made him feel comfortable.

"You make a persuasive argument, Meyer. Even if I'm wrong, we still think Hitler is getting help from somebody on those docks, and we need help."

"Were you wearing that uniform when you were looking for cooperation?" Polakoff asked.

"Yes, I was."

"That's part of your problem right there," Meyer said. "See, Commander, these guys have been running from men in uniforms from the time they were in grade school. The thing about being them is that *everybody really is out to get them.* That's why I'm trying to get out of certain businesses."

"If we weren't under so much pressure with the *Normandie,* we might have been more subtle," Haffenden said. "But the whip is cracking on us from the top."

"Moe told me you talked to Cockeye Dunn and Socks Lanza."

"And they told me to take a walk off the pier." Haffenden gave the details.

Meyer thought for a moment. "I know Socks. I met Cockeye years ago. He was with Schultz, who wasn't my kind of fellow."

"*Dutch* Schultz?" Haffenden asked.

Meyer said yes.

"What do you make of Socks?" Haffenden asked. "I'm told he's the boss of the Fulton Fish Market."

"Maybe he is. Maybe he isn't," Meyer said. "Just because you're the boss of one store, it doesn't mean you're the boss of every shop on the block."

"If I could cut to the quick, Meyer, our partners in law enforcement tell us that the Mafia controls the docks. We thought if we could get the support of its leaders, we might be able to make inroads to stop this sabotage. Given what's happening to the Jewish people in Eastern Europe, and given the desire of Italians to demonstrate their loyalty to the United States, we thought you could help."

Meyer shot Polakoff a glance immediately when he heard the word *Mafia.* Polakoff shuddered. Haffenden saw it, too. He thought he had blown it, which he would have if he had been talking to an Italian. They thought that word, *Mafia,* was a slur because it described a feudal system from the old country. The Jews didn't have a system like that. The Jewish mob guys were just trying to make enough dough to buy a house in Scarsdale and send their kids to good colleges. *First get on, then get honest,* Meyer liked to say.

Meyer finished his coffee. Collecting his thoughts. Buying time.

"There are a few things that I think are important for the navy to understand, Commander," Meyer began. "For one thing, there is no Mafia. It's a *bubbameisah,* a spook story to insult immigrants, especially Italians. Believe me, those men you met on the waterfront don't take to organization. I'm not going to insult your intelligence and tell you they're choirboys, but don't think of this ragtag band as you might a corporation or the Salvation Army. They are independent operators that form and break apart as self-interest demands."

"Is this your way of saying that Socks Lanza has no boss?" Haffenden asked.

"To say that a man is Socks's boss would be to say there is a corporation he works for. There is no corporation—this Mafia. But there is a man Socks respects—kind of a symbol for these fellows—and this man he respects is one of my closest friends."

"Do you think he's somebody you can talk to?"

Meyer hesitated. "A question for you, Commander. What do you make of these stories about rounding up Jews and sending them to working camps? What do they have them do there?"

"We don't know for sure, Meyer, but things are very bad in Poland, near Russia. We've heard reports about Nazi commandos killing lots of Jews."

"Killing? Not just putting them to work like in prison?"

"The stories are very bad. I wish I had something better to tell you."

"I'm from the Polish-Russian border. These could be my relatives."

"I'm sorry, Meyer."

"What are we doing to try to get at these Jews?"

"We're putting together forces to go after Hitler. That's why I'm here."

Meyer was less than encouraged. "One final question, Commander. If a man was able to help you, would you call him a patriot?"

Meyer could tell that Haffenden was not expecting this question. He looked around the restaurant before he spoke as if a busboy had the answer.

"Yes, I think a man who helped keep America safe would be a patriot," Haffenden said.

"Did you get any patriotism from Cockeye or Socks?" Meyer asked.

"More from Lanza. Cockeye's a real hard case."

Meyer explained, "Yes, but he's also a businessman who has a good reason to fear men in uniform who don't approve of how he makes his living. He's rough, but not impossible to motivate."

"What motivates these guys, Meyer?"

"Nobody wants to feel like a second-class jerk. They sure as hell don't want to feel like snitches."

"You wouldn't think they were patriots from my encounter on the docks. They think I'm the enemy," Haffenden said.

"That's a jungle instinct, but I understand it," Meyer explained. "The thing is, you've got to reframe this thing, reframe the snitch. See, if the men on the docks think they're talking to you, and they think you're the police, they'll feel like snitches, and then you're screwed. If they think they're talking to *us,* and that we're trying to *find* the snitch, well, then you've got an army."

Meyer had Haffenden's attention. "One more thing, Meyer. The identity of Lanza's boss . . . no, not boss, but rather this man Lanza respects. Your old friend. I assume that wouldn't be Albert Anastasia? I've been told to avoid him at all costs."

"Albert would be a big problem," Meyer said.

"More than that. To be frank, my people say he's a homicidal maniac."

This was completely true, but Meyer saw no benefit to conceding it. "He's a teddy bear, but a little unpredictable."

"So, who is this man Lanza respects?"

"That would be Charlie Luciano."

"*Lucky* Luciano?"

Meyer nodded, knowing that Haffenden was just pretending to be surprised.

"Isn't he in prison?" Haffenden asked.

"Framed," Meyer said.

"Oh, I'm certain that he was. Can you talk to him?"

"Sure, but I'm not your problem. I'll help you, it's patriotism. Poor Charlie's up in Dannemora doing thirty-to-fifty. There's a reason they call it Siberia. What's in it for him?"

"Well, I can't just go up there and set him free."

"No," Meyer said. "But you're asking me to make an unusual request, which I'm happy to do. You've got a man in prison—probably for the rest of his life. He's a tough man but, at this stage, bitter. I'll talk to Charlie, I'll even beg him if you want, but you never go to a Sicilian empty-handed."

"Do you have anything in mind?"

"Moe and I can bring him a spread of deli food, Italian sausage, and cannoli. I'd also like to bring a gift from you—goodwill."

Haffenden laughed. "Is it something I can order from Sears Roebuck?"

"This thing isn't in the catalog. Can you get him out of Siberia?"

"Somewhere more civilized," Polakoff said. "A little hope would go a long way."

"You really think this business about Luciano being a . . . symbol . . . that it's so important? How symbolic can a man be in prison?"

"Real symbolic," Meyer and Polakoff said at the same time.

Siberia

A DARK PADDY WAGON ARRIVED AT GREAT MEADOW PRISON IN Comstock, New York, at five o'clock in the morning. Nine prisoners had been awakened shortly after midnight in their cells at the Clinton Correctional Facility in Dannemora, New York, close to the Canadian border. The raw chill of the region gave Dannemora its nickname: Siberia. The prisoners had been handed boxes to pack their belongings and told to be ready for transfer in an hour.

In the rear of the paddy wagon, where they had been chained to steel benches—and to each other—the men questioned each other about what the hell might be going on. They expected inmate #92168, who had been working in the laundry in Siberia since his incarceration in 1936 on sixty-two vice counts, would have some answers, but he didn't. This inmate was not eligible for parole until 1956, which had given him plenty of time to think about his crimes in the sixteen hours each day that he was confined alone to his small cell. He kept coming up with the same conclusion: He had been framed by Prosecutor Dewey and a whore.

Meyer always had to hand it to #92168: He was a master of making the best of situations where most men would have given up.

Salvatore Lucania was born in 1897 in Lercara Friddi, Sicily, and came to America at the age of nine. He became an industrious street rat with a weakness for dealing in narcotics. One day when they were still in their teens, Lucania tried to shake Meyer down for money. He thought the Jewish boy would be an easy mark because of his size. Meyer told him to go fuck himself; then he asked Lucania to give him *his* money. Lucania laughed at Meyer and asked for the money again. Meyer told him to take his protection money and shove it up his guinea ass.

To normal kids, these would have been bad memories, but not to them. It was the beginning of a marvelous partnership. Soon, the "guinea" changed his name from Salvatore Lucania to Charles Luciano. Meyer shortened his from Suchowljanski to Lansky.

Luciano was still a legend, even in jail. A long time ago, he and Meyer moved aside some old Sicilians and put in a new system where the aim was making money, not discriminating by ethnicity. It wasn't always easy. One time, Luciano was kidnapped and knifed in the face. He walked away with a scar and a droopy eye, which became his trademark. This only made guys in his world respect him more, and it was when people started calling him Lucky because he'd survived it.

Luciano was a tough customer, but prison eats away at any man. Meyer couldn't imagine what Luciano must have been thinking when he was moved. Knowing Luciano, he was thinking, *Christ, they're gonna throw me in the electric chair.* Haffenden didn't screw around, Meyer thought. You never knew with government guys, when they started telling you secrets like you were old pals. But damned if they didn't move Luciano to a nicer place fast. It was a good thing, too, because Luciano was like Meyer—not a man who wanted to hear about good intentions. In their life, they didn't think any good would ever happen, so they weren't into hope, faith, and positive thinking.

When Polakoff got the call that Luciano had been moved, Meyer sent out one of the office girls to get food, then the two men drove up to Great Meadow. Warden Morhous set Meyer and Polakoff up in his meeting room. His secretary put their Manhattan spread out on the table. Smoked salmon, Italian sausage, an assortment of breads and cheeses, blintzes, and cannoli.

A few minutes later, the warden brought Luciano in. Meyer could see his senses were scrambled. There was no way he didn't smell this food from a thousand yards.

"Meyer?" Luciano said like a kid that snuck downstairs to take an illicit peek at the family Christmas gifts.

"You want the pumpernickel or rye?" Meyer asked casually. "Make up your mind. I don't got all day."

"What da fuck's goin' on here?" Luciano said, bewildered.

Meyer walked over to Luciano, who lifted his friend in the air.

"I been goin' nuts wit all dis comin' and goin'!" Luciano said. That's how he talked. One difference between the two mobsters was that Luciano never tried to improve his speech, just his clothing. Meyer liked good clothing, too, but he also studied vocabulary and proper speech.

"Ya gotta tell me what dis is all about," Luciano said.

Meyer pointed behind Luciano, who turned around and saw Polakoff.

"Jesus, Moe, what da hell?"

Luciano hugged Polakoff, and they all sat down. Luciano helped himself to some of the food on the table. A good start.

"You look good, Charlie," Meyer said. "A little thinner, a little gray up there."

With his mouth filled with food, Luciano said, "Ya don't got no gray, Meyer."

"I'm gray on the inside."

They all laughed.

"Let me tell you what this is all about," Meyer started. "So, Charlie, you know how we've got a war on?"

"Yeah, I read somethin' about it," the prisoner said mischievously.

"Did you read anything about all the ships being sunk near New York?"

"Just about a cruise ship. Read dat."

"Well, that's just one," Meyer said. "Anyhow, Charlie, it's the Nazis."

"Nazis?" Luciano said, his teeth grinding down on a thin slice of pastrami on pumpernickel. "It was prolly one-a our guys doin' it for the insurance."

"Don't event joke about that, Charlie! That's all we need people to think."

Luciano studied Meyer for a second, then shrugged. Meyer didn't like it.

"Anyhow, it was probably Nazis," Meyer reiterated.

"Get da fuck outta here! *Nazis?* In New York? Dat ain't right."

Polakoff said, "Charlie, the navy needs your help on the waterfront."

"Yeah?" he said as if it were a joke.

Meyer said, "They're not getting cooperation from some of our friends on the docks. They figure if they know you want them to cooperate, they will."

Polakoff stood up and said, "I'll let the two of you catch up. I'll come back when you're through."

"Thanks, Moe," Luciano said as Polakoff left. "Meyer, what can I do from my jail cell? I been gone a while, but guys like us don't shine to helpin' out da goverrmen."

"Not normally, no. But this is patriotism. See, we're talking about fighting Hitler, Charlie."

"I don't like da prick either, but what am I gonna do about it? And why da hell would I wanna help da goverrnmen given how dey framed me up wit dose whores?"

"I got to thinking," Meyer said. "Maybe if some of our friends thought you were getting out of Siberia, they'd want to help with the war effort. If they thought you're away forever, they may not want to help. But if they thought you'd be getting out, they wouldn't want Charlie Lucky upset."

"Ya know somethin' I dunno about me gettin' out?"

"For one thing, you're not in Siberia anymore, you're in Great Meadow. Step in the right direction. I told the navy that you needed some incentive, which is why you're here now. Besides patriotism, of course."

"A course, but here ain't free, Meyer."

"No, but it's goodwill. If you help the government, you'll have more chits."

"More chits, huh? I don't trust dese goverrmen pricks."

"Neither do I, Charlie, but it's not about trust, it's about leverage. The deeper we're into them, the more we can ask for."

"What, I help out wit dis, Dewey'll drop me off at Times Square in his Chrysler?"

"One step at a time, you follow?"

"Yeah, Meyer, I folla. Whose da guys on da docks dese days? Still Socks?"

"Yes, Socks. Cockeye Dunn, too."

"Whew, Cockeye. Forgot about him. He'll shoot ya for sport."

"Socks and Cockeye gave the navy guys attitude. The navy guy asked them about their patriotism."

"Cockeye knife 'em?" Luciano asked with a smirk.

"With his eyes, yeah."

"Did da navy talk to Anastasia?" Luciano smirked.

"No, thank God, they don't want him anywhere around this."

"He'll prolly ask me about it. Albert comes up here every now and then."

Luciano and Anastasia were a deadly mix. Anastasia brought out the gangster in Luciano. Meyer brought out the capitalist in him.

"Well, for Christ's sake," Meyer said, "don't say anything to Albert about this. See, Charlie, there's a problem with the Italians, which is driving this. The navy wants to know who they're with, you read me? America? Mussolini?"

"Lotta our guys like Mussolini, Meyer."

"What does that get 'em?"

"Don't matter what it gets 'em. It's the old country. It's blood."

"That doesn't get Italians a break from the Feds."

"Ya think da Feds'll ever give our guys a break? Roosevelt don't even remember all dat help we got fer him in New York in the ole days. Nobody knows better den you; you were da guy his man reached out fer."

"What do we have to lose?" Meyer asked.

"Easy fer you to say. I unnerstand what's goin' on wit da Yids over dere wit Hitler, but it ain't easy to sell Italians on Mussolini bein' some butcher. Besides, before dey locked me up, Moe tole me dey might send me back to Italy. I start goin' around doin' dirt to Mussolini, what's dat get me?"

"Look, Charlie, I follow. It's not like I'm asking you to come to some big rally. I want to hook you up with some of our old friends. Bring some of the Italians up here even. They want your blessing so they can crack down on the docks, make sure they know traitors aren't kosher. I'm worried what'll happen if Italians don't play ball with the navy. There's all kinds of noises about cracking down on Japs in America. And, who knows, maybe we'll get a pass on some of our other business."

"Dey tell ya dat?"

"Nobody proposed an exact deal, no," Meyer said. "But, when you've got business with somebody, you don't want that business disturbed. Like during Prohibition. The politicians that came to our speakeasies didn't want to bust us up. But this here with the docks is a hell of a chance."

Luciano leaned in toward Meyer. "Meyer, you was never a guy to troll around wit da broads, ya know? But if you was, you'd know dat ya don't pay a whore to screw ya, ya pay her to get lost. See what I'm sayin'? What are dese pricks gonna do wit us when dey're done wit us?"

"I see what you're saying, Charlie. The best thing we can do is be useful. Every man hits a point when he's not useful anymore, and all he can do is try to save a nest egg so he can fade away and have a quiet life when that time comes."

"In our business, we don't get to fade away," Luciano said. "And dose bundles a cash can't stop rollin' in or . . . ya know, we all got problems."

"I know, Charlie. What can I say? I'm going to do all I can to get you out of here."

"No matter how much we do, Meyer, dey'll say it wasn't enough."

"There will have to be a punishment to the government if they screw us."

"Right. Figger dat dey'll try to fuck us into da cost a services."

"Listen to you. Henry Ford I got here," Meyer said.

"I don't need to run no automobile company, Meyer. I'd give anything just to drive again."

The Ferret Squad

Socks Lanza didn't wear a jacket a lot, and it showed. He looked like a gorilla. He wasn't a dummy, but it was hard to get past his appearance. With a coat and tie, he looked like a fat kid in church whose mother told him to dress up for mass. He agreed to meet Meyer at the Hotel Astor in a lounge on the mezzanine level. If this meeting went well, Meyer would introduce Socks to Haffenden.

"I just got back from Albany. Spent some time with Charlie," Meyer said.

"Charlie?" Socks said. "Thought he was up near Canada, Meyer."

"We got him moved somewhere nicer."

"No shit?"

"We're working on a few things. Hopefully, we'll get him out one of these days," Meyer said.

"What are you workin' on?"

"A navy commander told me he sent some of his men to the docks. They were hoping to get some help watching for German spies they say are passing information to the Nazis who are sinking American ships."

"That's what the guy said to me, too."

"Charlie and I were talking. We need you to help out,

cooperate with them. The new district attorney, Hogan, and his man Gurfein, know what's going on. It'll really help out Charlie and set us right with the government."

"Does Albert know about this thing?" Socks asked. Anastasia.

"No. You know how Albert is. When you're a hammer, the whole world's a nail. This kind of thing isn't Albert's strength. It's low-key, not head-banging. The navy doesn't want him involved."

"What are we supposed to do, Meyer?"

"Look around for funny business, Socks. Maybe take some guys that may be a little odd out for drinks, see if they'll say anything."

"What if we find them spies?"

"Let me know."

"The docks get slippery." Socks shrugged. "People fall inna the drink sometimes. Like little fishes."

"What if they're bigger fishes?"

"You sayin' there are big Nazis here in New York?"

"Enough to help Hitler sink a couple hundred American ships," Meyer said.

"That many?"

Meyer nodded yes.

"That ain't right," Socks said.

Meyer nodded no.

"I'll ferret out whatever I can," said Socks. "But, so you know, I'm facing my own beef."

"What kind of beef?"

"They got me on an extortion and labor-fraud beef. I got parole for now."

Meyer asked, "For how long?"

"Dunno. You think if I help out on this, the judge will take a nap on my pinch? Like maybe Charlie'll get a break?"

"Maybe, but I don't know, Socks. I know that if we *don't* help out, it won't do you any good."

"May help though, right?"

"Sure couldn't hurt, Socks."

"No, couldn't hurt."

⁂

"I like the sound of that," Haffenden said when Meyer told him what Socks had said. They were at Haffenden's offices on Church Street.

"Sound of what, Commander?" Meyer asked.

"*Ferret.* I like the word. I think that's what I'll call our merry band—the ferret squad."

"You can call us the flying schlemiels if you want, as long as we do what we have to do for each other."

"Understood. Do you think Socks is against Mussolini?"

"No, I think he's against human beings," Meyer said.

Haffenden laughed a little. "So, do you think you'll be able to devote some real time to this effort?"

"Commander, I tried to join the army, didn't I? What does that show you about my commitment. I would have had to leave my business and my family—and maybe got killed—if they took me, right?"

"Right. Of course. Now, this Socks fellow . . . do you think he'll do something violent?"

"He's not a complicated guy, Commander, but he's been running things down at the Fish Market for years, so he's got some leadership in him on top of whatever else he is."

"Good, Meyer." Haffenden breathed in slight relief. "Outside of Hitler and Mussolini, we're not trying to hurt anybody."

"Of course not."

Lansky Condominium Balcony

Second Floor, Imperial House, Miami Beach, December 1982

"IS YOUR HAND GETTING A CRAMP FROM ALL THAT WRITING, JONAH?" Uncle Meyer asked me.

It was, but I fibbed, "No, I'm fine."

Bruzzer jumped up on his lap. Uncle Meyer brightened for a moment, then tugged at his neck.

"Do you want to rest?" I asked.

"I'll have forever to rest soon enough."

I wasn't sure how to respond to a comment so enormous, so I said, "This is an unbelievable story."

"What's unbelievable?"

"How poorly prepared we—the United States—were for the war."

Uncle Meyer shook his head. "America wasn't prepared, but I was." He wasn't kidding either. "Roosevelt was a great man. He knew we weren't prepared for the *first* World War, so he had all those dreadnoughts built when he was at the navy department. He knew we weren't ready for Japan or Hitler, but—and people now don't realize this—there was a lot of isolationist feeling in the country at that time. Charles Lindbergh, that Nazi lover, and all. Nobody here knew about the killing camps at the outset. Now we look back and think it was obvious that we had to deal with Hitler, but not then.

America's a big island, Jonah. That's a blessing because we're not surrounded by enemies. People didn't think it was their war, and you can't get people who don't feel scared to prepare. Why prepare? Nothing's going to happen to us. When the government can't get the people that need to be got, they get the people they can get. Your grandfather understands that, believe me."

"Let me make sure I understand something," I said. "This navy man, Haffenden, came to you. He said he needed your help, and you started on this path to help him."

"That's right."

I wasn't sure how I was going to word my next question, so after a few awkward windups, I just asked, "Why?"

"Why what?"

"Why help the navy? Why help America? All the government ever did to you, and my grandfather for that matter, is . . . you know . . . try to put you in jail."

Uncle Meyer narrowed his eyes at me. My heart jumped in my chest. This was not a man who was used to being asked questions, and I had to remind myself that I wasn't talking with my own grandfather. While Mickey was Uncle Meyer's doppelgänger, Mickey was also the man who raised me after my parents died, and who had gotten used to adolescent flintiness. I didn't imagine that Uncle Meyer had played such a role with his own children, at least not for many years.

He put Bruzzer down and leaned into me at the small table. My heart was still skipping. Something about his eyes. Not the eyes of your typical Miami Beach retiree. Everything else about Uncle Meyer's appearance bespoke the garden-variety *alter kocker*, but not his eyes. Gangster lamps. Eyes that had seen the blood spatter that had emanated from his orders and not blinked.

"Why help America? Is that what you're asking?" Uncle

Meyer said. "More than anything else, I wanted to be an American." His voice echoed against the concrete. "More than anything. It's why I tried to enlist in the army. It's why I registered as a U.S. citizen. Charlie Luciano didn't, which is one reason why he ended up the way he did. I thought I was more of an American than some of those blue bloods who bought my liquor, but kept me out of their country clubs!

"Another thing, Jonah. During that time, I had some good things going in the music business, distributing Wurlitzer jukeboxes. I also started buying land. These were legitimate businesses. Before the war I had committed myself to these kinds of things, but when the navy came around, I knew that I couldn't pursue everything I wanted to. I had to stay in certain things to stay close to certain types of men, men that needed to appreciate me, if you follow. To them, these legitimate ventures were what they called fronts, but to me they were the future. But, there's a saying, 'You can't dance at every wedding.' I couldn't do everything.

"And Hitler? He wiped out the town I was from. The whole town. I didn't know it for sure at that time, but the news kept pointing in that direction. I wasn't a very good Jew in many ways, but one thing I could do that these little yeshiva students couldn't do was fight."

Uncle Meyer was breathing hard now.

"Can I get you some water?" I asked.

"No, you stay sitting there. I just need to catch my breath a minute."

I sat for what seemed like forever, scribbling in the notebook.

When Uncle Meyer had composed himself again, he said, "I was very impressed with Commander Haffenden. I was not a man who was used to working for people. Hadn't in a long time. But something about Haffenden made me believe he was a great man. He had real *baytzim*. I didn't know how much he risked by coming to me until later, but he risked everything. The navy brass didn't want to touch men in my world, but they wanted the benefits of our services. Not Rad Haffenden. He got things done. And if you find a statue of this man anywhere, you let me know. But you won't. And he knew I was taking a risk, too."

"What did you see as being your risk?"

"Jonah," Uncle Meyer said, much more calmly now. "Did Mickey ever talk to you about working with the Italians?"

"Sure."

"What do you know about that?"

"I know there was tension. Mickey once told me the reason why the Italians pushed out the Jews was the nicknames. The Italians had Scarface Al, Joe the Boss, Charlie the Blade. The Jews had Sol the Worrier, Morty the Procrastinator, and Hymie the Kvetch. How scary would it be to owe Morty the Procrastinator money and hear him tell you, 'I'm gonna break your kneecaps . . . if I get around to it'?"

Uncle Meyer laughed. "Mickey may have been onto something. Can you imagine Hymie the Kvetch? 'I'm the meanest killer on the whole block, but my prostate's acting up.' "

After his quip, Uncle Meyer frowned, as if he regretted his brief lurch into shtick. "Even though they were partners," I began again, "Mickey was worried about the Italians thinking the Jews were getting all the money."

Uncle Meyer nodded. "Good boy. This is the Jewish curse. One of them anyway. At that time, in the 1940s, the Italians were on their way up in my world. The Jewish boys, well, our best days, with bootlegging and everything, were behind us, which is why I wanted to get into music, land deals, and not as much, you know, with the gambling.

"I had to tread carefully with my partners. I was like what they now call a chief executive. I ran things like our gambling business, but I had shareholders. Shareholders who didn't send out proxies, or when they did, those proxies came bloody. Shareholders who killed people. What does this tell you, Jonah?"

"It tells me you had to get good results, I guess."

"Don't guess. That's right, I had to get good results. There was another thing: I had to be very aware that many of the Italians didn't want me there. They resented that the whole thing wasn't pure Italian.

"So the war comes along, and a lot of the Italians are thinking, 'This ain't our war. Let Hitler kill the Jews. Fuck 'em. What do we want to get *our* asses shot off for?' So now, what, they're going to want this Jew, who's making a fortune I might add—they're going to take orders from this Jew who's telling them to keep a lookout for agents of people they saw as their brothers? Remember, Jonah, a lot of these Italians felt discrimination from our government."

"But you must have been glad that Charlie Luciano came on board, right?"

Uncle Meyer gazed out beyond me, I supposed, toward the ocean, which was to my back. His mouth twisted for a split second. I didn't know if he had aborted a smile or not.

"You're in politics, Jonah. I read a story that when they woke Reagan up the morning of his inauguration, he pulled the covers over his head and said, 'Do I have to get up?'"

I laughed, but I didn't know why.

"Do you know why he did that?" Uncle Meyer asked.

I shook my head no.

"Because, Jonah, now he's riding the tiger. Now he has to deliver, because if he doesn't, his ass goes back to making *Bonzo* movies in California. But me? Me, Jonah? If I succeeded, I'm the magical Yid. Indispensable. But if I failed? If I fell off the tiger? If I didn't help the navy? If I didn't spring Charlie? They would have made me into *kasha varnishkes*!"

III.

B-3

I'll talk to anybody, a priest, a bank manager, a gangster, the devil himself, if I can get the information I need. This is a war. American lives are at stake. It's not a college game where we have to look up the rule book every minute. . . . I have a job to do.

—Lieutenant Commander Charles Radcliffe Haffenden,
Naval Intelligence Unit B-3

Off the Record

Some coincidences in life, even if you put them in a book of fiction, will get you hammered for being cartoonishly unrealistic. During World War II, Meyer Lansky's family lived in an apartment building called the Majestic at 115 Central Park West. He had two friends who also lived in that building. One was Frank Costello, who succeeded Luciano when he went to prison. The other was Walter Winchell.

People said Winchell was the second most powerful man in America, after President Roosevelt, and there they were, the Winchells and the Lanskys—neighbors. Between his newspaper columns and radio broadcasts, Winchell reached 50 million Americans regularly, one-third of the country. Winchell touched all levels of society. He was friendly with Roosevelt. He liked to entertain the president with celebrity gossip and gangster stories. Meyer thought it was odd how men himself were interested in men like Roosevelt, but men like Roosevelt were also interested in men like Meyer.

In the 1930s, Winchell, who was Jewish, used to tip Meyer off to German-American Bund rallies, which Meyer would disrupt. Winchell got good tips about Nazi sympathizers and liked to publish dirt on them. He'd get a scoop with photos, and Meyer would get to put some anti-Semites out of commission and bank a favor with Winchell. Meyer didn't want Winchell to know yet about his work with the navy, but thought they might be able to help each other again. You've got to start somewhere.

In those days, Meyer traveled a lot. After prosecutors put Luciano away and collared Lepke Buchalter and some others, Meyer knew he had to get out of New York whenever possible. Meyer's legitimate enterprises were largely on hold because he had to keep his gangland partners happy with a reliable flow of currency. He had gambling operations all over the country—"carpet joints"—in South Florida and upstate New York. The Dodge Park Kennel Club in Omaha. Even new places in Havana, Cuba. Because of his travel, Meyer hadn't seen Winchell for some time. Plus, the isolationist movement in New York had died off.

Meyer knew Winchell's schedule—they were both creatures of habit—so he made sure to be in the lobby of the Majestic one morning when he knew Winchell would be there. Winchell was right on time. The two men began walking around the block. Meyer needed to strike a balance between offering him a little something and not making him too curious.

"Walter, I've been getting some reports from fellows on the docks about the big cruise ship that went down and who might have been behind it."

"No kidding?" Winchell said. "What are you hearing?"

"Well, I wouldn't want this to make the papers. Not yet anyway."

"I understand. Are you hearing that the Nazis had a role in the *Normandie*?"

"We're hearing stories about German spies. The Italians are keeping their eyes peeled. They're worried that people might think they're not loyal, but they're motivated to do the right thing."

"I hear Vito Genovese is helping out Mussolini," Winchell

said, which made Meyer shudder. "Maybe the Italians *should* be worried about how they're perceived."

"Believe me, they are. Vito is the joker in the deck, not the whole deck."

"How do you think I can help, Meyer?"

"People tell you things, Walter. Sometimes those things make the paper. I'm looking for any information about Germans in New York, Germans that may be up to no good. I can't say what I'll do with it, only that if there's any newspaper value in it, you'll be the first to know."

Meyer was just stating the obvious. What he really wanted was to see if Winchell was still game to *get* information to use in his columns.

"I hear things from time to time. You know, Meyer, I'm sure you hear things from time to time that may be of value to me."

"Yes, I hear things from time to time."

The only thing Cockeye Dunn liked more than shivving a guy in a barroom brawl was bossing the hustle and bustle of the docks. Most racket guys were lazy, wanted something for nothing, but Cockeye was industrious. He couldn't keep still. Like a shark, he was moving all the time.

Cockeye sometimes stood at the edge of the pier waving ships—cargo, fishing, he wasn't particular—toward land, regulating their speed with hand gestures. Today, he helped a group of stevedores unload cargo containers. He didn't know what was in them, and he didn't care. His work ethic won him the support of the men he had gathered for a disinformation campaign that Haffenden wanted set in motion.

A dozen of Cockeye's boys stood in a semicircle around him.

"All right, fellas," Cockeye said, "our navy friends asked us if any of our guys might have an extra room at home or in the basement for their outta-town guys to stay with 'em. See, they're tryin' to get some guys to blend in with us, but they'll really be spyin' on Germans because they know where some German spies are at. You don't gotta answer now, but if you got some room for a couple-a months, lemme know. You folla?"

The men listened respectfully, but their body language said that an accommodation like this would be a pain in the ass, which was just what Cockeye had in mind.

Domestic Affairs

"WELL, MEYER, I WAS SITTING AT HOME LAST NIGHT AND THE PHONE rang," Haffenden said one day in March at a secret office he kept at the Hotel Astor. "My wife, Mary, got it. It was my boss, Captain McPhail. He said, 'They got some bathtub gin going to church.' "

Haffenden had just been told, in code, that Nazi U-boats had destroyed a cargo of fuel crossing the Atlantic to aid the British. McPhail had roughed him up, saying, "I thought you had your boys in place."

Haffenden said, "So I told him we just got started, for Chrissakes. Miracles take time."

McPhail told Haffenden that he didn't have time.

Haffenden was under the gun. Socks and Cockeye had put the word out to their men to keep their eyes peeled for Nazi spies. They hadn't caught any yet, but maybe just getting talk going would scare some bad elements away. Losses in the Atlantic in the early spring of 1942 were still pretty bad.

"Commander," Meyer asked, "do you think there are other ways the Germans could be getting information about our convoys?"

Haffenden breathed in pretty deep and his face got red. Meyer wanted to ask him if he saw a doctor. Meyer was very self-conscious about health matters, and he thought Haffenden had a problem with his blood pressure. But Meyer had to be careful because he didn't know how Haffenden would take a question like that from a person he was just getting to know.

"Of course, Meyer. It's not like we have direct evidence that the leaks are all coming from the docks."

"What does Captain McPhail think?"

"Oscar's getting beaten up by Secretary Knox, who's getting his ass chewed off by President Roosevelt. Oscar was ready to retire until Pearl Harbor. He was all ready to fix up his house in La Jolla when they asked him to stay on. He's not a kid, you know. So now, in the twilight of his career, instead of going out as a great skipper from the last war, he's getting treated like all these shipwrecks are his fault."

"There's a lesson in that, no, Commander?"

"How so, Meyer?"

"Know when to get out. That's the lesson. Like Henny Youngman knows when to take a bow."

"Well, it's too late for McPhail to take that bow."

"I'm doing all I can, Commander," I assured him. "Socks and Cockeye are taking this very seriously."

Commander Haffenden reached into his drawer, shook an aspirin from a small glass bottle, and washed it down with a glass of water. "Meyer, anything you can do to bring me a moose head for McPhail's wall would be greatly appreciated."

Meyer woke up with a start on his living room sofa in his family's apartment on the third floor of the Majestic. Things at home were bad.

Meyer's twelve-year-old son, Buddy, was born with cerebral palsy. His younger son, Paul, was away at a military academy. His wife, Anne, well, it was hard to say what you would call her. In those days people just said somebody was meshuga or sick in the head. She blamed Meyer's business as a *schande*—a "shame" or "scandal" in Yiddish—that put a curse on their family.

Anne was standing above Meyer, and she dumped an armful of his suits and the *Z* volume of the *Encyclopaedia Britannica* on him. It was hard for him to imagine that he had ever found her to be beautiful, her strong features having morphed from being darkly bewitching to dark and witchy.

"Get the hell out of my house!" she yelled.

The fury boiled up inside him. It never ended with her. "What the hell is it now?"

"You know what now! *Everything* now!"

"What the hell does that mean?"

"It means go rob a bank, Jesse James!"

There was no talking with this woman. The idea of destroying his family was giving him trouble with his stomach, but he saw no way to save the situation. He was a problem solver, but he could only solve problems with a rational person. Here he was, lying on the couch with his clothes dumped on him by a madwoman. The hard thing to realize in life is that you just can't do business with some people. And you can't have some people in your life even if that idea goes against everything you believe. Anne probably felt that way about Meyer, too.

Buddy hobbled in on his crutches, his twisted legs dragging along the floor behind him.

"What's happening?" he asked, shaken.

Meyer glared at the poor kid as if the latest eruption were his fault. "Go back to your room!" he hollered.

"Only a legitimate businessman can yell at that boy!" Anne said, raising her fists.

Arnie Matthews was asked to stay after hours at Cockeye Dunn's dockside office. This was not an unusual request. Sometimes Cockeye or Socks Lanza had ambitious fishing crews that stayed out late because there were fewer competitors. Other times, Cockeye had other things going that were better done in the dark.

Matthews was one of the men Cockeye had asked a few weeks earlier to spare a mattress for a navy man. Of the dozen men Cockeye had approached, only two of them took the bait and volunteered. Matthews and the other longshoreman that stepped up didn't know it, but the men Haffenden had assigned to live with them were countersurveillance specialists; their mission was to see if they were being followed by German agents.

Matthews stood outside Cockeye's office alone, waiting for orders. When no one came, he started looking for Cockeye in his office and then in a workshop nearby. When he opened the door to the workshop, he heard a whoosh, then felt Cockeye's favorite crowbar strike him simultaneously in the gut and in the ribs, cracking two of them.

Matthews collapsed in shock, gasping on the grease-stained concrete floor, then was brought to his feet by two huge stevedores who dragged him out of the darkness to the foot of the closest pier. He could see almost nothing until he was right up against the river. That's when he spotted the two wooden flowerpots filled with some kind of mush.

Cockeye came out of the mist and nodded to the stevedores holding Matthews. They kicked their prisoner's legs so his feet stepped into the flowerpots. When Matthews felt the goop around his feet, he pissed himself because he knew now that he was standing in half-dried concrete. The pain in his stomach and ribs were footnotes now.

"What?" Matthews muttered, finding his balance.

"What nuthin'," Cockeye said as the hulking men let go of Matthews. "You been played, rat."

"What are you talking about?" Matthews groaned.

"The navy man living with you got followed by some Nazi spies. It's like they was tipped off a navy guy would be stayin' with you."

"I, I—"

"Ah, don't gimme that shit," Cockeye barked. "The navy got spies that followed you to Yorkville, meetin' with some of those Bund sympathizers that are startin' up again. You let 'em know you had a navy guy stayin' with you."

"I don't know—"

Cockeye belted Matthews in the face, the sharp edges of the keys sticking out between his fingers, puncturing the skin of Matthews's cheek. Matthews doubled over, his hands scraping against the concrete squishing around his shoes.

"I'm gonna make this the simplest thing your dumb ass ever done in his life: You tell me who your German friends are in Yorkville and we get you outta them shoes. You make pretend you don't know nuthin' one more time, you're getting' wet, permanent."

A few weeks after speaking to Walter Winchell, Meyer told the doorman in their building he wanted to see Winchell. The doorman said Winchell would be in the lobby of their building at eight that evening. He usually stayed out later than that when he was holding court at the Stork Club. Both men thought it foolish to meet in so public a place. Meyer got to their lobby a few minutes early and read the paper. A lot was in there about when and where America would first engage the Germans.

Winchell was always prompt. He came in from the street at eight on the nose. The two men shook hands and sat down.

"I've come into some information," Meyer said.

"I'm all ears."

"An American man loyal to the Nazis is giving a speech at a gymnasium in Yorkville next week."

"An American loyal to Hitler, these days?" Winchell asked.

"Believe it or not."

"Does this guy have brain damage?"

"I'm not sure, Walter. The guy we talked to thinks it's a recruiting mission."

"Recruiting for what?"

"I wish I could tell you," Meyer said. "I think the Germans are trying to get new people to help make more trouble here in America. You know how it is with termites: You think you killed them all, but you move a box in the attic and a whole bunch more crawl out."

"What's this bastard's name?"

"Willie Bauer."

"Willie Bauer," Winchell repeated, writing it down. "What happens next?"

"I was just thinking how during these times it might be nice for the public to see Americans taking action here on the home front."

"Patriotism is important."

Muscle was important, too, Meyer thought. It wouldn't be easy getting Italians for this. Besides, Meyer had plenty of Yids who would like to take a crack at these Nazi pricks. Winchell wanted what Winchell always wanted: a scoop. Meyer saw things a little differently. He would try to get Winchell his story, but what Meyer really needed was information that would be of use to Haffenden. The boys would have to lean on these Bund mutts for that kind of thing.

Meyer knew his limitations, which was why he had had a partner from the time he was twelve years old. Which was why he had Bugsy Siegel.

Hooray for Hollywood

MEYER DID WHAT HE ALWAYS DID WHEN HE HAD A SITUATION OUT OF his control such as his home life: Found a situation he *could* control. Improved himself. Built something. He had no patience for these weak-willed immigrant Jews he'd see schlepping down Grand Street whining, "America, ganef!"—America the thief—as if this country owed them something. *Deserve,* he thought; *who deserves anything?* His father was a man like this, a full-time victim who always had an excuse for his failure. Couldn't wait to list the reasons why his family lived in squalor. The kind of lemming that would have climbed into a cattle car when Hitler shouted, "All aboard!"

That won't be me, Meyer told himself.

Meyer sat at his favorite table in the back room at Ratner's delicatessen and restaurant. He had one of their famous onion rolls. Even though he always ordered the same thing, he glanced through the menu to see if the management had decided to serve the pastrami he loved. Being a "dairy" restaurant, Ratner's sold certain types of fish, but not red meats.

Meyer considered reaching for a second onion roll. He thought of himself as a man of great discipline, which was true, he supposed, in certain areas. He was strict about his diet, and personal and financial self-control. But he was a three-pack-a-day smoker. All men fooled themselves sometimes as to who they were.

As he thought about that second roll, Meyer saw the heads of the other patrons swivel toward the main entrance. Then came the hushed chatter. *Well, here we go. We've all got something we can't control.*

This is what always happened when Bugsy Siegel came into any place, the hubbub. Meyer favored back rooms for a reason. He didn't like drawing attention, and Siegel always drew attention.

Siegel was jaw-droppingly good-looking. He actually glowed. Tall for a Jewish boy of their generation, Siegel looked like a matinee idol with bright blue eyes and dark hair swept back from a side part. Meyer was furious when he heard Siegel was trying to get himself cast in motion pictures after he moved to Los Angeles full-time in 1941.

Meyer had encouraged Siegel to move out West. People said he was sent there to expand the mob's business, but Meyer just wanted Siegel out of New York because he drew heat, and Meyer didn't want to be that close to the bull's-eye. As he told Siegel after Charlie Luciano's prosecution, if the government wanted you bad enough, they'd get you even if they had to frame you. A Bugsy out West was a Bugsy not in New York.

Siegel was what Meyer's mother used to call a *vilde chaya*, a "wild animal" in Yiddish. How many times had Meyer tried to teach Siegel the laws of the universe? How their business and celebrity didn't mix. How, when the authorities thought the racket guys were having too much fun, they cooked up a pinch. How what goes around comes around. How, when the Yids looked too strong, the guineas resented it. Always make the guineas feel like you respect their muscle. Let them shoot each other down on the street and do time. Meanwhile, sock away your cash and quietly build up something legit. Look at Moe Annenberg. Sam Bronfman. That eye doctor Jules Stein out in Hollywood, who played those old Capone guys like a fiddle while he built up his thing.

The other reason heads turned when Bugsy Siegel entered a room was because he was kill crazy, an errant missile. Even so, when he looked in the mirror, he saw a prosperous sportsman, not the face of a madman. He was self-conscious of his Lower East Side roots in poverty, and any reminder of his street-urchin days and the reputation he had earned during that period drove him into a rage. Once he got going, if a man insulted him, Siegel was a locomotive off the tracks.

Once his work got going with the navy, and he knew that Nazi sympathizers were back on American shores, Meyer reached out for Siegel in Hollywood, who knew where he could find Meyer, who was as devoted to his routines, including his favorite restaurants, as Siegel was to his recklessness.

Before Meyer could stand up, his friend was onto him with a kiss to the forehead.

"Hi there, bubbie!" Siegel said to Meyer. *Bubbie* was a shortened version of the Yiddish term of endearment, *bubeleh,* and it was pronounced with the short *uh* sound, like *book.* This was not a term Meyer was used to hearing directed at him, but Benny was Benny, and Benny was special. "Look at you, Meyer. You look beautiful. I could go for you myself."

"See, Ben, I told you you'd go sissy out there in Hollywood."

Siegel sat across from Meyer and held out his arms. "What do you think of this suit? They call it houndstooth. Georgie Raft took me to his tailor on Sunset Boulevard." Siegel identified this famous street as if Meyer would be impressed.

"Sunset Boulevard," Meyer said. "Do you see me on Sunset Boulevard?"

"You kidding? The broads would love a tycoon like you. I'd tell 'em you're a big film producer."

"Benny, we've known each other since I'm twelve and you're eight. You think I'm going to swing from a chandelier like Errol Flynn?"

"Naw, not Errol Flynn. I know him. You're much better looking, Meyer."

"I look like the corner druggist."

"You could clean the floor with Errol. C'mon out, we could be the next . . . Laurel and Hardy." Siegel laughed. "We'd have our own shtick."

"We already have our own shtick, Ben."

"Right, I punch 'em in the nose and you take his wallet."

Meyer laughed. "Yeah? How'd you think that would look on film?"

"Beautiful."

"Then what? Two minutes later we're in the slammer."

Siegel spoke softly, as if he were seriously pitching this idea: "Georgie Raft makes all those tough-guy pictures and everybody loves him."

"Ben, we're not making pictures. We're making money, and the society people don't like how we make it."

"You worry too much." Siegel waved over a crusty old waiter.

Siegel ordered sable. Meyer ordered smoked salmon.

"A hundred years old, this guy," Siegel said as the waiter walked away. Meyer knew what Siegel was thinking: The waiter didn't titter like a schoolgirl taking an order from Rudolph Valentino. Siegel had what they called red-carpet fever, the notion that everybody was supposed to ooh and aah when they saw him, bow and scrape, or jump up and down the way they did for that skinny Sinatra.

"Ben, do you think it's all my imagination? Look how we live. Guns, police sniffing around. These aren't delusions."

Siegel had heard this spiel from Meyer before, and it never registered. Siegel saw these warnings the same way a kid sees a parent who tells him to stop jumping up and down on the bed or he'll get hurt: a useless warning about something that never happen. Meyer would never think, though, that Ben Siegel was a liability. Sure, he was violent and capricious, but careful men such as Meyer weren't quick on the draw, and in their world, sometimes you had to be.

"So, you're telling me that big ship was done by Nazis?" Siegel asked after Meyer told him what was going on.

"No, I'm telling you that people *think* it's the Nazis."

"Why don't we find the little bastards and sink 'em to the bottom of the East River? Are you hearing those stories about shipping Jews off to big prisons?"

"Sure I am, Ben."

"What the hell do they do with them there?"

"Who knows? Germans are businessmen. Maybe it's about cheap labor."

"I don't know, Meyer. There's talk about trainloads of Jews being sent somewhere like Thanksgiving turkeys. We ought to kill every German we find. Meanwhile, our motion-picture landsmen are too worried about their big German market to make pictures calling these rodents what they are."

"That's part of it, Ben, not all of it."

"What, you want to take the pricks out dancing?"

Meyer lit up a Parliament. "You're close, Benny. See, in order to find the guys you want to send to the bottom of the East River, you've got to take them dancing first so they'll tell you where the rest of them are."

"You want to take some Nazis dancing?" Siegel laughed.

"We've got our friends getting these Krauts liquored up and talking at bars all over town. We know about a meeting of the Bund in Yorkville this weekend."

"You want to bust 'em up?"

"Yes, but there's a special request. We need to interview the top guy, see about his contacts in Germany. See if he knows about the *Normandie* and who's getting info and fuel to the Nazis. The navy can't get a handle on a German spook they call Brahms, who's out there somewhere directing U-boats. Also, Mr. Winchell wants pictures. He wants to write about it like it's, you know, news."

"So our guys can't look like . . . our guys," Siegel said.

"They've got to look like real Americans who are fed up being pushed around by Germans. There's one guy you've got to pull aside. Willie somebody. I'll get it to you."

"What do we do with him after?"

Meyer shrugged.

Gym Class

MANHATTAN WASN'T AN IDEAL CHOICE FOR A NAZI RALLY, BUT SINCE the beginning of time, God has counted upon morons to do His bidding.

Two of Siegel's men followed Willie Bauer from the Warwick Hotel to the heavily German Upper East Side neighborhood of Yorkville. During the 1930s, Yorkville had been the turf of Fritz Kuhn, the leader of the German-American Bund. People called him the American Führer. Kuhn was, in fact, an American. He was convicted a few years ago of embezzling from the Bund when it was on its way down. As if being a Nazi wasn't bad enough, he was a ganef, too.

Willie Bauer was the scum that floated to the surface of what was left of the Bund. He was the kind of guy who liked Nazism for the shock value, or maybe the outfits.

In his midthirties, Bauer was a slight punk of a man who wore a crisp, military-looking outfit of no real affiliation. He was from Huntington, Long Island, but for the few Germans who went for this kind of nonsense, Bauer occupied them with a fake German accent.

When night came, Siegel's men, along with some fellows from Lepke Buchalter's old Brownsville East crew, waited in the shadows outside a middle school in Yorkville. A photographer named Vic who worked for Winchell was waiting nearby. The men watched through a window.

Siegel himself was not there. One of his guys, Seymour "Blue Jaw" Magoon, was the evening's master of ceremonies. His brute squad consisted of some thirty men, which turned out to be overkill since barely a dozen Nazi sympathizers, a bunch of young misfits, showed up.

Blue Jaw let the men file into the gymnasium, where punch and cookies had been arranged on cheap aluminum tables.

"This is *it*?" the photographer, Vic, asked, peering inside.

"Guess so," Blue Jaw said.

"Back in the thirties, Kuhn could draw hundreds," Vic said.

"Things change."

"This ain't gonna make a great picture."

"I been tole," Blue Jaw responded, "dat Winchell wants a picture, see, so you gotta get a picture."

"It'll be hard with only that many guys in the gym," Vic said.

"Lissename, Vic." Blue Jaw stood close to the photographer. "Meyer and Ben don't wanna disappoint Mr. Winchell. If you can't get a big picture with lotsa guys, get a small picture with a couple-a guys and put some words in dere about it bein' more guys, see?"

Cecil B. DeMille, this guy.

Once Bauer started speaking to his half-assed crowd, Blue Jaw moved his men in, shut the door of the school, and jammed a crowbar in the handles. He had a few others go around the back of the school to make sure nobody got out.

Vic loaded up his camera. Blue Jaw listened for a few minutes to Bauer's speech, which he gave against twin banners, one with a swastika, the other, Adolf Hitler.

"And ve must band togezzer to put down ze Bolshevik and da Jew vunce and for all!"

The cretins clapped.

Blue Jaw shot a look to his backup, Tick Tock Tannenbaum. "Hey, Tick, can you believe dis shit from a guy from Long Island?"

"I can't take another goddamn minute-a this guy," Tick Tock said.

Blue Jaw and the boys entered the bleak little gym. The New York Nazis looked up, stunned. Blue Jaw felt sorry for them and wondered if he should lay off. When he reminded himself where the order came from, he did his job.

"Just no bats!" Blue Jaw yelled.

Within the next five minutes, the boys knocked the tar out of these mutts. The wiseguys had handkerchiefs tied to cover their faces so people wouldn't recognize them from any photos. Tick Tock and a guy called Dasher dragged the hysterical Willie Bauer out the back of the gym, knocked him unconscious, and threw him in the backseat of a car. They took him to a warehouse in Brooklyn.

The next morning, Walter Winchell's newspaper was filled with pictures of a "huge" pro-Nazi rally that had been held the night before in Yorkville. Meyer and his guys had a good laugh about that. Vic had managed to snap half a dozen photos, which he put together in a way that gave the impression of a much larger turnout. This served everybody's purposes.

Willie Bauer woke up buck naked, doused with gasoline, and tied to a chair. Bugsy Siegel stood before him with a live blowtorch in his hand.

"You hold a Nazi rally in New York City? What are you, a fucking imbecile?" Siegel asked.

"Who are you?" Bauer asked foggily. And without the faux German accent.

"Who's got the blowtorch, schmuck?"

"What do you want?"

"Do all Nazis look like you, weasel?"

Bauer said nothing. Siegel nodded to Blue Jaw, who poured more gas on the captive.

"Is that gasoline?" Bauer cried.

"No, it's shaving cream," Siegel said. "We're going to give you a close shave, handsome."

"It's gasoline!"

"I'm going to make this very simple," Siegel said. "I've got a hard time believing you know bubkes, Bauer, and I don't have the time or patience to devote two seconds to somebody like you. When I get back to my friends who asked me to do this, I'm going to put my foot up their ass for wasting my time. Christ, I thought I was going to be meeting up with some hard-case spy. I can't believe it. Hitler's sinking hundreds of ships right off Manhattan and I'm interrogating the treasurer of the Chess Club!"

"Maybe guys like dis are all dey got left," Blue Jaw said.

Ben's mouth fell open. "Are you serious? It's come to this? I can't get over that Meyer brought me back for *this*. This guy looks like Donald Duck!"

Blue Jaw shrugged.

A furious Siegel fired the blowtorch up a notch.

"God, no!" Bauer cried.

Siegel placed the blowtorch against Bauer's earlobe and burned it to a nub. Because no gasoline had been poured there, it didn't light up. Siegel shook his head in disgust as Bauer howled his ass off.

Siegel pulled up a chair and faced Bauer directly. The blowtorch was still going.

"Now, Führer. May I call you Führer?" Siegel asked, but did not wait for an answer. "Thank you. Somebody thinks you've got information about some German spies. Personally, I can't believe that, but if you can't spin a good yarn in the next five seconds, I'm going to light you up like a menorah. And I'll tell you something . . . it won't be quick. I'll do you piece by piece. Now talk to me."

And Bauer did: "There are men coming from Germany."

"What men?"

"Ten, I think."

"Who are they?"

"I don't know their names."

"What are they going to do?"

"They are going to land on Long Island. Near the Hamptons."

"Nazis are landing in the Hamptons? You're shitting me! How are they getting here?"

"U-boat."

Siegel was confused. "What, a U-boat pulls up to the beach on Long Island and Hermann Göring walks up in his bathing trunks?"

"No. No. They will take a raft to the beach."

"Yeah, and?"

"They're supposed to come to the city. New York."

"How do you know about this, Führer?"

"I made the reservations at the hotels where they're going. The Governor Clinton. There's another one. I have it written down."

"When do these clowns get here?"

"June."

"*This* June? That soon?"

"Yes."

"Are they all going to New York?"

"No. There's another U-boat going south. I don't know where."

"What are these guys supposed to do? Take in a show on Broadway?"

"I don't know all the details. They wanted me to help find a warehouse."

"A warehouse for what?"

"I don't know, I swear."

"Did these guys burn up the *Normandie*?"

"No, no, they were in Germany."

"Do you know who torched that ship?"

"No, I swear!"

"Do you know how the U-boats are getting directions and fuel?"

Bauer's face was a blank, as if he couldn't believe the question. "Fuel? Fuel? I just figured they had ships for that."

"What about directions from the shore?"

"I, I don't know. From other boats I thought."

"Do you know the name Brahms?"

"Brahms? From music?"

"No, Brahms the Brownshirt."

Bauer screwed up his face, befuddled.

Siegel stood up. "Blue Jaw, what do you think?"

Blue Jaw shrugged. "I dunno, Ben. You look at dis guy and can't think dey'd trust him to pour coffee. But maybe that's why dey picked him, you know? Don't seem he knows nuthin' about no directions and no fuel."

"I don't know what to think. But if even half this crap turns out to be true—not the fuel, the other stuff—we'd be screwed if we didn't tell Meyer's navy friend, you know what I'm saying?"

Blue Jaw shook his head.

"This is your lucky day, Führer. If it were up to me, you'd be a slice of toast right now. But I've got friends who may want you alive, so I'm going to make a deal with you. You get to live, but if you try to go in the wind, you're going to get lit up good, you follow? You go right home to the address we have."

"Yes, yes, thank you," Bauer cried.

The next morning, Bauer was found tied to a tree in Washington Square wearing a greasepainted Hitler mustache, bright red lipstick, rouge and eyeliner, women's panties, fishnet stockings, and high heels. Vic the photographer, Winchell's man, was on hand to get the shot for the afternoon newspaper.

Getting a Break

MEYER MET COMMANDER HAFFENDEN AT HIS CHURCH STREET office and told him what Siegel had learned from Bauer. Haffenden wrote down every word. Meyer could tell Haffenden was excited and was pleased to be the bearer of this news.

For the first time since he'd got to this country as a small boy, Meyer felt that he was doing something for America. Even though people had started calling him a gangster even before Prohibition, he regarded it as slander by fools. He did not believe he was a criminal any more than Joe Kennedy was a criminal. Hell, Kennedy was bigger into booze than Meyer ever was, and Kennedy had become ambassador to England. Meyer did liquor business with Kennedy years ago, but Meyer was a gangster, not an ambassador. If you sell enough hooch, you can be a diplomat. Must be a volume thing.

Meyer could see, though, that Haffenden was also nervous. A huge amount of responsibility was falling on him, which is why he kept on Meyer, who genuinely felt for him and wanted him to succeed. Some things you do in your life because it's your job, but other things you do in your life because you believe you are doing a mitzvah, a good thing. While Meyer never believed that bootlegging and gambling were horrible things, he didn't kid himself that they helped America. The navy campaign was a different story.

He had other motivations, of course, besides patriotism. Socks began telling his men that he was trying to help Charlie Luciano get out of jail. He had to say things like that, but it made people expect that Luciano would actually get out. Guys started asking when Luciano would be free. In truth, Meyer had no idea if any of his work was going to help Luciano's situation. It was a crapshoot. Meyer became concerned that if the program with the navy was a one-way street, he'd be on the spot with the Italians before long. As long as the *vilda chayas* were getting their suitcases from the gambling rackets, he'd be all right. So much for the long-term John Q. Citizen businesses, for now anyway.

"Did Ben think Bauer was a crackpot?" Haffenden asked Meyer.

"Yes," Meyer said. "Ben said none of these guys were much."

"But Bauer said some Nazis were coming ashore in June?"

"Bauer said his job was to arrange for the men to stay at the Governor Clinton Hotel."

Haffenden rubbed his temples. His face had its red glow, but he was animated.

"Now, Meyer, I don't mean to sound ungrateful by asking this, but was your sense that Ben was, uh, leaning on this guy hard?"

"That's what Ben does, Commander."

Haffenden thought for a moment. "Sometimes men will say anything if they're pushed to their limits."

"I'm not an expert on this type of thing, but have to wonder why Bauer was so specific. Why didn't he name the Waldorf instead of the Clinton? Why did he pick June? Why did he say they were coming by a U-boat off Long Island and not just say they were going to be in New York, but that he didn't know how they were getting here?"

"You may be right, Meyer, but you can always flip that and conclude he had to say *something*, and what he told Ben is just what fell out of his mouth."

"The best I can do is bring you what I can bring you. I think we may be onto something here. If we are, we are. If we're not, we'll keep trying. Besides, we know where this jerk lives."

It was not lost on Meyer that Haffenden hadn't even asked if Bauer had said anything about the *Normandie*, but why press it?

Haffenden met with Socks Lanza separately to get a better feel for what kind of fishing boats he had in his fleet. Meyer didn't go to that meeting. He had to travel to Omaha to check on one of his investments, the Dodge Park Kennel Club.

Socks owned many fishing boats and had hundreds of independent fishermen he could turn to for help. He reached an agreement with Haffenden that the navy would install a new type of radio on a number of boats that would allow fishermen to talk to B-3 sailors to report anything unusual they saw in the waters around Long Island. Navy men would receive proper union cards and be put aboard certain vessels to see things for themselves.

Haffenden assigned men to spy on Willie Bauer to see if he made contact with anyone interesting. Meyer and his men would know soon enough if they had hit pay dirt or were in the shithouse with the navy. His stomach had been turning over something fierce, which wasn't helped when Frank Costello told Meyer when he got back to New York that Albert Anastasia wanted to meet with him. According to Costello, Anastasia had gotten word about the navy caper and wanted to know what was going on. He also was asking questions about when Luciano was getting out of jail.

Anastasia ran one of the five Italian groups Luciano had set up once the old "Mustache Petes," Maranzano and Masseria, were retired. The men who'd originally led that "family," right before Anastasia, were the Mangano brothers, who had since vanished from the planet. Do the arithmetic.

Anastasia's brother, Tony, had a big business on the pier, so he thought he had the right to know everything that went on, on the waterfront. Anastasia was kill crazy. People called him the Mad Hatter or the Lord High Executioner of Murder, Inc. Catchy names were fine for selling breath mints, but not for racketeers. One time, Anastasia had a man killed who witnessed a crime completely unrelated to his business just because he hated snitches. Anastasia was the last person Meyer needed on the navy account.

Anastasia was feeling his oats ever since Lepke Buchalter went to prison. Lepke, who was Jewish, and Anastasia shared the garment-district labor business. Lepke was every bit the killer Anastasia was, although he had a good business mind, too. But as long as Lepke was a free man, Anastasia had to tread lightly because Lepke wouldn't lie down to him. In later years, the Italians could pretty much have what they wanted when the Jewish boys got more focused on real business. In those days, though, men such as Bugsy Siegel, Lepke, Gurrah Shapiro, and the Purples in Detroit were perfectly willing to kill an Italian if he reached into a Jew's pocket.

Meyer agreed to meet Anastasia at a restaurant at the Park Sheraton Hotel, where Anastasia liked to get a shave and a haircut. Frank Costello thought it was best for him to stay away because he wanted to be in a position to play dumb with Anastasia if he had to.

Meyer had a few appointments that day, so he got Lilo to drive him to the hotel and told him to wait outside. Anastasia was a big man, more wide than tall. He had wild eyes, as if his big head would explode—a human hand-grenade. Everything he said came out like an ultimatum. He sat down across from Meyer and they both ordered some coffee. Anastasia wanted a Danish, too. Meyer always expected to see the limbs of a live creature dangling from Anastasia's mouth.

Anastasia said some of his men had heard others were helping out the navy on the docks.

"Yes, Albert, after that big ship caught fire in February, the navy approached us," Meyer said. "They asked if we'd keep our eyes and ears open for Nazi spies."

"So you said yes?"

"They wanted Charlie's support. I went up and visited Charlie and he thought it was smart to help out."

"Why did he think that?" Anastasia said.

"For one thing our country is at war, and we wanted to support the war effort. For another, Charlie was worried that the government believed Italians might be cooperating with the Nazis because of Mussolini."

"Fuck what the government thinks."

This guy . . .

The waitress brought the men their coffees.

"The government is pretty powerful, Albert. There's talk out West about rounding up Japanese people."

"Fuck the Japs, too, Meyer. You forget me and my brother run these docks?"

"C'mon, Albert. I've been working with Socks. This isn't any goddamn racket. Nobody's rooking you out of some cut, and we don't need extra trouble with the government if we can avoid it."

"Still, they're my docks and I don't trust those bastards."

His docks. Meshuggener. "It's not about trust. It's about helping our country, maybe catching a break, and helping Charlie."

"Helping our country? My guys don't see it that way. Italians are their brothers. The Yids don't have a fuckin' country that America's in a war with, Meyer."

"The Yids don't *have* a fuckin' country besides this one."

"How's that my problem?"

"Albert, this isn't about Jews and Italians, it's about Americans. It's about doing the right thing and the smart thing—"

"Yeah, Meyer? What's Charlie get outta this? His ass is rotting in the can."

Anastasia could not care less about Luciano's freedom. He was consumed with turf. Truth was, Meyer did bypass him, but he had to because Anastasia made Ben Siegel look like the poster child for lucid mental health.

Anastasia was also making noise because he wanted his men to think he was the emblem of loyalty—that whole Italian blood-oath thing, which none of the top guys really believed. Truth was, Anastasia was glad Luciano was gone. He wanted to be "boss of all the bosses," a moronic notion. Did the top executives of General Motors and Du Pont and Westinghouse get together and demand that the chairman of one of these companies be named the chairman of all the chairmen?

Anastasia also resented Meyer's bond with Luciano. Even though Luciano always valued Anastasia's muscle, muscle was a cheap commodity in their world. Having a business sense and making something of themselves was what Luciano and Meyer valued in each other.

"We are doing the best we can for Charlie, Albert, but we

have to show some results that help out the navy before they'll go to bat for us."

"You honestly think that's going to happen? You're smarter than that."

"This is the best shot we have. Do you have a better idea?"

Anastasia finished his coffee with an exaggerated sip that capped off Meyer's disgust with him. Sometimes the little habits make you realize how much you can't stand somebody.

"How about I burn another ship, Meyer?"

Meyer felt as if he'd just got kicked in the nuts by an elephant. "What the fuck are you talking about?"

"What if I told you some of our guys, maybe some of your guys, flambéed that ship?"

"The *Normandie*? Why the hell would you do something like that?"

"I might have had reasons," Anastasia smirked.

"What kind of reasons?"

"Maybe to get the navy to come to us for help? Maybe an insurance thing? Maybe as a favor to Mussolini? You don't know everything that goes on in New York, Meyer. And you're not Charlie's only friend."

"You're full of shit."

"Am I?"

"Nothing good can come out of talk like that. If the government even heard you joked about that, Charlie would never see the light of day."

"Relax, Meyer, they're never gonna find out a goddamn thing."

When they left the restaurant—Meyer paid—Anastasia looked poor Lilo up and down. "Who the fuck are you?" he asked the kid. When Lilo opened his mouth to answer, Anastasia walked away.

Hotel Reservations

MEYER DIDN'T BELIEVE THE *MAMZER* ANASTASIA. HE FIGURED ANASTASIA was just trying to torment him. If Anastasia burned the *Normandie* to draw the navy to men in the underworld, he wouldn't have been so angry that he was out of the ferret-squad loop.

Meyer couldn't be sure though, and he had heartburn for days. The newspapers always called them "organized crime." If only that were true, he'd have been a happy—and incredibly rich—man. In his world, everybody ran his own racket, and nobody told anybody else what he had going. Even though Meyer didn't have any evidence to believe that some gangland cowboys had blown up the *Normandie,* he didn't have any evidence to believe that they hadn't, and the thought sickened him given the potential consequences.

Meyer's work with Commander Haffenden and B-3 was beginning to take shape. The rusty fishing vessels had been patrolling the south shore of Long Island later than usual. During the spring and summer, fishermen wanted to take advantage of the weather to catch more fish or avoid going home to their wives. Something about these boats was odd, though, which would have been noticeable during the day if someone had been watching closely. But the men who should have been concerned with this irregularity were hundreds of feet beneath them.

The oddities on Socks Lanza's vessels were antennae that had been installed by B-3 agents. The ship-to-ship and ship-to-shore radios were good enough to allow fisherman to reliably report sightings of large seacraft in shallow coastal waters.

After midnight on June 13, 1942, Nazi U-boat 202, the *Innsbruck,* cut its diesel engines and turned on its quiet electric power plant and surfaced off the coast of Amagansett, Long Island. Four Germans in their thirties who had been on the submarine boarded a rubber dingy and rowed ashore in the fog along with crates of explosives and $174,000 in cash. As they buried the explosives in a dune, a twenty-one-year-old Coast Guard officer named John Cullen shone a flashlight onto the men, all of whom had, at some point during their lives, been U.S. residents. They all spoke English. In the darkness, Cullen was unable to see that the men were wearing German uniforms. They did this so that if they were captured, they could pass themselves off as defectors, not spies. This expedition was known as Operation Pastorius in honor of the first German immigrant to arrive in the New World in the 1600s.

"Who are you?" Cullen demanded.

"We're fishermen from Southampton," one of the men said. "We've run ashore."

"All right then," Cullen said. "You can come to our station and we'll find you some help." Cullen sniffed the air. "Were you using diesel fuel?"

Cullen heard a commotion a few hundred yards down the beach. "What's going on down there?" he demanded.

Worried now, a so-called fisherman grabbed Cullen. "Never mind what's going on down there," he threatened. "Do you have a mother?"

Cullen said of course.

"Well, I wouldn't want to have to kill you," the fisherman said.

The man making the threat, the leader of the four, was George Dasch, a weasel-faced German whose international espionage skills came from having once waited tables, bribed Cullen with $260 not to tell anyone about what he had seen.

"Forget about this, take this money, and go have a good time. My name is Davis. You'll be meeting me in East Hampton sometime."

Cullen took the bribe and returned to the Coast Guard station.

"They're here," Cullen told the B-3 officer who had been waiting, then surrendered the bribe money to the officer.

B-3 didn't collar the Germans as they came ashore because they wanted to see where they went. It took all of three minutes to find the supplies the men had buried on the beach.

The second leg of the spies' trip began when they got on a Long Island Rail Road train for Manhattan under the watchful eye of B-3 agents.

The four Germans—Dasch; a sad-eyed naturalized American named Ernest Burger; a thin-lipped hard case and former mechanic who had lived in Milwaukee named Heinrich Heinck; and jug-eared Richard Quirin, also a mechanic—split up once they found their way to New York City. Dasch and Burger were tailed to the Governor Clinton Hotel.

Given what was going on at home with his wife, Meyer had taken a room at the Waldorf. A few people who knew his situation knew where to find him. He got a call early one morning that his Nazi visitors had arrived. What kind of schmuck Nazi thinks it's a bright idea to invade Manhattan, where every other person's on his way to a bar mitzvah? he wondered.

When they got to their hotels, the Nazis threw parties. They spent a fortune on custom-tailored suits and big tips at fine restaurants. Dasch, evidently one of the great table waiters of the Third Reich, had chosen the Governor Clinton because he had once bused tables there and made his presence known to some of his old union buddies. These men, who reported to navy operatives (who had been given restaurant union cards since Frank Costello controlled the union), knew that they needed to tell Meyer's men about these developments.

Meyer contacted his friend Joe Adonis, who sent a team of professional women trained in the art of being impressed with unimpressive men. It always amazed Meyer that men could be fooled this way, not realizing a pro when they saw one, but "learning from experience" was the exception not the rule. Beauty is a gangster. Some things in life are governed by nature, not information. But Meyer wasn't complaining. The cash that he kept in a shoebox in his closet came from human weakness, and it was more than his grandfather the rabbi on the Russian border would have seen in fifty lifetimes.

George Dasch was at the bar at the Governor Clinton Hotel holding court with a woman who called herself Flo. She was tall and busty with light brown hair and angular features. Of the four girls in her pack, not only was she the prettiest, she was also the smartest. When talk turned to the war, the other girls made stupid, boozy remarks about liking a man in uniform, but Flo talked about specific developments that triggered Dasch's interest.

When one of the girls mentioned that the Allies would

whip Hitler, Flo said that Hitler was much more determined than Roosevelt.

"Do I detect a little accent, George?" Flo asked, once she and Dasch were alone at the bar. She stroked a gold cross that rested cruelly on the northern ridge of her freckled cleavage.

Dasch hesitated for a moment. "I'm afraid it's not a very fashionable accent these days," he said, trying to be bashful.

"I knew it! You're German. So am I." She let the cross fall in between two freckles.

"No. Do you speak German?"

"No, silly. I was born here in New York. My parents are from Ulm. They live in Yorkville now."

"I know Ulm. I know people there. I've heard of Yorkville. What is your last name?"

"My name is Florence Mueller."

"There are many Muellers in Germany."

"You would be surprised, George, how many there are in America, too."

"Do you have brothers in the military, Flo?"

"No, only sisters. I think if I had brothers, my father would shoot them before he let them serve in the American army."

Dasch cocked his head, surprised by Flo's strong feelings. "I'm sure he would not do that."

"You don't know my father, George." She took a sip of her drink. "So, why are you in America?"

"My aunt is ill. My parents are old. They wanted me to come and see her. It's very sad."

Flo put her hand on Dasch's. "I'm sorry, George. Family things are very worrisome." Something about the touch of an attractive woman lobotomized a man. It was strange how a feminine beauty's skin made a man feel like a conqueror when the touch of a less appealing woman made him want to call the police.

"Yes. You have no idea what I had to go through to get here. With the war and everything."

"I don't think there will be a war for much longer."

"No, why?" Dasch asked, intrigued.

"I think the Americans are running scared. People here didn't want this war from the get-go. Not that they like Hitler; they sure don't. They just didn't think it was their war. It's a good thing the action is so far away. If anything terrible happened here at home, I don't think we could stand it. A sailor friend told me that as scared as Americans are, the Germans are too scared to get close to our shores."

"Scared?"

"That's what my sailor friend Philip says. He tells me everything."

"Don't be so sure, my dear Florence."

Dasch ordered another round of drinks. The bartender had been instructed to fill Flo's glass with only juice or club soda, but to drop a tranquilizer provided by B-3 into Dasch's drink.

"So, are you really on a top-secret mission?" she purred.

"Do you want to go on a mission with me?" he said, real suave.

"It depends. Could I help you assassinate Roosevelt?" She winked.

Dasch was shocked. "I am not a violent man, Flo. I would never do such a thing, but I'm sure I'll think of something."

They went to Dasch's room, where he fell flat onto his bed. Flo fished a slip of paper from his wallet, which she handed to a man waiting in the next room. That man took the paper downstairs to the handsome blue-eyed fellow waiting to interview Dasch in the hotel's boiler room.

Shopping Spree

George Dasch found himself tied to a chair in the basement of the hotel in the less-than-tender arms of Bugsy Siegel and Blue Jaw Magoon.

"You heard of the Arsenal of Democracy, Dasch?" Siegel asked, pulling up a chair as Dasch blinked awake.

"Yes," Dasch barely uttered.

"Well, you're lookin' at it."

Dasch shivered.

"You speak English pretty good so I'm gonna lay out your options for you real clear," Siegel said. "Blue Jaw, please."

Blue Jaw held Dasch's wrist on a small table. Siegel picked up a ball-peen hammer and smashed the small bones of the German's hand in two strokes.

Siegel and Blue Jaw left Dasch to his sobbing for a half hour while they made themselves comfortable and split a corned-beef sandwich, sliced lean the way health-conscious Siegel liked it, with Russian dressing and coleslaw.

When they came back, Siegel said to Dasch, "My friend and I can drive you out into the country where some friends of ours would like to meet you—guys whose families are from Germany and Poland—Mr. Shapiro, Mr. Berman, Mr. Tannenbaum, Mr. Strauss, Mr. Alderman, Mr. Levine, Mr. Magoon here. To name a few. If you want me to go over those names again so you can familiarize yourself, I'd be happy to. Thoroughness is one of my virtues.

"We were hoping to make a whole weekend out of it," Siegel added, finishing off a pickle. "Maybe even a long weekend, invite some other friends. If you like barbecues, you'll like this place.

"Now, my friend Mr. Lansky, who has been working with the American government, he's no fun. He doesn't like parties. He thinks I ought to keep an open mind. Did I mention that he came over to America from the Russian-Polish border where his grandfather was a rabbi? Anything you want him to know about how his relatives are doing over there? Never mind. I'm sure when your Gestapo friends went into Poland they didn't disturb the synagogues or anything, which will come as quite a relief to Mr. Lansky."

Dasch wept. "Please."

"What, are you trying to tell me, that Mr. Lansky's relatives in Poland and Russia aren't safe and sound?"

Siegel leaned in to Dasch and winked at him conspiratorially. Siegel spoke softly, "See, George, between you and me, Mr. Lansky is not a worldly man. All he knows is dollars and cents. You know how *those* people are, right, George? It's just about the money, am I right? Because I like you, I'll tell you what: I won't tell Mr. Lansky about what's going on in Poland if you agree to pick up that phone right there and call a man, Mr. Hoover, at this phone number, and tell him where he can come and pick you up. Do you know who Mr. Hoover is, George?"

Dasch nodded no.

Siegel looked at Blue Jaw. "I swear to Christ, I can't believe the Jews are running away from these guys."

Turning back to Dasch, Siegel said, "Hoover is America's top policeman. If you call him and tell him where to pick you up right now, I won't take you to our barbecue. Now, if you don't cooperate with Mr. Hoover and tell him where all your friends are and what your plans were, he'll just call me back and I'll pick you up. Being as how we're friends and all. And then we'll go out into the country for some fresh air, okay?"

Dasch sighed. "I am not a hero. I had second thoughts from the beginning. I did not want to do this."

"What was the big plan, George? We found the dynamite out on Long Island, so if you hold back . . . oh, George, if you hold back . . ." Siegel nodded like a mother disappointed that her child hadn't finished his broccoli.

"No, I'll tell you! I'll tell you!"

Siegel threw a pot of cold water on Dasch. As soon as he caught his breath, Dasch told Siegel about Operation Pastorius.

"I've got maps in my room," Dasch began.

"Maps of what?" Siegel asked.

"Defense plants. We told Berlin we were going to use the dynamite at a few defense plants. One in Philadelphia. Some railways in Ohio. A hydroelectric plant near Niagara Falls. We had a factory, the Aluminum Company of America, in Pennsylvania. Penn Station, too."

"Which Penn Station? There are a few."

"Newark. In New Jersey," Dasch said.

Siegel and Blue Jaw shook their heads as they listened.

"We were never going to go through with most of this," Dasch said. "We just wanted to live in America."

"A regular patriot," Siegel said. "I feel tingly. What else?"

A bridge on the East River. Hell Gate Bridge."

"You were gonna blow up the Hell Gate Bridge on the East River? For Christ's sake, how many people were you gonna kill?"

"It wasn't so much killing. It was to scare Americans."

"Well, my Nazi friend, it probably would have worked," Siegel said.

"Berlin didn't believe Americans had the stomach to keep fighting."

"How do you know what Berlin thought?"

"Because I was trained in Berlin. On a farm nearby, actually. The Nazis laughed at how long it took Americans to get into the war."

"That's because Americans don't like war; Americans like war *movies*. There's a difference. It's like in my business. Everybody wants to be a tough guy. Everybody wants to pull a gun—like this one," Siegel said, brandishing a .38-caliber revolver. "They want to point it at a guy, watch him shit his pants. But they'll never pull the trigger. See, Georgie, they want the killer swagger, but they don't want to draw blood. You know what I'm saying?" Siegel asked, pressing the barrel of the gun against Dasch's eye.

"Please," Dasch pleaded.

"But that's what America's really about—something for nothing."

Siegel withdrew the piece of paper that Flo had taken from Dasch's pocket.

On one side of the paper was a handwritten list of department stores. Siegel read them aloud:

Sears Roebuck
Abraham & Straus
Altman's
Gimbels
Lazarus
Magnin's
Neiman Marcus
Saks Fifth Avenue

"You like to shop, George?"

"No, not really."

"Then why the list of department stores?" Siegel pushed.

"They were names given to us in Berlin."

"Yeah? Why these places? There are other department stores. Why not shop at Macy's?"

"It wasn't on this list," Dasch said.

"I see that, George. Why not?"

Dasch just nodded no in desperation.

"Don't insult me, George," Siegel said, getting right in Dasch's face so that he could feel Siegel's corned-beef breath. "Say it and get it over with."

"They are Jewish names," Dasch admitted through his tears.

"Really?" Siegel said, glancing at the list again as if he hadn't known. "Sears isn't a Jewish name."

"I don't know. The owner I think was Rosen-something."

"Rosen-something. I don't know him. Is he related to Silver-something? I'll be damned. What was going to happen at these places?"

"We were told to put bombs in them."

Siegel raised his eyebrows in perverse admiration. "Not a bad idea, Georgie. You should see the bills my wife racks up at Saks."

Dasch did not smile at Siegel's quip, which was perhaps the first wise thing the ex-waiter had ever done in his life.

"Tell me, Georgie," Siegel continued, "what did you think the Jews would do when you blew up their stores, just sit there and bleed?"

"I don't know."

"Is that what they're doing over there where you're from, just sitting and bleeding?"

"I don't know."

"I *do* know, pal, and I'll tell you. From now on you'll be

dealing with a different kind of Jew. No more yeshiva boys. Now you meet *shtarkers*."

"*Shtarkers?* Like strong?"

"That's me, bubbie. Did you guys burn up that ship on the Hudson?"

"What ship?"

"The *Good Ship Lollipop,* for Christ's sake. The *Normandie,* ass."

"No, no," Dasch answered. "We were not even in the country when that happened."

"That doesn't mean you didn't help with the plans."

"No. I never heard anything about that ship."

Siegel pinched Dasch's cheek. "You're so full of shit, Georgie."

"No, I swear."

"You didn't do it for the insurance juice?"

Blue Jaw laughed at Siegel's question.

"Insurance and juice?" Dasch asked, puzzled.

"Jesus. Forget about it already," Siegel said. "It doesn't matter anyhow. Now, what do you know about how those Nazi submarines get fuel?"

"I don't know about fuel. I know the U-boats leave from France."

"But they don't turn around to go back to France every time they need gas," Siegel said.

"No, I suppose they don't," Dasch said blankly.

"What about convoy routes? How do the U-boats know where our ships are going?"

Dasch's eyes widened in terror. "Convoy routes? I-I don't know."

"Who directed your U-boat to Long Island?"

"I-I don't know. I am not a U-boat captain."

"Are you getting cute with me, asshole?"

"No, no, I swear. I am not cute."

"No, you're not cute. Have you heard of a Nazi called Brahms?"

"I don't know him."

"That's not what I asked you, George," Siegel said. "I asked if you had heard of him."

"I have heard him mentioned, yes."

"Well?"

"Brahms is the name the Abwehr gives to an agent in America who directs some of the U-boats. They say he is some kind of monster, a giant who has killed many people. That is all I know, I swear."

Siegel thought about it. Why would Dasch have disclosed so much—including the bombing of department stores—but hold back on the *Normandie* and fuel supplies? It didn't make sense unless Dasch didn't really know the answers. It's not as if they all operated according to one central plan any more than the rackets did. After all, Meyer didn't know everything Siegel was into.

"A little birdie told me you have some friends who came with you in that clown car of a U-boat," Siegel continued, kicking Dasch in the knee.

Dasch looked into Siegel's baby blues and decided to surrender entirely.

Dasch nodded. "A man named Burger. Burger's at this hotel, too."

"Good job, Georgie, but we've got Mr. Burger. He was very cooperative. Know what I think, Georgie? I think you and your buddies were Hitler's garbage. If you succeeded, you succeeded. If you failed, nobody would miss you."

Dasch frowned. "That may be true."

"Where are your other friends?"

"We came with two others. They are staying at the Martinique."

"The Martinique. Good. Anything else you want me to know? What about this Riverside address? Last chance, Georgie." This was the address on the back of the department store list.

Dasch studied Siegel's eyes. Siegel always knew when people were doing this. They were soft eyes, not killer eyes. Perhaps if Siegel had wild killer eyes, Dasch would have been less frightened. There would have been a certainty to his predicament. But this was strange, this handsome man with feminine lamps talking softly to him, alternating between endearments and jamming a gun in his face. When Siegel had called for Blue Jaw to restrain Dasch when Siegel smashed his hand with a hammer—without any of the facial contortions that one might expect would accompany such viciousness—Dasch had realized he was up against a madman.

What Siegel learned in the next few minutes made him want to kill Dasch on the spot, which he could have done and sat right down and had a blintze. But Meyer had specifically told him to keep Dasch healthy. Siegel later said to Meyer, "God love you, little man. You always have some brilliant reason to keep some motherless worm alive."

Sand Crabs

MEYER CALLED COMMANDER HAFFENDEN THE MINUTE MEYER knew he had the spies in hand. When Haffenden answered his phone, Meyer said, "We caught some sand crabs." At his Hotel Astor offices a few days later, Haffenden told Meyer that B-3 had confirmed that the Riverside Drive location on Dasch's paper belonged to Dasch's handler, who, in turn, communicated with a Nazi spymaster who was directing U-boat fleets from a coastal location. *Brahms?* Among other things, Haffenden had learned that the Nazis planned to direct a new fleet of U-boats off the coast of New York. These particular U-boats would have platforms attached to them they could use to launch small rockets into New York City, setting it on fire.

"I'm no military man, Commander, but is something like that possible?"

"According to our friends in England, they've got photographs of U-boats with platforms attached along the coast of Norway, which is under Nazi occupation. Besides, Meyer, we were skeptical about what your men were saying about Nazis landing on Long Island until we saw it with our own eyes. Now Hoover's in the mix."

"That's good, I suppose."

"Yes," Haffenden said. "That's very good. And, Meyer, thanks. This ferret squad of ours sure has caught a few rats."

"You're welcome, Commander. I hope I can bank this for Charlie."

"You can sure bank it with me. I'll do my best to see if I can cash that check up the line."

On June 17, 1942, four additional German saboteurs landed on a beach near Jacksonville, Florida. Within days, J. Edgar Hoover's FBI men fanned out and captured Edward John Kerling, Werner Thiel, Hermann Otto Neubauer, and Herbert Hans Haupt, who all had American relatives and spoke English. The men led the FBI to the stash of supplies they had buried on the beach believing, naively, that their cooperation would allow them to claim deserter or prisoner-of-war status to gain a measure of leniency. When the FBI found these supplies—explosives, including detonators disguised as pens and pencils—all thoughts of mercy evaporated.

By the end of June, all of the saboteurs were in a Washington, D.C., prison to be tried by a military commission. Meyer paid his neighbor, Walter Winchell, a visit to give him the tip.

Winchell had a lot to say in his exclusive about how J. Edgar Hoover had caught the Nazi spies, but he didn't identify them by name:

HOOVER'S G-MEN CAPTURE NAZI SPIES IN NEW YORK, FLORIDA

FBI Infiltrated Gestapo High Command in Berlin to Crush Spy Ring Planning to Kill Americans, Sabotage Economy

Winchell's article referenced an anonymous source that indicated that some of the spies were linked to the destruction of the *Normandie.*

When Bugsy Siegel saw the story, he went nuts. Meyer didn't. He never expected he'd get any public recognition—and *wanted* Winchell to kvell over Hoover. Meyer was more interested in Haffenden's feeling that Meyer, personally, was fulfilling his promises. Haffenden didn't even care that Hoover got the credit because the navy brass was, for once, appearing to be on top of things. Plus, Winchell was excited he got the scoop.

The eight German saboteurs were convicted in a military court. They pushed for a civil trial, but President Roosevelt would have none of it. As commander in chief, he had the final say in their treatment. The president agreed to commute Dasch's sentence to thirty years, according to Winchell's truthful source, because he implicated a few of the other men in the *Normandie* attack (even though it was a lie). Burger got life in prison.

On August 8, the eight convicts were having breakfasts of bacon, scrambled eggs, and toast in their cells at the District of Columbia jail. The tribunal's presiding officer and an army chaplain burst in to tell each of the men of their sentences: death for the six other saboteurs. The six men were immediately led out of their cells in alphabetical order and strapped to a chair facing a one-way mirror. J. Edgar Hoover and members of the military tribunal were there. One by one, the men were hit with forty-five hundred volts of electricity. Fourteen minutes later, each body was covered up and wheeled out on a gurney in front of the next convict, who was then brought in to meet his own fate.

The Germans' bodies were placed in cheap pine coffins and buried in a potter's field near the Industrial Home School for Colored Children in Washington. The wooden grave identifiers were stamped with the men's inmate numbers, 276, 277, 278, 279, 280, and 281.

Winchell quoted President Roosevelt in his story about his decision to execute the spies. He said America wouldn't tolerate "mush hounds" as leaders. The subtext, Winchell and Meyer knew, was that by zapping these bastards pronto, they would never get to present evidence that they hadn't been responsible for torching the *Normandie*. The press did not initially report that only six of the eight spies had been executed; there were reasons to let the public, not to mention the Germans, believe they were all dead, and Winchell was pleased to help the American cause.

These were good times for Winchell, and his support for the war effort came out in various ways, including an Irving Berlin song called "How About a Cheer for the Navy." Winchell was no longer just chronicling celebrities, he had become one, an objective he shared with Benny Siegel, but not Meyer Lansky.

When Meyer was riding up the elevator to go to his room at the Waldorf after his meeting with Haffenden, he started having a terrible feeling in the pit of his stomach. He was not one of those people who believed for long that anything good can really happen, or that good deeds were rewarded.

During his tutoring session, his hotel telephone rang. It was Moe Polakoff. He said he had gotten a call from "our friend upstate." Luciano. Polakoff said Luciano was ranting, demanding to be told what the hell was going on. He had read about the German spies being captured and executed. He figured the ferret squad had something to do with it. He wanted to know when he was going to get out of the can. Polakoff assured him that they were doing their best, but Luciano said he wanted to see him. Meyer, too. They had to go, of course, if only to try to calm him down. So Meyer's satisfaction over helping to catch the spies didn't last long.

Things were about to get a lot worse. They almost always did. But at least the ferret squad had a new pawn: B-3 had decided to put George Dasch to work—for the Americans.

Meyer and Haffenden went for a walk in Central Park. Meyer was pleased to learn that Dasch's life had been spared. Dasch was, after all, more valuable alive than dead to all parties.

"The question," Haffenden said, "is how to make use of him to get Brahms. We can't have Dasch go to his handler and say he knows about ship movements. He just won't buy that after all the coverage."

"That's not how I would go anyway," Meyer said.

"What do you propose?"

"I haven't thought it through yet, Commander. But there is one thing I've always been able to count on in tricky situations."

"And what is that, Meyer?"

"Greed."

Going to Work

GEORGE DASCH, ALIVE AND GRATEFUL, SAT ALONE IN THE CRAMPED basement of a house in Larchmont, a leafy suburb of New York City without the self-congratulation of its sibling Scarsdale, where Bugsy Siegel's wife and two daughters lived. He had been driven there blindfolded an hour before by two government men after being transported from Washington, D.C. Dasch was told he could remove his blindfold once he was left alone. His hosts let him stew for an hour to walk around the basement and study the heating ducts. It was not lost on him that the only exit was the stairs the G-men had gone up when they abandoned him.

The basement door opened. Dasch first saw the sharply pleated pant leg of someone he'd hoped he would never see again. When the matinee-idol-handsome man stepped into the light, Dasch wished for a moment he had been executed with his compatriots.

Bugsy Siegel held out his arms as if he were greeting one of his young daughters. "Bubbie!" he said to Dasch.

"Please don't hurt me."

Siegel frowned. "Hurt you? Why, Georgie, we're partners now."

"What are we going to do?"

"Have a seat."

Dasch complied while Siegel found another chair and sat across from him.

"Well, George, the good news is you get to live. But the even better news is we get to work together on a special mission! Can you believe it? I'm very happy about this personally because I felt we became very close when we met last time. I'm actually very sensitive, which is something that not a lot of people know about me.

"Anyhow, I'd like to introduce you to a friend of mine from the navy, Commander Haffenden. He's going to tell you about our new adventure."

Siegel went back up the stairs and returned with Haffenden. Dasch stood up.

"Sit down," Haffenden ordered Dasch.

Haffenden took Siegel's chair as Siegel paced behind him.

"Mr. Dasch," Haffenden began, "you know that your friends were electrocuted a few days ago."

"Yes, I know. I was shown their bodies."

"And you know that you are lucky not to have been one of them?"

"Yes, I know."

"And you know that between my capabilities and those of Mr. Siegel that if you don't cooperate with us, your good fortune could find itself reversed?"

"I know."

"Good. Now, Mr. Dasch, tell me, who was the man you were supposed to meet, your main contact or handler—the one on Riverside Drive—when you got to the United States?"

"His name is van Voorst. Or, at least that was the name I was told."

"Have you met him since you have been here?"

"No."

"Why not?"

"We were captured."

"Are you aware that the newspapers have reported that *all* of the spies were executed?"

"No."

"Do you know why that is, Mr. Dasch?"

"No."

"I'll tell you why," Haffenden said. "We want people to think all of the spies were executed. We want your friend van Voorst and this fellow called Brahms to believe this, too. This way they'll think you are more valuable than we both know you really are. As I think you know, Brahms is the man who has been providing Nazi U-boats with information about our convoy movements. Your Mr. van Voorst may be the one relaying information from someone at the docks to Brahms. Is there anything else you want to tell us about Brahms?" Haffenden withheld the little nugget that B-3 had found at least one of the waterfront agents, Arnie Matthews, who had ultimately led them to the Long Island landing.

"I don't know much. We were told he was . . . a giant with a very scarred face."

"What else?"

"That he knew very well the communications, and that he was a Waffen SS man. Very violent, tortured Jews or Germans that were sympathetic to them."

"That's all the more reason to catch him," Haffenden said.

"What would you like me to do?"

"I would like you to go to van Voorst. I want you to tell him that you were the spy that got away, that not all eight spies were caught and executed. Tell him that your plan, the one to blow up different targets in America, is no longer possible because the Americans have seized your matériel and know the targets."

"Then of what use am I to him?" Dasch asked.

"I think you need to be worried about that, Mr. Dasch. You need to worry about that for your sake, and you need to show van Voorst that you are worried. You can also tell him that one of your contacts presented an opportunity, an opportunity that you're not so sure about."

Dasch looked beyond Haffenden and saw the alley-cat movement of Bugsy Siegel's shadow waxing and waning beyond the lone bulb that feebly lit the basement.

"What is this opportunity?" Dasch asked.

Siegel reached into his breast pocket, causing Dasch to recoil. He breathed a sigh of relief when Siegel dropped a wad of $100 bills on his lap, then retreated back into the darkness.

Haffenden said, "We'd like you to tell van Voorst that one of your contacts is in the importing business and that he is going to have some very valuable shipments coming in from, well, wherever. The only problem is that they need to pull their boats into secret locations on the East Coast near New York. See, they don't have the communications equipment to get the job done because the Americans control all of the communications command centers and are monitoring the coast.

"If there were some way that someone who had access to communications equipment—and who knew how to avoid detection—could simply guide these motorboats into secret locations without being seen, there would be a great deal of money in it, as much as thirty thousand dollars in the next few months."

"What are these boats carrying?"

"If van Voorst asks you, just show him the kind of money you've already been paid just to ask your contacts. There's five thousand dollars in that wad Mr. Siegel just handed you."

"All yours, bubbie," Siegel chimed in helpfully.

"All this money, just to help guide some boats around?" Dasch asked.

"All that money," Haffenden answered.

"It must be something pretty important."

"That's not yours to determine, Mr. Dasch," Haffenden said. "We all need to supplement our income somehow, wouldn't you agree?"

"I guess so."

Dasch sat staring at the bills in his lap. Haffenden could tell that Dasch had probably concluded that the shipments would contain narcotics, the only thing that could fetch that kind of dough.

Truth was, there were no drugs and there would be no boats. Haffenden wanted to float the idea that he was corrupt because it would validate why he seemed to be in business with a man like Bugsy Siegel, not to mention that one of the first things Haffenden had learned in spy school is that one's enemies were preternaturally inclined to believe *their* enemies were uniquely venal. Haffenden's vagueness certified the subtext of all of these things all toward one end: rattling the cages to see if the charade led to Brahms, who might be intrigued by the promise of a fresh windfall. Indeed, after years in hiding, he might think he deserved such a jackpot.

"Mr. Dasch," Haffenden began again, "you'll need to believe in this opportunity that we're giving you with all your heart and soul, because if you don't, when we win this war, we will pay your father, Klaus, and your mother, Mitzi, and your sister, Eva, and her daughters a visit. And once we've visited with them, you will spend a very long time as the guest of my friend Mr. Siegel. His will be the last face you see, not mine."

Siegel stepped one last time into the light for Dasch to behold. The madman hadn't been kidding: This was a different kind of Jew.

Siegel and Haffenden went back upstairs.

"Did I do all right, Commander?" Siegel asked.

"You were fine, Ben."

"I hope we're helping you out the way you wanted. Meyer's taking this awful seriously. This sure is different from my other jobs."

"Me, too. With my other jobs, they were . . . jobs. It's hard to feel strong about selling biscuits," Haffenden said.

"Selling biscuits? Is that what you did, Commander?"

"I was once the sales manager for the National Biscuit Company, Ben. So many of the things we do every day are just going through the motions. Selling biscuits, basically. It doesn't do any harm, but it doesn't do any good. The thing about this project is that nobody's doing anything like it. It's attacking the Nazis in a way they're not expecting, really helping us where we're vulnerable."

"That's all you'll say?"

"Secrets are kept for a reason, Ben."

"People think when you keep secrets, you're doing something wrong."

"That kind of conspiracy thinking goes back to the beginning of the country, people seeing the king's agents everywhere, whispering to each other that we're really not a democracy after all. The thing is, when you're up against someone as dangerous as Hitler, you can't knock on his front door."

"You never know, maybe if you put it that nicely." Siegel winked.

"I'll tell you one thing. George Washington didn't put it nicely. You can't imagine the spy operations he had going during the Revolution."

"And I thought he just chopped down cherry trees and apologized."

"You don't get to be the commander of that rabble by going tent to tent telling all those toothless hard cases, Mother-Goose fables about honesty. Old George didn't hesitate to have spies and deserters lined up and shot. Washington looked like a king, but he could be vicious. Lincoln was folksy, but if you were a threat to his agenda, you'd get a visit from some mean hombres. Still, it's hard to see Washington and Lincoln getting all dressed up in black and messing around with men who creep around in the night."

"We're a nation of men who creep around in the night, Commander."

The Pinch

MEYER'S SON BUDDY TOLD HIS FATHER HOW IT HAPPENED.

Anne Lansky answered the door bloody-eyed at six in the morning after she heard the three loud knocks. Anne had heard these knocks before. She put on her bathrobe. She took one look at the plainclothes detective's badge, rolled her eyes, and said, "He's not here."

"We're looking for Meyer Lansky," the detective said. A uniformed officer stood behind him.

"He moved out," Anne said.

"Who's at the door?" Buddy asked, hobbling up on his crutches.

"Go back to bed, Buddy," she ordered.

Buddy saw the cops in the hall. "What do the police want, Mom?"

"The police want what they always want. They want criminals, and there aren't any criminals here." Anne then said to the police, "If you want a criminal, there's another tenant in this building, Frank Costello. Maybe he'll know about whatever god-awful thing you're looking into."

Anne slammed the door and went back to bed.

Later that morning, Meyer was midbite into his toast at

Lindy's when he felt a clap on his shoulder. He looked up, still chewing.

"Meyer Lansky?" a big man with greased-back hair said. He threw his badge on the table.

"Yes," Meyer said.

"I'm Detective Young. You need to come with me." Two uniformed officers were with him.

"Am I under arrest?"

"Not now you're not. C'mon, let's go."

"Where do you want me to go?"

"We're going down near the financial district."

"You're taking me forcibly to Wall Street? I'll give you investment advice right here."

"C'mon, Lansky."

"If you guys are who you say you are, you'll tell me right now where we're going."

Detective Young shot his best tombstone eyes at Meyer. Meyer shot him his own tombstone eyes back. *Fuck him, mine are better.* Meyer thought Young shuddered a little. *Good, dip into that fear bank a little.*

"Attorney general's office. State of New York."

"Now, was that so hard, Young? I have to pay my tab."

"Right, you wouldn't want to steal from somebody," Young said.

"You're right. These people work very hard." Meyer wasn't kidding. He put a few bucks down on the table, picked up his hat, and left with Detective Young.

Wolfie's Restaurant

Miami Beach, December 1982

After my initial interview with Uncle Meyer the morning after I got to Miami Beach, I went back to the Singapore to organize my notes and go for a run. A local radio station was playing back-to-back Bob Dylan songs. I didn't usually think of Dylan as an aerobic musician, but I did get lost in his lyrics, trying to figure out what he was saying. It was easy for a young person to suffer the misapprehension that Dylan was trying to tell him something.

One Dylan song in particular, "It's Alright, Ma (I'm Only Bleeding)," got me wondering. A line in it had long been the object of my fascination: "He not busy being born is busy dying." How could a person be busy dying? Don't you just die? Outside of killing yourself, there wasn't a hell of a lot you could do. The strange thing was that given what I was doing here with Uncle Meyer, the lyric suddenly made sense: By summoning all of his faculties to tell me what he had done during World War II, Uncle Meyer was, in fact, *busy dying.*

The schlepper Hymie Krumholtz came to the Singapore at five. Then we swung back to pick up Uncle Meyer for a ride to Wolfie's restaurant, famous for deli food. I got a kick out of how early these old people ate dinner. Given that I was raised by my grandparents, my biorhythm could easily accommodate this schedule.

Krumholtz pulled into the driveway of the Singapore in the same tan Chevrolet Malibu he had driven when he picked me up at the airport. Not your average Mafia staff car. I entered the Imperial House and met Uncle Meyer in the lobby and helped him out to the car.

Krumholtz drove at the speed of smell. We were practically going in reverse. What should have been a quick hop to Wolfie's took fifteen minutes. As we inched closer to the restaurant, I was disconcerted to see a line around the block. I vaguely recalled that Wolfie's didn't take reservations.

"Whoa," I said, craning my neck around.

"It's always a *kesselgarten*. Don't worry about it," Uncle Meyer said.

Krumholtz stopped outside the entrance. I got out on the street side and walked around to help Uncle Meyer out of the car. He was having difficulty, and it took me a minute to get him on his feet. He held my arm as we approached.

The people in line tittered when they saw him as if he were Aerosmith. Their eyes then slid over to me. Their faces were masks of puzzlement. I supposed they had expected a scary-looking *gavone*, not a collegiate-looking kid in a V-neck sweater and khaki pants. A few of them waved to Uncle Meyer, who nodded from behind big sunglasses.

A large man was waiting at the entrance holding the door open. The decibels audibly lowered as we made our way inside to Uncle Meyer's booth in the back. I overheard one man who had a problem with voice modulation say, "If any other Jew on the planet had cut in line like that, we'd be saying kaddish."

"Good evening, Mr. Lansky," a waitress named Betty said. "The usual?"

"Just the soup. My appetite isn't so good."

"I'm sure it'll be back in no time," Betty said. "Who's this handsome young man?"

"My nephew, the future president of the USA." Even though the whole statement was ridiculous, it made me feel good. I was a sucker for anybody who expressed an interest in adopting me, lies included.

I stood. "I'm Jonah Eastman."

"So, Jonah, is your appetite better than your uncle's?"

"I don't need to look at the menu. I'll have matzo-ball soup and a corned-beef sandwich with Russian dressing and coleslaw."

"How'd you like that for an appetite, Betty?" Uncle Meyer said.

"We'll send up all the corned beef he wants to the White House after he's elected."

I actually had the youthful grandiosity to fleetingly envision this.

"Jonah, what's on tap for tonight's lesson?" Uncle Meyer asked.

"Um, well . . ." My head was saturated with a million fragmented thoughts. "Were you scared about the police coming after you?" Good, Jonah. Dazzle Meyer Lansky with your probing questions.

"Are you kidding? I was shitting my pants."

I laughed out loud. I don't know what I was expecting him to say. Maybe I thought he'd have some scripted Edward G. Robinson gangster line: *Nyaa, see, I knew I'd beat da rap, da bums. Nyaa, nyaa.* (Maybe that was Bugs Bunny.)

"What happened with the police?"

"We'll get there, kid."

"What made you get a bad feeling after all your progress?"

"That's how I get when things are going good."

"Did you think your work was done at that point?"

"Not by a long shot. Our ships were still being lost even though things were better. We hadn't found Brahms, who was directing the U-boats smack into our ships. Anastasia was a wild card with his talk about blowing up the *Normandie*, and Charlie was still in jail. Then there was Benny Siegel, who decided he was James Bond, going to personally wipe out the Third Reich."

"What did he do?"

"Ben had a fling a few years ago with an American broad who became an Italian countess, Dorothy DiFrasso. He went to Italy with her on what he called a fact-finding mission. I think the only facts he found were under her dress. He even met two of her guests: Hermann Goering and Joseph Goebbels. He came to Charlie and me with an idea to kill them. Mussolini, too. This was Ben. He'd go in and out of his *mishegoss*. Never understood what leads to what. Like how the Japs lost the war when they bombed Pearl Harbor."

This didn't make sense to me. "I don't follow."

"There's an old joke. A guy goes into a bar with a pile of dog shit in his hand. He says to the bartender, 'Look at what I almost stepped in.' He's got dog shit in his hand, see. What I'm saying is that the Japs were impressed that they bombed us, but didn't figure Roosevelt would come at them with everything we had, including men like me who under normal circumstances they wouldn't have touched with a ten-foot pole. The Japs picked up dog shit at Pearl Harbor."

"Did Ben try to go after Mussolini?"

Uncle Meyer evinced a slight smile. "In his own way. He had the countess tell the dictator that she was friendly with an 'American scientist' who had developed a new explosive that would be useful in combat. Mussolini, whose hold on power was shaky, invested in the new 'miracle' technology. He had his agents give Countess DiFrasso fifty thousand dollars as a down payment. Schmuck.

"The countess and Benny showed up in the Italian countryside to demonstrate the new bomb. Mussolini was disappointed to see a pathetic little puff of smoke come out of whatever the hell it was Ben tried to blow up. He demanded his money back. Ben said he'd get right on that. Instead he gave the fifty thousand to a young fellow who was running guns to Jews in Palestine."

"Did Ben go to Italy just to swindle Mussolini?"

Uncle Meyer's face grew serious now. He shook his head no. "Ben and Charlie had their own thing going. Dope. Because of how they lived, they needed quick cash. They had a weakness for that business, which I wouldn't touch. I didn't see what they had going behind my back as a betrayal; I saw it as a relief.

"That's also why I was so worried about what I was hearing about how the *Normandie* was torched for the insurance. See, Charlie and Ben liked . . . real *crime* crime. I was no yeshiva student when we were kids, but as I got older, I didn't like the rough stuff. I didn't see booze and gambling as crimes, Jonah. I saw them as businesses that society people would have been rewarded for if they could turn a profit at it, which they eventually did."

"But you didn't actually think Charlie and Ben were responsible for the *Normandie*?"

"Hold your horses, kid."

Hmm. "How did you find out about Ben and dope?"

Uncle Meyer took a sip of his coffee and cleared his throat. "When Ben got back from Europe, he started running his mouth about the Italians. He said he'd been to Sicily with his countess friend. He said that the Sicilians hated the Nazis and didn't like that Mussolini got in bed with them. The Sicilians were angry that the Nazis were all over their country. Ben said that just because the Italians are partners with Hitler, it didn't mean the Sicilians were. Ben said, 'Look at their history, Meyer, how they deal with invaders. They let them think they're in charge, but they run their own thing when nighttime comes.'

"I asked Ben what he was doing in Sicily and he got all *farmisht.* He came up with some nonsense, but I figured it was drug business. But I learned something about Sicily that gave me an idea later on. But first, I had to try to smooth things over with poor Haffenden after the roust with the cops."

"What did you do?"

"Pulled every idea out of my ass I could. I had Haffenden bring his men and their wives to the Copacabana."

"I've heard of that place."

"Yeah, what did you hear?"

"'Copacabana.' It's a Barry Manilow song."

"Is he that rock-and-roll singer?" Uncle Meyer asked.

I wasn't sure how to answer that. Barry Manilow wasn't exactly a headbanger. So I just said yes.

"Frank Costello owned the Copa, a fancy nightclub. Not officially, of course. One night, we closed the Copa to the public. Only Haffenden and his B-3 men and their wives and girls could come in. We didn't tell them what to expect, just that it would be a special evening."

Uncle Meyer was more animated telling this odd diversionary tale than with anything else he had imparted so far.

"Everybody came in looking all nice, the men in their uniforms, the women in beautiful dresses. I had never seen such a nice, clean-cut group of people. You should have seen the look on their faces when the curtain opened up and they saw Tommy Dorsey himself. Tommy played his most popular selections like 'I'll Never Smile Again,' 'Swing Time Up in Harlem,' and 'Yes, Indeed.'

"About an hour into the show, Tommy begged the audience's

indulgence. He explained that show business was tough and how it was nice to give a new kid a break, let him try out a couple of songs. Didn't the audience agree? They all clapped very friendly, not knowing what to expect.

"This young, skinny kid, midtwenties, comes onstage, probably five-seven. Weighed about one hundred and twenty pounds dipped in tar. His hair was a dark brown mop combed straight back in a pompadour. Under the bright stage lights, you could see a scar on the left side of his face beneath the corner of his lip, and running along his jaw to his left earlobe, which was partially missing. The scar was interesting to men and women in a different way. The men thought it made the kid look tougher than he would have been without it. Women thought it made him look vulnerable. 'Who hurt this sweet boy?'" Uncle Meyer laughed a little. "Somebody told me he got the scar and the chopped-up ear when he was born from a pair of forceps. No matter how big he got, he never did anything to have it fixed. He would make photographers for his albums take him from his right side. But the thing that really jumped was these blue eyes he had—"

"Francis Albert?"

"That's our boy. You should have seen the look on the girls' faces, Jonah."

"Mickey introduced me to Sinatra when he played at the Golden Prospect, but I never noticed the scars you mentioned."

Uncle Meyer, busy dying, grew wistful. Betty put our orders down on the table. When she left, his eyes misted and he became otherworldly, as if the Angel of Death himself had imparted an eleventh-hour poetic capacity to this old hard case.

"I don't know, kid. I guess as nature took command of Sinatra's appearance, the scars of that Jersey pier town of his vanished into the ages, and the cover-up was complete."

IV.

America Ganef

MEPHISTOPHELES: *If you care to join forces with me for life, I shall be very happy to oblige you on the spot. I'll be your companion and, if I suit, I'll be your servant, your slave.*

FAUST: *And what do I have to do in return?*

MEPHISTOPHELES: *There's plenty of time for that.*

—GOETHE, *Faust*

Joker in the Deck

FRANK COSTELLO ANSWERED THE DOOR IN A SILK BATHROBE, APPEARING kingly. The plainclothes detective flashed his badge.

"Yes, gentlemen?" Costello said in his croaky voice.

"Mr. Costello, we'd like you to come with us for questioning."

"Questioning about what?"

"We'll deal with that downtown."

"Downtown where?"

"Lower Manhattan. State Police."

"I been drivin' too fast?"

"Don't worry about it, Frank."

"You're not gonna tell me what's goin' on?"

"Downtown, Frank."

Costello shrugged. "You mind if I shower and shave?"

"There's no time for that, sir."

Costello was particular about his appearance. So he went into his bathroom, showered, shaved, and put on his suit and tie.

Fuck downtown.

Socks Lanza was beheading fish on a counter at the Fulton Fish Market when three police officers, two plainclothes, one uniformed, stormed in and badged him.

Socks read the badge. Detective Marshall. New York State Police.

"What'd I do now, Marshall?" Socks asked, wiping a large knife on his bloody bib.

"We need you to come in for questioning, Socks," Marshall said.

"What'd I do now?"

"It's something about the docks. You hear anything about what's going on, on the docks?"

"Yeah. I hear there's fishies on the docks," Socks said. "And the water over there's all wet."

"I'm sure that'll impress the attorney general."

Socks was thinking, *They screwed us. I knew they was gonna screw us.* "You know Gurfein?"

"Don't know any Gurfein," Marshall said.

And why would he? Gurfein was with the New York City district attorney's office. Marshall was New York *State*. "Who you with?"

"Attorney general of the State of New York."

Socks took off his homicidal bib and waddled from behind the counter. "You know something, Marshall?"

"What?"

"If you was in the old West, you'd be Marshal Marshall."

"You learn that at Harvard, Socks?"

"Nah. Part of my stand-up act inna Catskills."

"I'll look forward to your show. Now, come with us and get in the back of the car."

When Meyer got down to the Manhattan office of the New York attorney general, he saw Costello and Socks sitting on a bench next to a couple of pickpockets. If this weren't such a serious situation, he would have thought it was a pretty amusing sight. Two uniformed police officers were watching them from across the room.

"Top of the morning, Meyer," Costello said.

"Good morning," Meyer said. "Do you know what this is about?"

Socks said, "Something about the docks. I told 'em I heard that docks have water and fish around 'em." Socks chuckled at his wit.

"I don't get this New York State beef. They just showed up," Costello said. "It's gotta be about the docks if they got Socks here. But state? Don't make sense. Anyhow, Meyer, they said they got your wife outta bed. She was real annoyed."

"She's always real annoyed," Meyer said.

A man in a suit came out of an office and introduced himself as Inspector Arthur Sparrow of the New York attorney general's office. He said that his specialty was labor fraud.

"What the hell's labor fraud?" Socks asked. "Pretendin' you're a laborer? I got plenty-a them."

Sparrow ignored him and asked Socks to come with him.

The men were each taken into separate interview rooms. After an hour of waiting, Meyer opened the door and asked if he could have a newspaper. An officer said no. He asked if he could have a piece of paper to write on. An annoyed-looking officer tore a piece of paper from a pad and gave it to him. Meyer went back to the interview room and kept himself busy with algebra.

Finally, Sparrow came in with a stenographer. He did not apologize for making Meyer wait. Keeping Meyer waiting was a measurement of success to a man like him.

"We're looking into allegations of racket activity on the waterfront," Sparrow said when he sat across from Meyer.

Meyer said nothing.

"Did you hear me?"

"Yes, sir."

"Do you have interests on the waterfront?"

"No."

"You seemed to know those men out in the waiting area."

Uh-huh.

"How do you know them?"

"They're friends."

"You don't have business with them, Lansky?"

"No."

"We've got people who say you have business with them."

"They're wrong."

"Mr. Lanza says he works with you on some business on the docks."

Meyer knew this was a lie. "He may have me confused with someone else. I have no business with him."

"What about Lucky Luciano?" Sparrow smirked.

"We were friends. We worked together during Prohibition."

"What did you do with him during Prohibition?"

"We owned an automobile company."

"What did you do with the automobiles?"

"We drove them."

"I understand that, but you drove them to what end?"

"To get from one place to another."

Sparrow gritted his teeth. "Did you transport liquor?"

"We just drove things from place to place. We liked the fresh air. You realize, Mr. Sparrow, Prohibition's over? My attorney is going to be very annoyed if you brought me here for a history lesson."

"I decide what to ask, not you, Lansky."

"Ask whatever you want, but I don't know what you're talking about."

"But you do know Lanza?"

"I told you I did."

"It's come to our attention that you and Mr. Lanza are working on some kind of project on the docks. Something involving the navy."

Polakoff's voice echoed through Meyer's skull. *Less is more.*

"Sounds like you are just fishing on those docks."

"I'm doing more than fishing. Some of your boys like playing with fire, don't they? We know exactly what you're up to."

Meyer knew Sparrow didn't know what his gang was up to, but that he knew something. The thing about playing with fire cut Meyer to the bone even if it was just a figure of speech. That line of questioning was bad news. It meant that the *Normandie* questions didn't die with the Long Island saboteurs, and of course he had the lunatic Anastasia running around as if he did the job to boost his hoodlum image with his crew. Meyer didn't need to be in criminal jeopardy to have a shit storm on his hands. The success of his ferret squad was based on secrecy. If Sparrow started poking around, it would be bad for Meyer, bad for Luciano, and bad for America.

Meyer leaned in closer to Sparrow and asked, "Do you consider yourself a patriot, Mr. Sparrow?"

"What are you talking about?"

"I am asking about your patriotism."

"Of course, I love my country. What—?" Sparrow glanced at his stenographer.

"Do you respect the laws of this country?" Meyer asked.

"Of course I do—"

"Do you respect our men in uniform?"

"Wait, who the hell are you to question me?" Meyer figured Sparrow was trying to save face with the stenographer.

"I'm a patriot," Meyer said. "You, sir, are not. If you were, you would know better than to drag an honest citizen who loves his country into a police station just because you can. If you don't intend to arrest me, I'm leaving. If you do intend to arrest me, call my lawyer, Moses Polakoff, and tell him why."

Costello, Socks, and Meyer went straight to Polakoff's office after the unpleasantness. Polakoff heard them out and took notes.

"He's cage-rattling," Polakoff said. "My concern at the moment isn't criminal exposure, it's the navy matter you've gotten into. Do you know about a man named Harry Bridges?"

"He's that commie longshoreman outta San Francisco," Costello said.

A leftist rabble-rouser, Bridges ran the International Longshore and Warehouse Union, or ILWU. The ILWU was the West Coast version of the International Longshoremen's Association, Socks and Cockeye's union. The mob's union. The two unions hadn't really ever stepped on each other's toes given their geographical distance, but there had always been the possibility of a rivalry as the labor movement gained political power nationally, and even socialists dreamed of empire.

"Commander Haffenden called me," Polakoff said. "He's hearing rumblings from his sources that Bridges is going to make a play for the ILA. He's telling all kinds of stories about gangsters on the piers, the *Normandie,* and so forth."

"Son of a bitch!" Socks said.

"What did you tell him, Moe?" Costello asked.

"I told him I didn't know anything about it, but that I'd tell you. I didn't know about this New York attorney general development when I talked to Haffenden. We'll need to report this to him."

"That's all I need is another pinch," Socks said.

"It's worse than that," Meyer said. "If there's an investigation and Harry Bridges moves in on the ILA, the navy will drop us like a hot potato. You can't just start educating new management on something like this. That's bad for you, Socks, and worse for Charlie."

Socks asked, "What if Haffenden drops us like a hot potato?"

Polakoff said, "He doesn't want this blowing up either."

"That's true," Costello said. "Better he should hear from us than think we're pulling a long-con on him."

"Strange, don't you think?" Meyer said. "That this Sparrow shakedown happens at the same time Haffenden gets word about a union move?"

"Never occurred to me," Costello said sarcastically.

"You need to talk to Haffenden, gents," Polakoff advised.

On the way out of Polakoff's office, Costello waved Meyer into the restroom. He turned on the faucet so hot water was coming out strong and steam was rising.

Costello moved in close to Meyer. "How's everything on our special project?"

Meyer knew what he meant. Meyer and Costello were the only two who knew about a certain little sideshow.

"Coming along slowly, Frank. Sit tight, pal."

"You pull this off, I owe you big."

"Forget about it."

When Socks returned to work, his men were panicked. They confronted him about the "bust." The more Socks denied it was a bust, the more the longshoremen were convinced they were in play. They demanded to know when they were all going to get pinched. Most of these guys had guilty consciences, for good reason.

"Nobody's getting busted for nothing," Socks said.

"I dunno, Socks, guys is talking," a longshoreman known as Bugle said. "You got that beef, I know—"

"I'm on appeal," Socks said sternly.

"I know, Socks," Bugle said. "But we dunno when that gets pulled and you go away, see? Now, we's hearin' crazy talk about our guys burning up that ship. We's hearing from some guys that when Harry Bridges comes to town in a couple-a weeks, he's gonna take us over 'cause of all the corruption."

"What some guys?" Cockeye demanded.

Bugle handed Socks a business card, then walked away with the others, save Cockeye.

Socks showed the card to Cockeye. "Whattayou make-a this?"

Cockeye studied the card. "Allan Kurtzman. Never heard-a him."

"Me neither."

"Guy got balls," said Cockeye.

"Maybe. Or maybe he's got somebody here with us who's tellin' him he got a shot of takin' over, ya know, Cockeye?"

"Was wonderin' about that myself."

Commander Haffenden called Murray Gurfein in the district attorney's office and told him about Sparrow and the New York attorney general roust. Gurfein asked if Haffenden would give him a couple of hours to check things out, then stop by his office.

When Haffenden showed up, he found the rackets prosecutor upset. "Well, Commander, let it never be said that everybody in government knows what they're doing and is working from one concerted plan."

"You're telling me, Murray? I'm in the military."

"Here's the situation. This roundup is straight out of the attorney general of New York State. State. We didn't know anything about it and we don't control it. Governor-elect Dewey and his team operate on their own agenda. That's the long and short of it."

"Why is Dewey taking this on now?" Haffenden asked. "He's going to be sworn in, in a few weeks."

"We don't know that he's even aware of it, just that it's coming from the state level," Gurfein explained. "For all we know, it started with the Democratic AG for political reasons. I wish I knew more, Commander."

Haffenden became tense. "What does this mean for Socks, Murray? He's still free on whatever it is your people have on him."

Gurfein got edgy, too. "Now, Commander, when this whole thing started, we made it very clear that there would be no leniency for these racket guys."

"I don't know, Murray . . . Socks is doing good work. He's got those dock guys terrified, looking for Nazi snitches everywhere, which is what we wanted. . . . Your boss, Hogan, worked for Dewey. Isn't there anything he can do? Put in a call?"

"Call Dewey and tell him we've enlisted Luciano? I don't think so, Commander."

Haffenden breathed heavy the way he did. Gurfein felt sorry for him because he thought Haffenden was sick. He couldn't help but wonder what Haffenden's payout would be from working with a bunch of hoodlums.

"What do you recommend we do, Murray?"

"Off the record?"

"Of course."

"For one thing, you need to understand that this state investigation could trigger questions about why Socks is still walking the streets with an extortion conviction. The danger of working with these characters is that even if they're not guilty of everything state thinks, they're sure as hell guilty of something. I'm even hearing some noise that Luciano may have had Siegel or Anastasia light the fire on the *Normandie*—"

"That's bullshit, Murray!"

"Probably so, Commander. But this isn't about forensics; it's political. If Bridges succeeds with his union play, the state's shenanigans are vindicated. If he fails and becomes a political liability, well, there you go."

George Dasch sat on a bench in Washington Square watching for pigeons and Nazis. The pigeons were easy to spot; the Nazis, not so much.

Several minutes after the appointed hour, a thin man with an Ichabod Crane Adam's apple and dressed in a drab business suit sat beside him. "Good afternoon," he said, betraying a slight accent.

"Good afternoon."

"It's a nice park, isn't it? Although I prefer Yorkville," Ichabod said.

Yorkville. The German section of town. *Bingo.* "I do, too. I'm new here."

"You're a lucky man, Dasch, getting away and all."

"I know it, van Voorst. I just went out for cigarettes when they came for Burger. Luck was all it was."

"So, what now?" van Voorst asked. "Hail the next U-boat back to Berlin?"

Dasch explained that he was at a loss about what to do now. He was stranded in America. He couldn't possibly start scrounging for explosives and finish up what the Pastorius saboteurs had set out to do.

"No, Dasch, that's no longer an option."

"Could I be of some use to you?"

"I don't know, can you? You seem like a sad sack. That isn't exactly a useful skill for an agent."

"I cannot pretend, van Voorst, that I am a master spy. The only thing I seem to be good at while I've been in America is making money."

"How do you make money, Dasch?"

Dasch explained that his friends in the waiters' union had him doing deliveries of some kind. He said he had been making short trips delivering chemical supplies to a warehouse in northern New Jersey, and he was paid handsomely for this seemingly menial task. The problem was that this job was coming to an end.

"Why is that?"

"I do not have details," Dasch explained. "I only know that my friends have been unable to receive shipments here of whatever it is they're getting in New York because they can't get anything through the docks."

"Is this narcotics?"

"I do not ask. It may just be supplies for the process. But there is so much money involved that I think it may be what you said. But it is over. I don't know how to bring boats and their cargo into New York."

"Must it be New York?"

"Nearby at least."

"What kind of money are we talking about?"

Dasch told van Voorst that he had made $5,000 so far.

"In the short time you have been here?" van Voorst asked.

"Yes."

"I would not get involved in making deliveries—much too dangerous—but what if I could find a way to bring boats into this area? Not New York, but close. What kind of money could I make?"

"I don't know. I could ask—"

"Don't mention me, Dasch, when you talk to your friends. Just ask what *you* could make, and I would take something from your portion."

"I will do that. I don't know how I will make a living with what's happening. If I could just get this kind of money for the next few months, I might be able to disappear."

"That should be worth something to you, no?" van Voorst asked.

"It would be, yes—if you think you could find a way to get boats quietly here. Wait one minute." Dasch turned away from van Voorst, reached into his pocket, and peeled off ten $100 bills. He gave them to van Voorst. "This is one thousand dollars. You will check on a way my friends could bring boats in?"

Van Voorst quickly stuffed the cash in his pockets, got up, and walked away.

Hitler on the Hudson

HAFFENDEN WANTED TO MEET RIGHT AWAY AT AN OUT-OF-THE-WAY place. He told Costello, Socks, and Meyer to come to a Chelsea pier in casual clothes. A Coast Guard boat took the men for a spin around Manhattan, which was pleasant in the late autumn. They met on a small, covered deck.

Haffenden looked pale in the sunlight, his skin like wax. Meyer had never seen him look so shaken. Haffenden had always said there would be hurdles, but it was with a twinkle, as if everybody knew the right guys would win in the end. Not today.

"A stevedore in Harry Bridges's union floated up on Fisherman's Wharf in Frisco yesterday morning," Haffenden began. "They won't give me too many details other than to say they think the guy was killed and that it was meant as a warning to Bridges."

"I don't mean to bring everybody down, but word on my docks is that Anastasia's been making noises about hitting Bridges," Socks said.

When Meyer heard that name, he felt as if DiMaggio had whacked him in the *kishkas* with his Louisville Slugger.

"Albert's sayin' that?" Costello asked.

"Yeah," Socks said.

Meyer thought Haffenden was going to die on the spot. Costello said, "Commander, that ain't gonna happen so don't you worry."

Haffenden breathed in as if he were desperate for oxygen. "For Christ's sake, Frank, you have to sit on Anastasia. If Bridges even gets a hangnail, we're *all* finished. Nothing else means a damned thing if somebody blows Bridges's brains out all over the Fulton Fish Market." After a beat, he added, "And another thing you should know: My brass and Murray Gurfein are hearing rumors about Anastasia being involved with the *Normandie*. Maybe Ben Siegel, too."

"It's a load of shit," Meyer snapped. "Believe me, I've talked to them."

"Who the fuck knows?" Socks said. "Albert can be two-faced."

"Just keep an eye on your men, Socks," Costello ordered, clearly unhappy with Socks's free association.

Socks said okay. "But I can't go pushing around Albert."

"Meyer and I will deal with Albert," Costello said.

"Damn well better," Haffenden said. "But what about Bridges? He's still coming to town in a couple weeks. Very charismatic, like a preacher. The man's a demagogue. He doesn't need to produce a body to say somebody killed one of his men. A guy like that could just say that some old stevedore who happened to have died did so under suspicious circumstances."

"Ben Siegel says Bridges isn't connected with any outfit," Meyer said.

"The nerve-a the guy!" Costello said. They all laughed. Well, not Haffenden. "What do you know, Commander?"

Haffenden explained that Bridges was from Australia. "Very radical."

"How radical?" Meyer asked. "*Communist* radical?"

Haffenden said that he didn't know yet. "All I know is that Bridges has been giving speeches about cleaning up the unions from mob influence."

"I don't blame him," Costello said with a smirk. "The mob they got out in San Francisco wears ballet tutus."

"Sounds like they need a real mob, guys who wear pants," Socks said, his belly heaving.

"This is serious, boys," Haffenden said. "You really helped tighten things up on the docks, but we need to keep it that way. We've got a lot of reasons—all of us—why we want our ferret squad to stay healthy. All I know is our ships have to come and go across the Atlantic unmolested, and we can't have Hitler cruising up and down the Hudson willy-nilly."

The Navy must be planning something big. We had better be a part of it, Meyer thought, *or we're out on our immigrant asses.*

"I can't stress this enough," Haffenden added. "No goddamn Anastasia or Siegel stunts! Then Sparrow finds the crime he's looking for, and we're all screwed."

"Nothing will happen to Bridges in that kinda way," Costello said.

Meyer had known Costello long enough to know that he wasn't too confident about Bridges's safety, but what else could he say?

As the boat pulled into Chelsea, a shared sense of dread filled the men. With only spasmodic light in an edgy Manhattan, the greatest city in the civilized world loomed like an undead Frankenstein.

I Like Arson

BEFORE SUNRISE, IT LOOKED AS IF IT WERE GOING TO BE ANOTHER routine day at the Fulton Fish Market. Nothing seemed to be off-kilter. Fishing vessels dumped their catch on the dark, wet docks; gruff New York voices echoed, sounding as if they were picking a fight over nothing; everything, from the men to the unpainted buildings, was slippery; even the wharf smells had a slickness to them.

At sunrise, Socks Lanza was chased down by one of his men who told him about a protest at the entrance gate. When Socks heard the news, he felt his blood drop like a cinder block.

When Socks got to the gate, he was relieved to see the protest wasn't big. But something was strange, though, about this crowd with ILWU placards with messages such as ILA=I LIKE ARSON, ILWU FIGHTS FOR YOU, and HARRY BRIDGES' VISION, NOT BROOKLYN BRIDGE'S HOODLUMS. The protesters were almost all women. Ugly, frizzy-haired women, but women.

Fucking brilliant, Socks thought. Bridges sent broads.

Cockeye was on the scene within minutes.

"What the fuck?" Cockeye said.

"The prick sent broads," Socks said.

"What prick?"

"Bridges. He sent broads."

"What for?"

"'Cause we won't whack around a bunch-a broads," Socks explained.

"Why the hell not?"

"Because they're broads, Cockeye."

Cockeye looked at the screaming women. "They don't look like broads."

"They don't look like perty broads, but they don't got what we got."

"Whattaya mean?"

"You know, down there," Socks said.

"Look at 'em," Cockeye said. "How'd you know what they got?"

"C'mon, no messin' around!"

Cockeye, the great one-trick pony of the waterfront, stepped toward a large, mop-headed woman holding a sign that said NO ILA CROOKS.

"Careful, Cockeye!" Socks said.

"Yeah, yeah." Cockeye got nose to nose with the woman and asked, "Who sent ya?"

"Nobody," Mophead said, stepping back.

Everybody's tough from a distance. "Harry Bridges didn't send you?"

"We came ourselves because we believe in the cause."

"Yeah? You just woke up this morning and decided to do a little good?"

"What do you care, you pyro?"

The only thing these guys hated worse than being accused of something they really did was being accused of something they really didn't.

"You're insultin' my men is what I care. Now get the hell outta our market!"

"This is public property," Mophead said, pleased with her legalism. What she didn't get was that certain things in life were settled out of court.

"Where'd you get shit like that?" Cockeye asked, grabbing the woman's sign. Mophead resisted. A few of her cohorts came to her side and attempted to peel Cockeye off her.

"Cockeye!" Socks yelled, stepping forward to help the women pull Cockeye away.

"What the fuck, Socks?" Cockeye let go of the woman.

"This is just what Bridges wants!" Socks said.

"Yeah, well, let's give it to the son of a bitch." Then Cockeye, true to his nature, which was rooted in the belief that getting in the last shot was his mission on earth, leaned into Mophead and pushed her to the ground.

A photographer snapped Cockeye in midlunge, and the ugly, but female, Mophead fell backward. The scene could only be seen one way, and the newspaper's caption editor summarized the photo:

THUGS!!!

Meyer met Anastasia at the barbershop at the Park Sheraton. It wasn't a planned meeting; Meyer just knew Anastasia's routines. Costello and Meyer agreed that if Anastasia thought Meyer was coming to *him,* even seeming to wait on him, it might stroke his ego. Costello thought it would be better that Meyer did it because Anastasia always resented sharing the garment rackets with a Jew, Lepke. They figured if Meyer was solicitous, Anastasia might feel as if he had won the Yid-guinea struggle.

Meyer took a seat in a guest chair in the barbershop as Anastasia was being dusted off.

"Here for a shave, Meyer?" Anastasia asked when he saw him.

"Just waiting for you, Albert. I wanted to run something by you."

Meyer could see Anastasia's chest puff up as the barber was attending to him, with Meyer waiting like a handmaiden.

"Let's talk on the street," Anastasia said, self-satisfied.

The men walked outside and Anastasia asked Meyer what was on his mind.

"I was talking to some of the guys on the docks who said they heard you've got a marker on Harry Bridges," Meyer said.

"What if I do?"

"Christ, Albert, do you have any idea what that'll do to all of us? He's untouchable."

"What happened to the Meyer I knew when your guys took out Maranzano?"

"Bridges is a civilian—and a celebrity. You can't touch him, Albert. Now, we're told they're looking into a murder of one of Bridges's longshoremen. A message job, I'm told. We have to do everything we can to make sure Bridges doesn't get hurt."

"Yeah, yeah, yeah."

"I'm not kidding, Albert. This is the Dutchman all over again wanting to clip Dewey—"

"You gonna do to me what your boys did Yid-to-Yid to the Dutchman, Meyer?"

"Come on, Albert, this isn't about me. This is all of us."

Anastasia stopped cold. "Meyer, go to the library and dream up some of your respectable Chemical Bank high-finance bullshit. Leave the fuckin' street to me."

In the late afternoon, as van Voorst drove across the George Washington Bridge into New Jersey, a small civilian airplane took off from a private airport near Hoboken. The German's Buick traveled at an unimpressive speed southeast toward central New Jersey. The navy pilot at the controls of the plane noted van Voorst's direction, greatly encouraged. Assuming this was not a feint, it told B-3 that Brahms's location was, perhaps, on the central Jersey coast.

The pilot followed van Voorst for another twenty miles before a panic hit him. The sun was rapidly setting over the rolling hills near Flemington. If van Voorst continued southeast—and east was a virtual certainty because that's where the Atlantic and its hostile inhabitants lurked—he would hit the Pine Barrens, the vast woodlands that comprised more than one-fourth of the state. The Pine Barrens were the Sherwood Forest of the Garden State, a mysterious and, some said, haunted wilderness said to be populated by albinos and native "pineys," not to mention the Jersey Devil, the hideously deformed thirteenth child of an old woman named Leeds. There was also a legend about a man named Ong who tossed his hat up into the air only to have it get caught in a tree branch, which shifted like a lever and caused him to fall into a hidden opening in the earth.

Who knew what to believe? Regardless, the pilot's worst-case scenario came true: The sun was setting, and van Voorst had indeed disappeared beneath the impenetrable trees. As the pilot turned his plane back toward north Jersey, he removed his flashlight and made a note in his airman's journal that would prove to be more hopeful than he had initially recognized: *Brahms—South Jersey Pines.*

It made perfect sense. The Pine Barrens were so isolated that even the cops avoided going there, which was why the old bootleggers such as Mickey Price operated their stills in those woods, not to mention used it as a graveyard for inconvenient witnesses and obsolete personnel. Not only was it an ordeal to find anything in the pines, there was nothing anybody *wanted* to find. Moreover, while the Pine Barrens ran to the west almost to Camden and Philadelphia, they stopped to the east just before the Atlantic shoreline.

The Game Moves North

COCKEYE'S LITTLE PERFORMANCE, DECKING A WOMAN, WAS EXACTLY the kind of thing that shook Haffenden to his core. It seemed as if every time the ferret squad made a little progress, another threat was thrown down at them. The Cockeye mess was a self-inflicted wound.

There had not been one act of sabotage on the New York waterfront since the ferret squad got going, something Haffenden reminded Meyer of when they met at a greasy spoon in Brooklyn, far from where anyone could eavesdrop.

"Ship losses are falling," Haffenden said. "We only lost three or four ships last month. Last year at this time, it was two, three dozen a month."

"Progress is progress."

"The thing is, Meyer, I didn't want to say that in front of Socks or Cockeye. Guys like them could start bragging about it, or thinking they could make more demands. I know you're getting pressure from Luciano, but you understand better than the other guys do that I can't start making demands of the government before I have more results. A man is just as good as his last miracle."

"Do you have a miracle in mind, Commander?"

"Potentially. But there's something I think I should tell

you." Haffenden frowned. "We have reports that the Nazis are executing Jews in towns in Poland, including near where you're from."

Meyer felt flames behind his eyes. "Executing how?" he asked through his teeth.

"Shot in front of ditches that they were made to dig. Whole towns, we hear."

Meyer felt a burning in his stomach. "What can I do?"

Haffenden explained that the British and American navies were on the verge of a breakthrough in direction-finding equipment that would expedite the Allies' move on Europe.

"I don't really understand these gadgets myself—other than to say that if they work, they'll go a long way toward cleaning up the Atlantic once and for all. It's called radio detection and ranging, or *radar* for short."

But, as always, there was a problem. A company near Boston called Reslex made the radar. The navy suspected that the Nazis had a spy inside Reslex who was keeping Berlin informed of developments and, maybe, even sharing designs with the enemy. The navy found telephone calls had been made from Reslex in the Boston suburbs to a pay telephone on one of the local piers. The U-boats didn't have great direction-finding technology either and had been relying mostly on naked-eye observation of Allied ships.

Haffenden focused his concern: "If the Nazis get these gadgets, at the very least they'll be able to track us tracking them. At most, they'll be able to track us even better and hit us harder."

"How do you think I can help, Commander?"

"We haven't had a lot of success with the Boston ports like in New York. But it's the same kind of thing with the piers, you know, the guys that run things. I was thinking that maybe you could get the word out to any contacts you may have in Boston that something big is going on with Reslex. Maybe a shipment going out of Boston harbor of Reslex radar gadgets. That way, the rat on the dock may get excited, alert his Nazi friends. We might start to see some activity."

"Radar, huh?" Meyer said. "This company, Reslex, they're onto something?"

"I think so."

"Are they a company that sells stock?"

Haffenden scrunched up his face. "I think so."

"When a company like this makes something that's a winner with the military . . . what happens?"

"They get big contracts."

Meyer nodded, but kept his gaze on Haffenden to try to read him.

"Where are you going with this, Meyer?"

"Just that you need to think of your future, Commander."

"Oh, I don't know, Meyer. I'm not cut out for financial schemes."

"Okay. It's good that you know that. Never go against your nature. But if you do, have your wife buy the stock in her name."

When Haffenden left, Meyer brooded on the massacre of Polish villages. He conjured a memory from his boyhood of a rabbi, whose limbs were strapped with ropes, being torn apart by Cossack horses. Then he went into the men's room and threw up blood.

Inside Man

AT A NONDESCRIPT BUILDING IN A SUBURB NORTHWEST OF BOSTON, A skinny man in a laboratory jacket, Dr. Ochsman, stood at the head of a conference table and drew on a large pad of paper fastened to an easel. He was happy to report that Reslex had finally perfected a three-centimeter-wavelength radar that could detect U-boats. It had also, in partnership with ITT, developed an upgraded high-frequency direction-finding, or huff-duff, set that would improve on what the British had been using in recent months.

These systems would be ready for distribution to Allied forces in a convoy departing from Boston next week. Everyone congratulated each other. The good feelings were as much about patriotism as they were about the likely spike in Reslex contracts once America won the war.

One of the men at the table, Will Moody, didn't understand a word of what Dr. Ochsman was saying, but it wasn't his job to understand. His job was to make Reslex's customers happy. It was important that Reslex developed innovative products, but what mattered most to Moody was that the customers got these products in a timely fashion. To do this, he was one of the few people at Reslex who cared more about what the little people thought than the company's brass did.

Despite the top-secret nature of their work, people were people, life was boring, and the moving of goods from Point A to Point B was just like baggage handling at airports. The little people in this chain may not have had the talent to invent gizmos, but they sure as hell could see to it that they never reached their destinations.

When the meeting was over, Moody did what he always did. He returned to the shipping office and set the wheels in motion to transfer a new product to Naval Logistics personnel within the next two weeks. Moody reached into his uniform and pulled out a key that he wore on a chain around his neck. He then unlocked his desk drawer, where he kept his manifest. The way he held his key so closely conveyed a personal guarantee of the transfer's safety.

It wasn't.

Moody had left the meeting having taken everything that Dr. Ochsman had said at face value. Yet, in a bigger way, the whole meeting had been a lie.

The agent from Berlin, whom Moody thought of as Mr. Reich, hadn't relied on him for regular intelligence. Berlin had told Mr. Reich that a defense contractor in Boston had developed an important device that would be delivered to the Allies via Atlantic convoys. Berlin wanted to snatch it, but if they couldn't, the next best thing would be to make sure the Allies never got it.

Mr. Reich had approached Moody months ago with $5,000 and a simple request: to tell him if and when he became aware of any special movements of Reslex products that might be destined for naval convoys going out of Boston. Moody, in the kind of self-serving gesture that comes with snitching, told Mr. Reich that he would not betray any secrets about Reslex's technology. In his mind, he was only temporarily crossing a line in order to save for the educations of his grandchildren. He had seen some of the American propaganda discouraging greed, but in his mind, he did not fit the description of a greedy man. Greedy men wanted furs for their molls and a thick bankroll to flash around those dens of iniquity such as that awful Copacabana. *That* was greed. But a churchgoing man looking out for the welfare of his family? Well, small compromises needed to be made in life in the service of a larger good.

"Of course not," Mr. Reich said sympathetically. "I would never ask such a thing." Always make them feel that you don't believe they're rats.

Never mind that Moody had been in no position to betray technological secrets—Mr. Reich's mission was simply to determine when and how Reslex's fancy doodad would be shipped. Moody met Mr. Reich in Harvard Square and shared the dates that the cargo would be transferred from Reslex to the navy. Moody took an additional $5,000 from Mr. Reich and returned to the suburbs feeling as if the vagaries of the information he had betrayed somehow made the transaction something other than what it was.

Meyer knew Boston well. The Lanskys had lived there a few years ago when Buddy was having treatment from a Dr. Carruthers at Children's Hospital. They returned sometimes for checkups, and Meyer thought it would be good to combine some father-son time with his latest ferret squad mission.

Meyer quizzed Dr. Carruthers about Buddy's condition. For Meyer, as a man who thought arithmetically, the bottom line of these medical discussions was always the same sum: zero. Buddy Lansky would never walk like a normal boy, and there wasn't a damned thing that medical science and Meyer's money could do about it. These sessions were all about going through the motions of hope. Maybe there was some value in that, but it didn't register in Meyer's mind.

After meeting with Dr. Carruthers and seeing to it that Buddy was reasonably occupied, Meyer was picked up by a Cadillac and driven to the waterfront suburb of Revere, five miles northeast of Boston, to a restaurant owned by his old bootlegging partner Hyman Abrams. Meyer remembered that Hy made efficient use of dockside labor and even lived near one of the piers.

Hy Abrams was a squat, chubby-faced former street tough with a thick forest of dark, unruly hair piled on his head. Like Meyer, Hy liked games of chance and owned gambling places such as the Wonderland Dog Track in Revere. Later he became Meyer's partner, along with Mickey Price and some others, in Las Vegas casinos such as the Sands.

Hy and Meyer shook hands when they met in the restaurant. They weren't like the Italians with all that hugging and kissing nonsense, which Luciano could never stand either. This was business, not a bar mitzvah.

After Hy dismissed the restaurant staff, Meyer shared with him the basics of his work with the navy. He made it seem like more of a security assignment than a spying program. Meyer respected Hy Abrams, but Arnold Rothstein had warned Meyer during Prohibition (using a crude sexual analogy) that you never knew the complete history of alliances of your partners. Even if your business associates didn't mean to commit treachery, you never knew what they might pass along for sport.

"In a way, Hy, it's up to guys like us," Meyer said. "You know what I'm talking about. Our *mishpocheh* in Hollywood are too busy trying to be goyim. The Italians will only go so far, plenty of them are loyal to Mussolini."

"I see what you're saying, Meyer. Have you talked to any of

our landsmen in other places? Moe Dalitz? Mickey Price? Longy Zwillman?"

"Mickey and Longy are doing their part. Moe joined the army—"

"No shit? I hope the government appreciates it."

"They don't, Hy. We're on our own like we've been from the start."

"Do you believe what they're saying about massacres of Jews in Poland?"

"And Russia."

Hy stiffened. "I'm from Russia. Still have people there."

"Then let's stop waiting for Louie B. Meyer to get off his Catholic ass." Meyer got down to business: "There's a company out in the suburbs here, a defense company, that's shipping out some important weapons parts in the next few weeks. From what I understand, the materials go to the docks in Boston and then get shipped up the coast and will end up on a navy convoy going across the Atlantic."

"You're a regular John Paul Jones, Meyer," Abrams said.

"I'm doing what I can, Hy. Do you still have contacts on the docks from your days at Harvard?"

"Sure, but it's not like it was when we were running rum. One of Joe Kennedy's old dock guys we used to move our product, Timmy Shea, right here in Revere, comes into my place from time to time. Haven't seen Kennedy in years now that he's a big statesman." Hy rolled his eyes. "You can steal a hell of a lot more with a Harvard degree than you can being a Heeb from Russia with a bar mitzvah scroll. Shea and I still get on pretty good. Are we talking about security, eyes and ears, or are things going to get personal?"

"Here's what I'm thinking, Hy. If this Shea fellow could tell his guys to keep an eye out for anything funny, that would be a start."

"But, Meyer, you know how the docks go. Word gets around fast, even if you tell people to keep their mouths shut."

"My guy at the navy says that's all right," Meyer explained. "They say if there's rumors going, it keeps away the Nazi saboteurs."

"Is that what they're worried about? Sabotage?"

Meyer shrugged. "They want to make sure whatever gadgets this Boston company makes gets on those boats."

"And they think there's mischief going on to prevent that?"

"Yes."

"What happens if my guys up here catch a Nazi spy?" Hy asked.

"Zol zein mit glick." Yiddish for "lotsa luck."

Hy Abrams reached out to Boston dock boss Timmy Shea, who told his men to look out for German spies. The buzz caught the attention of the spy, the mysterious Mr. Reich, who had a contact or two on the New England docks. The German's assets on the pier confirmed for him what his Reslex informant, Moody, had told him about the impending special shipment.

Three trucks, smaller than both Moody and Mr. Reich had anticipated, left from Reslex's shipping docks on a frigid Sunday evening in the late winter of 1943. They arrived on schedule to the Northern Avenue Fish Pier in South Boston, which Mr. Reich dutifully relayed to his handlers. Berlin instructed him to report back as soon as he knew the ship with the Allies' valuable cargo had departed Boston.

Graveyard of the Atlantic

MR. REICH WAS FEELING GOOD ABOUT HIS SUCCESSFUL COMMISSION of espionage, so he took one of his wharf spies to a nice steak dinner.

"I'll tell you, Mr. Reich," the Rat said. "If you thought what I got you on this Reslex deal was sweet, I've got more coming your way."

"That's very welcome news," Mr. Reich said. "Do you have a new source?"

"I think so," the Rat said archly.

"Who is this man?"

"She's a woman."

"Really?" Mr. Reich said, intrigued.

"In fact, she'd like to meet you after dinner. Maybe you could tease her out a bit."

"I can do my best."

After dinner, Mr. Reich followed the Rat to a waterfront warehouse.

"Where's your girl?" Mr. Reich asked.

"She's coming."

Indeed she was. Mr. Reich heard the clop-clop of high heels. His heart raced. A snitch *and* a lay.

When he turned and saw her, Mr. Reich was momentarily

surprised. She was wearing high heels all right, but she was a gargoyle, thick, solid like a linebacker. The Rat grabbed Mr. Reich from behind to restrain him as the longshorewoman slit his throat with serrated knife. Afterward, the woman made a phone call from a pay phone in Dorchester to a restaurant in Revere.

The owner was put on the line.

"Yeah?"

"It's done."

Mr. Reich's lifeless body was found on a public Chelsea pier the following morning. Berlin, perfectly capable of monitoring newspapers, was interested to read the headline in the *Boston Globe:*

UNIDENTIFIED MAN FOUND WITH
THROAT SLIT ON CHELSEA PIER

Possible Labor Strife Cited

The Nazis knew better than to buy the line about labor unrest. In fact, Berlin felt that by Mr. Reich's having the decency to be murdered on the eve of the shipment of the Allies' great new technology, it confirmed the enormous value of this cargo.

Admiral Dönitz was salivating.

The navy had a merchant ship bearing the logo of the Northern Tide Fisheries Company leaving from a pier in Chelsea and heading northeast at ten knots toward Halifax, Nova Scotia. The SS *Northern Tide* was followed by three heavily armed chase craft.

The *Northern Tide* signaled its status using nonencrypted transmissions about its plan to dock briefly in Halifax then hook up with a large and slow-moving convoy scheduled to depart at the same time from Sydney, Nova Scotia.

The Nazis knew it would be an important convoy, so Dönitz dispatched more U-boats to the North Atlantic. Three wolf packs. The wolf packs were communicating by radio; sometimes these transmissions were encrypted, sometimes they weren't. They allowed the navy convoy of six ships to quietly make their way two hundred miles east of Nova Scotia, then the lead U-boat, U-130, gave the command to converge. The wolf packs raced closer to the American convoy.

Deep within the narrow bowels of U-130, the German sailors had been underwater for so long that they identified each other primarily by their stench. If the smells could have been injected into a torpedo and launched, they would have decimated the Allied navies. The crew all had beards now and looked more like Moroccan pickpockets than Hitler's Aryans. U-130 had been spending a fair share of its time hiding on sea cliffs ever since its "happy time" heyday in the early months of 1942. With the fierce pushback of U.S. and British naval forces, and the refusal of Dönitz to withdraw from the North Atlantic, the wolf packs had lost their enthusiasm for surface-and-attack strikes. With the news of this important U.S. convoy, the German sailors' dreams of glory were flooding back. They did not know that they were about to play a new role.

They were targets.

U-130's Captain Wertz was sending regular transmissions to Admiral Dönitz, who was encouraged by what he learned. The Germans had finally drawn a bead on America's magical technology, which, according to recent intelligence, had something to do with direction-finding. If the Nazis could seize it or destroy it, they could perhaps resume their "happy time."

"You've got to give it to the Americans," Dönitz transmitted. "With all their love of their coloreds and kikes, they know their science. Roosevelt must have more German blood than the Führer cares to admit."

A transmission came from Dönitz's headquarters in Lorient, France, alerting U-130 that more ships were in the American convoy than had first been anticipated. More U-boats were needed. Dönitz ordered U-130 and its squadron to proceed to a strange island, basically a sandbar, about 110 miles southeast of Nova Scotia. When the name Sable Island was transmitted to Wertz, he took a few minutes to respond.

Sheisse. "Are you sure?" Wertz asked headquarters.

"Affirmative."

Wertz, despite his misgivings, gave the directional orders.

Sable Island was shaped like a boomerang, about twenty miles long and a mile wide. It was known for two things. One was its feral horses. The other was its lethality. It was the proud home of hundreds of confirmed shipwrecks, right on the continental shelf. Foggy with vicious and unpredictable currents and frequent, terrible storms. Even though he was a cold, calculating captain, Wertz, like most sailors, had a superstitious streak. There was no way he could ignore a place known as the Graveyard of the Atlantic.

Given the value of the target, some risk-taking was unavoidable. The U-130 squadron had been dispatched to be the lead wolf pack of three to stalk the American convoy from the northern side of Sable.

What Wertz did not know was that a squadron of British and Canadian Algerine class minesweepers had begun crawling along the southeast coast of Sable Island. The minesweepers had been chosen not only for their function, but because they sat low in the water, which made them harder to see.

While the crew of U-130 had been sliding beneath trillions

of gallons of seawater, they nevertheless received bulletins from Dönitz's headquarters. Not only did they know the war was going poorly, they had heard about the diversion of resources to the annihilation camps of Eastern Europe. Many were troubled by this. They were, after all, warriors, not butchers. Even if what they had heard was one-quarter true, it could not be a sign of military strength.

"Battle stations!"

Captain Wertz's anxiety was entirely rational. The Americans knew the exact location of the U-130 wolf pack. The U.S. convoy alerted an antisubmarine air wing based in Gander, Newfoundland, which scrambled. As the wolf packs moved toward Halifax, the Algerine minesweepers moved eastward and curved around to the northern side of Sable Island.

From his stalking position, Wertz ordered the designated U-boats to surface and move in the night toward the jackpot. Wertz feared they had been detected, but did not betray his fear to his crew and the other wolf packs. The Germans would not recognize their fates until the U.S. minesweepers and airplanes released their depth charges.

The explosives detonated seconds apart. The first blast struck the U-boats like God shaking a carbonated drink. The vessels shook only a few feet in each direction, but did so at a speed that destroyed any sense of balance or direction. The second blast forced the vessels straight down as if they were in an air pocket. The crews felt their gonads shoot through the tops of their heads as the boats' helmsmen fought to stabilize their rapid descent.

U-130 was damaged, but not mortally. A move against the American convoy was impossible. Now it was about survival. The disorientation was so acute that every vessel was on its own. Wertz knew he couldn't escape to the south because that was the Graveyard. He knew he couldn't head west because he now realized they were being tracked by the Allies with far better technology than the Germans had known existed. He couldn't go north because that's where the convoy was, and Wertz figured it was well-protected by now.

Wertz ordered U-130 east. It was the best of his bad options. The remnants of two wolf packs submerged and traveled east beneath the Algerine minesweepers. The Algerines released hedgehog clusters—small, but powerful, underwater bombs.

Wertz did not know exactly how the other U-boats in his fleet had responded to the hedgehogs, but his sense of impending doom when he got Dönitz's orders had been validated. Sometimes it's perfectly reasonable to believe men are trying to kill you.

Now Wertz was being killed, and he knew it. Several hedgehogs struck U-130 as it hovered near the ocean floor. The first explosion rocked the craft, sending men flying into the unforgiving steel. The second explosion ripped open the submarine. Frigid seawater gushed in at a terrible speed and filled the crew's lungs.

Wertz was spared another terrible fate: knowing his death had been planned with the help of a diminutive Jewish-American mobster by way of Poland, and that the American convoy departing Halifax had contained only barley.

In truth, the Reslex radar technology had been aboard U.S. warships for several months, having been shipped in stages by garbage trucks to waste-transfer stations in Boston, then by textile trucks to Norfolk. The navy didn't, of course, want the Germans to know about its improved technology. The navy never deliberately let specific U.S. ships be sunk, but the Allied commanders thought that more lives would be saved in the long run if the Nazis concentrated their U-boat war in the northwest Atlantic and let the bulk of the convoys, with the new radar equipment, pass safely to the Mediterranean theater from Norfolk.

The presentation that Dr. Ochsman of Reslex had given to his staff had been factually correct, but the swindle was that the radar breakthrough had just occurred. Reslex had not suspected anyone in particular in their shop of being a rat, but the navy wasn't taking any chances. U.S. Naval Intelligence had insisted that Reslex deliberately mislead their regular chain of custody, which was carried out with the con that had fooled their own shipping director—and snitch.

As disappointed as Berlin had been with the lousy stream of intelligence coming out of New York, they had been faring better in Boston. This was because the navy had *wanted* the Nazis to feel good about Boston, which lured Hitler's U-boats to the North Atlantic to be pummeled into shipwreck history.

Still, it was premature to rejoice. The two greatest military mobilizations in human history lay ahead and would need an unprecedented quantity of supplies, the bulk of which would flow across the Atlantic. This haunted Haffenden's dreams because there would be no final push against the Nazis in Europe as long as Harry Bridges was poised to restaff the Eastern waterfront and the ogre Brahms was free to direct the U-boats that remained from his hidden nest in America. In an absurdity that must have engendered much laughter in the heavens, the fate of civilization rested upon a handful of weary sailors and patriotic crooks.

Sailors with Tommy Guns and Fedoras

THE KID PULLED HIS DARK CHRYSLER INTO A GAS STATION IN QUEENS. An attendant hopped out of the small office and asked the young driver what he wanted.

"Fill 'er up," he said. "And shine up that windshield, wudja?"

As the attendant got to work, a bakery truck pulled up to another pump. A stocky man with days of beard stubble in laborer's clothes got out of the passenger side. He shoved the attendant aside as he wiped down the windshield and stuck a snub-nosed .22 revolver through the Chrysler's open window and popped two off in the kid's temple. When he slumped over, the stocky man reached in and put a slug in the driver's ear. Then, as if the poor boy's fate were uncertain, he shot another round into the back of his head.

The half-cleaned windshield was matted with blood, brains, and bone.

The attendant called the police and reported that a tall, slender Negro in a tailored suit killed the unsuspecting driver. But later he had a different version when Meyer's men paid him a visit.

Commander Haffenden's boss, Captain Oscar McPhail, made himself comfortable in one of Haffenden's guest chairs. McPhail looked like an actor who would play an admiral. Or president. Or even a king. McPhail had been a navy man for forty years and had commanded battleships. He had been set to retire when the trouble started out on the seas, and they asked him to stay on until the navy put together war plans for the Atlantic and the Pacific. As much as McPhail loved his country and the navy, he knew, even better than Haffenden, that their very identities on this planet were on the line. Who the hell wanted to go out as the man who let Hitler into Brooklyn?

McPhail had supported the formation of the ferret squad, but he was a snob who held his nose at dealing with racketeers. He liked the dividends of the ferret squad—Navy Secretary Knox credited McPhail for recent successes—but he wanted to sweep Operation Underworld under the rug, pronto.

McPhail knew this wouldn't be easy. Given General Eisenhower's plans for Europe, withering pressure came from FDR to ensure the safety of Atlantic shipping routes. For this to happen, Harry Bridges would have to be decommissioned. Whatever wariness McPhail might have felt about the ferret squad, he was a realist who understood that the bastards you know are better than the bastards you don't.

"This Bridges thing is an incredible turn of shit luck," Haffenden told his boss.

"Things have been looking up though lately," McPhail said.

"That's my point. We make progress and then Bridges comes along and takes a baseball bat to a hornet's nest. I'm dreading what we're about to hear."

The men were meeting to listen to a speech Bridges was giving from his home base in San Francisco in advance of his upcoming trip to New York. CBS radio was carrying the speech live. Even though both sailors knew Bridges was an Aussie, hearing his voice for the first time was a jolt.

"He sounds like he's from outer space," McPhail said. "I can't imagine that's going to play well with your friends on the pier."

"Who knows, Captain? We sure as hell didn't see Bridges coming in the first place, how do we know what could come out of his visit? It's a big unknown. I don't like small unknowns, let alone big ones."

The first part of Bridges's speech was turgid union chest-thumping. The New York longshoremen might like it for morale, but it wouldn't trigger their self-interest. It didn't take Bridges long to get to his pitch.

"The worker is the backbone of this nation and any nation, but the worker cannot work with a broken back. He cannot work when he is off in a strange land getting shot at by men who only mean him harm because they are in the service of a government that does not value their lives.

"I will soon travel to New York to meet our brothers there. Our brothers are free to decide how their interests will be represented. I've spoken in recent months to many of our ILA friends, who have shared with me their distress at the stranglehold gangsters have over their union. Why, the gangsters even force our brothers to get their hair cut at mob-owned barbershops near the docks and pay extortionate sums of money.

"Our brothers in New York want a change and are rightly considering striking against the shippers who happily climb into bed with crooks. Who can forget what happened not so long ago when an independent group of women concerned about working conditions protested at the Fulton Fish Market. What did they get for their exercise of free speech? A savage beating by ILA thugs!

"And a man, Bobby Miles, who had toiled by my side for almost twenty years, turned up dead in San Francisco Bay, a note on his body warning our union to stay away from East Coast gangsters.

"Then there's that mysterious fire that ruined the great ship *Normandie*. The ILA wants everybody to think the Nazis did it. Nazis in New York? Nazis are about as likely to come to New York as an American couple is likely to honeymoon in Berlin!"

The sound of a large crowd laughing could be heard over the radio.

"And how can we trust our government, a government that sentenced the German defectors who came to New York to die before giving them the benefit of a fair trial? Why was the government in such a hurry to silence these men?"

Haffenden couldn't take it anymore. He stood up and angrily twisted the radio dial off.

"He's a madman," Haffenden said, throwing his arms in the air. "He thinks the Third Reich just wanted to play a harmless game of croquet until Roosevelt woke up on the wrong side of the bed and decided to meddle!"

"When exactly is the bastard's road show?"

"Coming to New York in a week," Haffenden replied. "I can see the cartoons in the paper now if this blows up: sailors with tommy guns and fedoras."

"What's he talking about, a man turning up in the Bay?"

"Some poor guy probably fell into the drink by accident, and Bridges calls it a homicide."

"Well, then, here's my question," McPhail said. "Just because Bridges is making noise, that doesn't mean the ILA boys in New York will go with him, right?"

"Let's be honest: Some of the things Bridges is saying are true, Captain. There *are* gangsters at the wheel in New York.

I don't know how else to say it: They may be gangsters, but they're our gangsters."

"Can Lansky sit on that cowboy Siegel?" McPhail pleaded. "And that other maniac, Anastasia? Good Lord, that's all we need! Presumably you can take care of this commie creep without killing him?"

Haffenden decided not to tell McPhail about how serious the Anastasia threat was, and he sure as hell wasn't going to mention his suspicion that maybe Anastasia had something to do with that man's death in San Francisco Bay.

"It depends how you define *kill.* Do I have the order?"

McPhail stood up and left Haffenden's office.

Typical.

On the Spot

Meyer was not up to driving to Great Meadow to see Luciano, so he decided to ask Lilo if he would take him, and bring Polakoff, too. Lilo was always on time, but not today. Meyer called his house. His poor immigrant mother was sobbing, "They kill-a my boy, they kill-a my boy!"

Meyer was distressed by this news. He went to the Majestic and took the elevator up to Costello's apartment. Costello wasn't awake yet, so his wife, Loretta, woke him up.

As well as Meyer knew Costello, he hadn't seen him look so disheveled since they had hidden out from Masseria and Maranzano in '31 at a farmhouse in New Jersey. "What the hell is it, Meyer?" he asked, concerned.

"Our kid, Lilo . . . you know, my driver. He didn't show up this morning. His mother was crying how somebody killed him."

Costello took a deep breath and squeezed his eyes closed. "Fuckin' Albert!"

Now Meyer was really dreading this trip. Polakoff didn't seem too excited about it either. It was something they had to do. Frank sent some men over to be with Lilo's family; he asked one of his Prohibition-era strong-arms from the Bug and Meyer mob days, the hulking Phil "the Stick" Kovolick, to drive.

Meyer couldn't speak for the first hour thinking about a young life snuffed out for no good reason. He also felt terrible for Luciano and thought the way most people think when they see someone close to them suffering: There but for the Grace of God go I. He couldn't imagine being in jail for so long. As they drove up to Great Meadow, they eventually started to talk about what else they could be doing to get Luciano out.

"The problem is, Meyer," Polakoff said, "it's not like Charlie was doing five years. They could look the other way at something like that. But thirty-to-fifty? Commutation's a hard sell—especially since Judge McCook has tossed out every application I've made for a sentence reduction."

"Be honest with me, Moe, have we delivered or have we delivered?"

"Sure you've delivered, but the problem is leverage. The government really doesn't have to do anything for us if they don't want. And now you have Harry Bridges and Albert Anastasia circling like sharks."

"So why bother doing all we're doing? Outside of the patriotism."

"Because, Meyer, the deeper you get the government into this thing, the more they might be motivated to appease you."

"Well, Moe, Haffenden knows at some level that we've got Walter Winchell out there, who could blow this thing up, but once we drop that bomb, we lose the leverage."

"Do you think you can get the Bridges thing under control?"

"Do you really want the answer to that, Moe?"

"No, sir, I do not."

They got to Great Meadow Prison in time for lunch and waited for Luciano in the warden's conference room. Meyer brought Italian and Jewish delicacies from Manhattan. Luciano wasn't hungry, though. He looked thin and pale, an appearance that exaggerated his scarred face and droopy eye in a way that made Meyer think of a greyhound that had barely survived a vicious dogfight.

"What da fuck's goin' on, Meyer?" Luciano said. "I did my end-a da deal. I'm readin' in da papers dat they're plannin' some big invasion."

"I know, Charlie. I understand," Meyer said. "I've got some things in the works. You just have to be patient."

"Patient? I been in a dungeon for eight fuckin' years! Now they're talkin' about deportin' my ass if I get out. Dat's pretty fuckin' patient in my book."

You were convicted of being a vice lord, which you are, Meyer thought. Even though Dewey had nailed him on trumped-up charges, the things Luciano really did were a lot worse than peddling broads. Still, every man in the clink thought he'd been framed.

"Here's the situation we're facing—"

"Yeah, tell me da situation," Luciano said, swatting a sourdough roll away from him. It fell on the floor.

"They want more from us, Charlie," Meyer tried to explain. "Like you said, they're planning a big move."

"Sounds like dat next move don't include me and you? Outta sight, outta mind, ya know, Meyer?"

"Believe me, I know."

"Didn't ya say a long time ago dat a guy's gotta stay useful, and when he ain't useful, he's clipped?"

"Something like that."

"I knew dey'd fuck me."

"The scene has changed, but the game's still on."

"But dey don't need us no more. What, Eisenhower needs Benny Siegel to be a one-man invasion of Germany? What can we do for dem now? What do you think, Moe?"

Polakoff said, "There's only one thing we can do because we don't have a lot of juice. We can try to help them one more time, Charlie."

"Bullshit, Moe. I ain't helpin' 'em do jack no more. Can't we grease somebody already?"

Polakoff threw up his hands. "That's not something I could ever be involved with, Charlie. You know that."

Luciano looked at Meyer, as if to say, *That's something* you *could be involved with.*

"I'm trying, Charlie," Polakoff added.

Luciano looked as if he had just been kicked in the gut with a steel-tipped boot. Meyer told Polakoff that he wanted to talk to Luciano alone and it would be best for his own protection if he left the room, which he did. Meyer looked over his shoulder. It was a habit from a life spent in restaurants and on street corners where you never knew who was listening, only that somebody always was. Meyer got up from his chair and walked around to the other side of the table to sit almost nose to nose with Luciano.

"Here's how I see it, Charlie. I understand how you think our thing didn't work, but it did. It's just like investing back in a business, only we didn't get the payout yet. We had more freedom to do business than we would have if we blocked the navy, see? And we don't know about you yet. I know how you want it, Charlie, but in this life, you've got to do what's doable. We all thought America would be the answer, and it may be someday, but how can we live our lives getting chased around all day long? We need our own country, and I think we can get it in Cuba. Maybe we can get you into Cuba. Just stay calm as much as you can. Don't give up."

"Prison's all about giving up, my friend. Meantime, I got Albert tellin' me he'll spring me by greasin' some judge. He says he can clip dat Bridges punk."

Meyer wanted to shoot Luciano then and there. "Goddamnit, listen to me, Charlie! Here we are working with the government, helping them, and bringing them deeper in debt to us. So, what, then Albert comes in like a bull in a china shop and he's going to drop a wheelbarrow of cash on a judge? Then he's going to shoot down Harry Bridges, one of the most famous people in the country, like a dog? This morning, Charlie, the poor kid who drives for me and Frank got hit in front of his house."

"Which kid?"

"Lilo—"

"Lilo? Da kid was like sixteen when I got sent up. He used ta do errands fer my mudda."

"That's what I'm saying."

"Fuckin' waste."

"That was Albert's way of telling Frank and me—and you—to go fuck ourselves. If we don't get this business under control, they'll send your ass back up to Siberia in a heartbeat, and I'll be right behind you. Did you know that Albert is running around saying he torched the *Normandie*?"

"Tole me dat, too, Meyer."

"Albert's full of shit. He's like Benny, he doesn't think around corners like us. What's his logic, that he burned that ship so the navy would come to us for help? If that's the case, why did we keep him miles away from this operation? If that was part of his game, wouldn't the navy have come to him? Well, they didn't, Charlie. They didn't want him anywhere near this, made a special point of it even. He's just all crazy that he *doesn't* have a hand in this. If the navy ever thought he did something like that with the ship, we'd all be finished, bullshit or no bullshit. . . . Albert sees you here in prison, he knows you're upset, so he feeds you a line about trying to get you out. His *mishegoss* could kill us all, Charlie."

"All I know is he dropped a bundle on my sister and tole me it was from the insurance he got from lightin' up dat ship."

"That cash could have come from anywhere. He's just blowing you kisses, Charlie."

"Why do you think he's doin' dat, Meyer?"

"Because, Albert's running around New York like he's your guy. He's making money hand over fist, building a new mansion over in Jersey. Your name's currency for him, but do you think he wants your ass back? Everything he's doing is to keep you right where you are."

Luciano put his head in his hands. "Okay, I read ya. So what now?"

Meyer put his hand on Charlie's shoulder. "We've been playing the asset side of the ledger, being helpful. Now, we play the other side. Throw them off-balance by throwing them liabilities."

"Dey gotta have some hurt. Ya talkin' about Haffenden?"

"No. His tit's in the wringer, too. If we can get the right people shitting their pants, they'll look at the balance sheet and want to be flush again. That won't happen unless they see the downside. But we have to get them in deeper first, help them with something bigger. You know, the harder they come . . ."

Luciano gave Meyer a friendly slap on the cheek. "So, Meyer, you gonna take all a hundred twenny pounds-a your Yid ass and invade Washington, D.C.?"

"Hey, Charlie, when you tried to shake me down on Delancey Street when we were kids, you didn't get a dime."

"Yeah, but I also laughed my ass off. I'm thinkin', 'Dis little midget just tole me to go fuck myself!' You ain't dat scary, Meyer."

Light came through the warden's window and onto the table where they had set down the food. *Look at us,* Meyer thought, *a Norman Rockwell painting.*

"You know what's scary, Charlie?" Meyer said, catching a ray in his hand. "Sunlight."

On the way out of the prison, Meyer stopped for a cigarette to talk to Polakoff.

"The guy you've been negotiating with in Dewey's outfit . . . you think he's approachable?"

"Do you mean approachable by an attorney like me, Meyer?"

"No, Moe. By . . . somebody else. Like me."

"The guy I deal with is straight law. There's a political guy with Dewey though. He's a different story. You understand I couldn't be involved in such an approach."

"Leave the political guy to Frank and me. You do what you do with the legal."

Cheesecake at Rumplemeyer's

MEYER WENT INTO AN ICE CREAM PARLOR IN THE ST. MORITZ HOTEL on Central Park South called Rumplemeyer's. Red Levine sat at a small table finishing a slice of cheesecake. With orange hair and freckles at middle age, he looked about as scary as a soda jerk, but looks were lethally deceiving.

Meyer and Levine had shared a pinch together for felonious assault when they were kids. Levine had knocked out plenty in his day. Even more than Bugsy Siegel. Siegel was violent, but he was not a *cold*-blooded killer in the true sense of that phrase. He was a *hot*-blooded killer, which led to trouble. Levine kept it all very businesslike.

Levine did a lot of the heavy work in the Castellammarese War of 1929–31, which is what put Luciano in the Mafia's top job. It was good for all of them. Even though everybody liked to talk about the war against the old "Mustache Petes" being an Italian thing, a lot of the rough stuff was a Hebrew affair. Meyer figured, let the Italians take the headlines, as long as his guys got the dividends.

"I'm sorry I'm late, Red," Meyer said.

"It's okay. I like their cheesecake. You want some?"

"I'm all right."

"Always got that self-control, huh, Meyer?"

"It doesn't mean that I don't want it, Red."

"Sweet tooth. My one vice. You need something done, Meyer?"

"Yes. There's a labor leader, Harry Bridges, causing us some problems. We think he's trying to get his hooks into Socks's operation."

"Anybody checking out Bridges?"

"Yes, but I may need you to keep an eye on him. He needs to stay healthy. Anastasia may have one of his torpedoes take a shot at him. That can't happen."

Red said okay and added, "What's wrong, Meyer?"

"They're killing our people over there, Red. The Nazis are lining them up and shooting them into great big holes."

"You know that for sure?"

"Yes, Red."

Meyer stood up to leave and placed a few bucks on the table to cover Levine's cheesecake.

"Meyer?"

"Yes?"

"Just no rough stuff on the Sabbath, okay?"

Levine was an observant Jew who wouldn't kill on the Sabbath.

"Of course not, Red."

One Sunday night, Walter Winchell went into the lobby of the Majestic. The doorman told him he had his newspaper.

"I've already read it today, thank you, Foster," Winchell said.

"This is the evening edition, sir."

"I've already read it, thank you," Winchell said impatiently.

"I don't believe you read *this* edition, sir," Foster insisted. "Another tenant of the building wanted you to read it."

Winchell followed Foster into a tiny office behind the front counter. He removed a manila envelope from a desk drawer and placed it inside the newspaper closest to him.

"Thank you for persisting, Foster. I'm sorry I misunderstood you."

"My pleasure, Mr. Winchell."

Winchell hurried up to his apartment and ripped open the envelope. He told Meyer later that he shook with delight.

"Meyer, Meyer . . . ," he said aloud, as if the envelope contained a treasure map.

Which it did, in a way.

Two dozen dissenters from Socks Lanza's ILA showed up to Webster Hall on East Eleventh Street in Manhattan to hear Harry Bridges speak. They had been under the impression that they would be meeting more ILA members that shared their unhappiness with their union's current leadership.

About two hundred of their ILA brothers had already arrived. They had been gathering since sunrise, making signs to protest Bridges's visit.

"Whattayou think Bridges is gonna say that's gonna make rainbows in Central Park and boidies choiping all over the place?" Socks asked the dissenters.

Cockeye Dunn led the crowd in laughter. Mean laughs.

Minutes before the appointed hour, a dark Chevrolet sedan pulled up to the curb. People could see Harry Bridges's tan, weathered face in the rear window. At first, Bridges smiled broadly when he saw all the longshoremen, the crowd he'd been promised. When Bridges heard shouts of "Commie Frisco queer!" and "Pinko traitor!" and read the signs (such as WELCOME TO MANHATTAN, COMRADE) demanding he get his ass out of

New York, he knew he had either been conned or deluded about the coronation he would get in the East.

Bridges was surprised, but megalomaniacs never learn. So, he stepped out hoping that the applause was hiding beyond the first wave of men or, if not there, maybe in the auditorium of Webster Hall.

A thickset *gavone,* who looked like a snowman with a few days' growth of beard, shifted in the crowd. He began to mirror Bridges's steps, but from among the spectators. The Snowman was nervous, which he showed by repeatedly reaching into his pocket as if to make sure something important was in there. The Snowman didn't know it, but, as he was tracking Bridges's movements, a more sure-footed chap in a fedora was tracking *him.*

The man in the fedora had little regard for human life if that life conflicted with his contract. Maybe the Snowman was planning to take a whack at Harry Bridges, or maybe he wasn't; the man in the fedora wasn't too worried about a blue-ribbon panel critiquing his work.

As the Snowman appeared to close in on Harry Bridges, his hands in his pocket, the man in the fedora stepped forward and stuck a shiv in the Snowman's lower back. The Snowman felt the cold steel puncture his kidney and crumpled like a paper doll. His assailant evaporated into Manhattan.

At the same moment that the Snowman fell, a grim-looking man in a boxy, gray suit stepped forward, flashed a badge, and introduced himself to Bridges as an agent of the FBI. Two sedans pulled up beside Bridges's automobile, blocking it against the curb. More agents got out and surrounded Bridges. The leadman on the sidewalk, the one who had just badged him, said, "We're bringing you in for questioning, Mr. Bridges, regarding alleged un-American activities on your part, including your leadership role in the Communist Party of the United States and your use of the ILWU as a vehicle to undermine the American war effort."

Bridges forced his mouth into the kind of smile men get when they're really about to piss themselves. When Meyer saw the picture of the grinning Bridges in the newspaper, he wondered why people who were completely screwed did this. Maybe it was something the brain told you to do to protect you from feeling pain. Politicians did this when they were shouted down, comedians did it when they were heckled, and rejected lovers did it when they were jilted. *See if I care,* was the fudged message, even though they cared a lot. To their core, in fact.

Was the Snowman Harry Bridges's would-be assassin or just another New York lug that caught the wary eye of Red Levine? Who the hell knew? Collateral damage. Besides, it wasn't the Sabbath.

Go Home, Harry!

EXCLUSIVE

LONGSHOREMEN PROTEST VISIT BY COMMIE FRISCO UNION BOSS BRIDGES

G-man Hoover Detains Pinko Aussie Harry Bridges Before He Can Speak Moscow Links *Exposed!*

BY WALTER WINCHELL

New York—This morning, members of the New York–based International Longshoremen's Association (ILA) protested the arrival of their nemesis, Australian Communist Harry Bridges, boss of the San Francisco–based International Longshore and Warehouse Union (ILWU).

Bridges, who intended to speak about the corruption of our hometown ILA and incite a strike against American shipping concerns, was forcibly detained by a squad of FBI honcho J. Edgar Hoover's men before he could even enter Webster Hall at East Eleventh Street in Manhattan. ILA officials believe Bridges was hoping that a strike would lead to a folding of ILA into his ILWU.

As Bridges was pushed into the rear of G-man Hoover's

dark sedan, the Communist yelled, "This is the work of Roosevelt's corporation running dogs!"

Hundreds of men from the ILA turned out wielding homemade placards reading, "Go Home, Harry!"

When reached at his Washington, D.C., office, Congress of Industrial Organizations (CIO) chief John L. Lewis said, "Our job is to listen to our members, not to tell them how to think. If they like what Bridges says, that's fine. If they don't, that's fine also."

Bridges has long been suspected of being a Communist, however, the radical union boss has consistently denied it. After weeks of investigative reporting, however, the *New York Evening Graphic* has come into the exclusive possession of documents that prove for the first time that Bridges has been an active member of the Communist Party of the United States for many years, even serving on the national Central Committee using an alias.

"I was shocked and appalled to learn of Mr. Bridges's Communist Party affiliation," said ILA dock boss John "Cockeye" Dunn in a statement provided to the *Graphic*. "We had been looking forward toward a frank and constructive discussion with him during his visit."

FBI Director Hoover spoke to the press briefly once Bridges was ushered inside the Federal Building.

"The information that has come to light about Mr. Bridges is very disturbing. He is not being charged at the moment, but the FBI has discovered irrefutable proof that he is an active member of the Communist Party in our country and even one of its leaders approved by the Kremlin. We also have evidence that Mr. Bridges has direct ties to Moscow, and we will be questioning him about this shortly," Hoover said.

Bridges opposed American entry into the war and declared President Franklin D. Roosevelt and British Prime Minister

Winston Churchill "warmongers" for inciting hostilities against Germany, whose intentions he had deemed peaceful.

In an unusual twist, the *Graphic* received credible information that Mr. Bridges had been feeding Communist disinformation to an investigator in the New York State Attorney General's office, one Inspector Arthur Sparrow, who had harassed decent, hardworking American businessmen in the shipping trade at the behest of the ILWU.

A *Graphic* photographer captured a meeting between Mr. Bridges and Mr. Sparrow at a park adjacent to the Flatiron Building on Fifth Avenue (pictured below).

When contacted for his comment, Mr. Sparrow's secretary said that he was "on holiday."

The weekend following the Bridges blowup, Meyer went into the Majestic to pick up his sons to take them to dinner. He met Walter Winchell in the lobby, and they rode up the elevator together.

"That was a helluva scoop," Winchell told Meyer. "My boss renewed my contract. He'd been saying I'd been getting a little thin lately."

"It's always about proving your usefulness, isn't that right, Walter?"

"I guess it's the same way in every business, Meyer."

"Tell me about it."

"Thanks for thinking of me for that one. I owe you," Winchell said.

"It's patriotism is all. I'll call you for coffee."

Meyer got off on his floor. Winchell knew men like Meyer were always banking their chits. And Meyer had every intention of cashing his in. He knew Winchell enjoyed their arrangement, but thought he seemed nervous when they got off the elevator, as if he were thinking about how many bodies might have gone to the bottom of the East River because of their little capers—and the circumstances under which he'd end up being one of them.

The Bridges roust was the last laugh Socks Lanza was to have for a while. All of the noise about labor racketeering caused District Attorney Hogan and Rackets Bureau boss Gurfein to come under fire about why a convicted felon such as Socks was walking free in the Fulton Fish Market. His extortion conviction was upheld. Socks spent the rest of the war in prison, and the dockside ferret gentry fell under the command of Cockeye Dunn.

Local Boy Made Good

THROUGHOUT THE MONTH OF MAY 1943, AMERICAN BOMBERS WERE destroying Nazi U-boats with a vengeance. The wolf packs had terrorized U.S. and British ships in the Atlantic in 1941 and 1942, and the Americans were suddenly enjoying their reversal of fortune. The Atlantic had become a duck shoot thanks to the code-breaking advancements.

Captain McPhail and Haffenden met at their Church Street offices.

"Rad," McPhail said. "We broke an Enigma cipher a few days ago. I think you'll want to hear it."

"Is this going to make me an admiral or get me sent to Alaska?" Haffenden asked.

"Just listen to these little love notes from Admiral Donitz to Berlin and from Berlin to Dönitz." McPhail read:

> May 26, 1943, Dönitz to Berlin—Presence in North Atlantic impossible to sustain. Supplies and fuel from American East Coast choked off due to neutralized vessels. Depth charges from U.S. B-24 aircraft counterattacks destroying seacraft at insurmountable rate. Information flow from human sources loyal to Führer

all but inoperative. Improvements in US/UK direction-finding capability betraying wolf-pack locations at great cost. Spike in waves of antisubmarine aircraft (B-24, B-17, PBY Catalina, Sunderland) render it impossible to remain on surface. Initiating immediate retreat of most fleets from North Atlantic theater pending improvement in conditions.

May 26, 1943, Berlin to Dönitz, Lorient, France—You must answer for prior assessment of Drumbeat that enemy aircraft would not be effective antisubmarine weapons.

"It's all over when it degenerates into blame," Haffenden said.

McPhail's cable report was as good a pat on the back as Haffenden would get in their racket.

"Rad," McPhail asked, fidgeting. "Have you heard anything more about your friends and, you know, the *Normandie*?"

"There's nothing to it, Captain."

"Good Lord, I hope not."

Haffenden and Meyer met at the navy's Hotel Astor offices to celebrate the crash of Harry Bridges. Haffenden showed Meyer the Dönitz transmissions, then poured himself a drink. Meyer declined, asking for club soda. He asked how Haffenden thought his "favorite G-man," Hoover, felt about the Bridges bust-up. Haffenden said that Hoover was pleased.

"I'll tell you, Commander," Meyer said, "the law and newspapermen are the same: They always have to screw somebody. As long as you give them somebody more interesting to screw, you're all right."

"Speaking of getting screwed, have you heard anything more

about Ben, Charlie, and . . . you know . . . the *Normandie*?" Haffenden asked.

"Only that there's nothing to it. Nothing at all."

Meyer had been told this, but with the government sniffing around, who knew what would turn up?

"I'm still taking flak on it, Meyer. Gurfein's asking. Sparrow's little harassment play may be dead, but now Feds are making noises about an inquiry, and McPhail's been throwing me jabs. I don't think I need to tell you what would happen if they find something."

"No, you don't."

Meyer felt his stomach convulse. Goddamned ulcer. He was getting a goddamned ulcer. Meanwhile, he had to keep pulling stunts out of his ass to keep useful. They threw Socks in the slammer, didn't they?—and nobody had done more than Socks. Meyer put down his club soda and wound up his pitch. "I think I have another thing for you."

Haffenden seemed tense all of a sudden. "I appreciate that, Meyer, but remember the Hippocratic oath."

He wasn't sure if Haffenden was serious. "The doctor motto?"

"Yup. First do no harm."

"I read you now. You don't want to push it."

"Right. We're in deep, Meyer. My bosses were happy with the results up to when Harry Bridges entered the picture, but if the wind blows the wrong way, we'll all be liabilities like *that*." Haffenden snapped his fingers. "Especially if we don't bring Brahms's head in on a plate soon."

"The Bridges thing worked out, though," Meyer said.

"What can I tell you? They want to close this book before somebody reads it."

"Well, Commander, maybe I can help you. On another front, that is."

"What have you got?"

Meyer turned over the newspaper that he had folded on the side of the table. The headline read:

PATTON EYES SICILY

Other Attack Points Considered

Meyer held it up for Haffenden, knowing he had already seen it. "It seems like General Patton wants to invade Sicily."

"There are other possible targets, but your intelligence gathering is astonishing, Meyer." Haffenden winked.

"Why Sicily?"

"I suppose it's a base for striking at the Reich by air and Italy by land and sea. If we get Sicily, it's only a matter of time for the Krauts."

Meyer smiled, which was rare these days. "What will determine where exactly an invasion happens?"

"Lots of factors, among them where we're likely to have the fastest success."

"All right, do you know anything about Sicily, Commander?"

"A little. What do you know?"

"I know they don't like being invaded. Terrible history of being raped by the conquerors. Arabs. Greeks. Spaniards. Barbarians. French. It's why the Mafia started: to make it tough on the invaders."

"Patton doesn't want to conquer Sicily, Meyer. If that's where he ends up going, he'll be looking for a foothold against the Nazis."

"Invaders always say they've got noble reasons. Do you think Patton will show up and Sicilians, with their history, will get down on their hands and knees and say, 'Thank you for invading our country. Would you care for some linguine puttanesca, General?' No, they'll say, 'Why is your invasion different from all the others?' Then they'll play with the road signs and send Patton's army marching right into the opening in Mount Etna."

"Patton can be rather persuasive."

"Maybe, Commander. But is Patton so brave that he will want a hard fight when he could have an easy one? I've never known a leader who wants a fair fight when he could have one with an advantage."

"And you could help deliver that advantage, Meyer?"

"The Mafia in Sicily are like cockroaches. No matter who invades, they'll still be there in one form or another. And Patton will have to deal with them. The Mafia can make it easy for their guests or they can make it hard. They may hate Mussolini, but it's all tribal. Mussolini is the cousin they don't like but they'll live with because he's blood; Patton's the bully from across the street. Does Patton want accurate maps or does he want to drop bombs on churches?"

"I thought Mussolini crushed the Mafia in Sicily."

"They don't die; they adapt."

"You think you could help Patton in Sicily?"

"Not by myself. I need Charlie."

"Charlie, huh?"

"He's getting ornery, Commander, and he's starting to get other visitors. I need to keep him happy. He feels he's paid his dues."

"Brahms is still out there," Haffenden said.

"Are you telling me that's all on us? That doesn't strike me as kosher."

"No, no, it's not all on you. I'm just under the gun with Brahms out there and the big push we're planning. How do you think Charlie can help, Meyer?"

"Charlie came to America from Sicily, a little town south of Palermo. To Sicilians, he's a local boy made good."

"Made good, eh?"

"Like I said, it's tribal."

"But, Meyer, is that local-boy-made-good stuff enough to get us help?"

"No, it's not enough. But, see, Charlie has business with some of the old bosses there. It's a closed society. They only trust each other, and Mussolini didn't throw them *all* in jail. Charlie has done favors for some of them, and they have done favors for him. Barter. Sicilians won't help out of loyalty; they'll help return favors because it's good for business."

"Do you think you can guarantee that?"

"Guarantee? No. It's a war, Commander, there are no guarantees. But, there are *odds*. That's a game I know, one I can bet on."

"Patton would be lucky to have you." Haffenden chuckled.

"I hear he's nuts."

"But Eisenhower says he always delivers. Sometimes that goes hand in hand."

"Believe me, I understand. Ben Siegel is the same way. You never know when he's going to pop off, but he's not afraid to get his hands dirty."

"The thing is, Meyer—and I say this as a navy man—when you've got a loose cannon rolling around the deck, it's only a matter of time before it pops off and hits your own ship."

Hard Sand

HAFFENDEN SAT AT A CONFERENCE TABLE COVERED WITH MAPS OF Sicily along with two guests. One was a Sicilian immigrant named Frederico Adamo. Adamo was in his thirties and worked on the Atlantic City piers as an honest laborer. He had operated a fishing boat in Castellammare del Golfo before coming to America and finding a job working for a seafood company owned by Mickey Price. He had relatives in Sicily.

The other man was Navy lieutenant Anthony Marsloe, who had changed his name from Marzullo. Marsloe, a lawyer who had worked for Dewey, was a language whiz and an authority on Sicily. He was Haffenden's preinvasion point man dealing with the Sicilian immigrants that the ferret squad had identified for the navy.

"I give crabmeat for missus," Adamo told Haffenden, sliding across a thick paper bag of delicacies.

"She will love it, Frederico. Thank you very much." Haffenden spoke loudly, as if volume would overcome Adamo's bad English, and set the bag down beside him.

"Lieutenant," Haffenden asked, "what have you learned about how Sicilians feel about Hitler and Mussolini?"

Marsloe turned to Adamo and asked him in his Sicilian dialect to talk about Sicilian attitudes.

"Sicilians no like Mussolini, no?" Adamo said, adding something in Sicilian.

"What he's saying, Commander," Marsloe said, "is that not only do Sicilians not like Mussolini, but that the Germans and Italians don't like each other."

"What does that mean on a practical level?" Haffenden asked.

"It means that Sicily is a very fragile confederacy at the moment," Marsloe explained. "It's not a rigid top-down occupation. The Nazis are in some places, and the Italian army chiefs are in others. The Sicilians resent the Italians because they see them as their relatives working for the Nazis to occupy their homeland."

"What about fear?" Haffenden asked.

"Fear of what, Commander?"

"Fear of betraying their occupiers."

Marsloe posed a question to Adamo in Sicilian.

Adamo responded in English. "Sicilians strong. No like Mussolini. In front of Italian army, seem nice. When Italian turn back, not so nice."

Marsloe asked Adamo if some beaches were particularly accessible. On the map, Adamo pointed to the southern coast where the beaches were flattest.

"Castellammare. Other places. They high. To shoot gun down at beach. No good to come there. Gela. Licata, more like floor. Hard sand." Adamo made a horizontal gesture with his hand.

"You still have contacts in the fishing industry in Sicily?" Marsloe asked.

"Many fishing boat. Many friends, family."

In mid-May 1943, Haffenden's B-3 men flew to the Algerian coast with maps of the Sicilian shoreline and a fresh list of Sicilian contacts in key cities including Palermo, Gela, Castellammare, Corleone, and Messina. They provided Naval Intelligence with even better maps and photographs of potential landing sites and inland roadways. Patton's commanders were also supplied with the identities of fishing-boat captains that their former associates in America had once worked with, as well as the names of their boats. Under the direction of Marsloe, U.S. and British amphibious personnel on submarines in the Mediterranean made contact with Sicilian fishermen, arranging for Allied agents to be on board to monitor the movements and transmissions of Axis ships. A new generation of direction-finding equipment from Reslex was secretly installed on Sicilian fishing vessels.

Meyer felt as if he were turning into Talleyrand with all the diplomacy missions he was going on these days. This one took him to Atlantic City, Mickey Price's home base, where Mickey arranged for Meyer to meet with a political adviser to Governor Dewey at the Traymore Hotel. The subject was Luciano.

Meyer went to a suite on the top floor where a collegiate man in his thirties answered the door.

"I'm Mr. Smith," the man said.

"Mr. Smith, allow me to introduce myself. I'm Mr. Jones." Meyer looked as much like a Mr. Jones as Roosevelt looked like Louie Armstrong.

Mr. Smith did not smile, he just nodded. He asked if Meyer wanted coffee, but he declined. He wanted to get in and out of here as fast as possible. He made sure to keep his statements vague in case this guy got cute. They sat across from each other on comfortable sofas.

"I understand that Mr. Polakoff and one of my colleagues have reached a standstill regarding your friend's status," Mr. Smith said.

"Yes. Is the problem that you don't have enough political pressure from the navy or federal government to move this along?" Meyer asked.

"That's part of it, Mr. Jones. The president himself could demand the action you are hoping for, but my boss couldn't just let that happen with a snap of his finger."

"Okay, I think in figures, so bear with me," Meyer said. "If I heard you, one figure in your equation has to be more federal pressure to help my friend."

"That's right. My boss needs to feel like he's banking a note from much higher up, like he's doing a favor for somebody high up in the government. He's got his own ambitions, as I'm sure you realize."

"Yes, I do. You also said, though, that even with the pressure from high up, you weren't sure about commuting my friend's sentence."

"That's true, but it's not impossible."

Meyer thought for a second. What did Mr. Smith mean that *it*—freeing Luciano—wasn't impossible, besides, of course, that he wanted a bribe, which went without saying? The question was, would a bribe go up to Dewey? Meyer decided not to ask. He'd just increase the grease and let Mr. Smith sort it out.

"Let me ask you this," Meyer said. "Is it possible that you might enjoy a goodwill gesture and then my friend does *not* get to see the outside?" In other words, bribe the prick and get screwed.

"Not if a goodwill gesture was very sincere."

Meyer rubbed his temples for a moment and thought through what he wanted to say. "Let me ask you about another option, Mr. Smith."

"Another option?"

"Yes. One you might find more attractive."

"All right, I'm listening, Mr. Jones."

Meyer told him what he had been thinking.

Mr. Smith said he was surprised.

"I understand that," Meyer said. "As you can imagine, my friend doesn't trust our government."

"I appreciate that. Now, I just want to be sure that your feelings of goodwill toward me will be equally as sincere in this new scenario, Mr. Jones."

"You can count on it."

Poolside at the Imperial House

Miami Beach, 1982

BERLIN HAD ITS BROWNSHIRTS, BUT MIAMI BEACH HAD ITS CONDO Commandos. I was sitting with Uncle Meyer inside the Lanskys' poolside cabana watching retirees assert their waning vestiges of earthly power with gratuitous admonitions to other people's grandchildren to (a) stop running by the pool; (b) stop jumping into the pool; (c) stop splashing in the pool; (d) stop eating by the pool; (e) take that drink out of the pool; (f) not go into the pool with suntan oil; (g) stop doing somersaults off the diving board into the pool; (h) not take that kid with the diaper into the pool; (i) not walk so fast with that straw because it was liable to put somebody's eye out; (j) put some kind of weight on that book before going into the pool because it was liable to blow off the table and put somebody's eye out. There must have been a veritable epidemic of poolside ocular impalings among South Florida Jews.

One valuable sociological lesson I gleaned was that pool-related admonitions to vacationing children were not made only by retired dentists, but retired gangsters as well. When I was walking Uncle Meyer to his cabana, he barked, "Cool your jets," to a six-year-old running with an inner tube. What,

I wondered, would Bugsy Siegel have done to a kid like this had he lived into old age?

A bar mitzvah–age boy sprouting three chest hairs was being disciplined by a nasty-looking old woman for jumping into the pool before having waited the Old Testament–decreed one hour for proper digestion before getting wet. This woman was evidently not his grandmother because the boy's grandfather sprang up to defend him. Under Condo Reich rules, one was permitted to discipline other people's grandchildren, but if one's own grandchildren were disciplined for a similar infraction, it was like the siege at Masada.

All of this brought me back to my own boyhood, when, as a risk-averse child, my idea of a badass was a boy who went into the pool after *not* having waited the Talmud-decreed hour for proper digestion after eating. If a kid violated the Proper Digestion covenant, what was next, murder?

I point these things out because it was against this backdrop of jaw-dropping banality that Meyer Lansky spent his final days telling a fellow mobster's grandson how he helped polish off the Third Reich.

Uncle Meyer was now sitting in the shade in a beach chair wearing a sweater with a blanket covering his legs. His sunglasses eclipsed his sunken face. I sat beside him at a table with my Woolworth's notepad. He was glancing at a new edition of *Time* magazine that had named the computer its Man of the Year. A photograph showed something called the Apple Macintosh.

"How the hell can a gizmo be Man of the Year?" he asked.

"I was wondering the same thing."

"Do you have one of these, Jonah?"

"No, I don't."

"I'm a dinosaur," he said.

"I'm not much better off."

"Ah, you'll learn. So, where were we?"

"It doesn't seem like the navy supported Commander Haffenden very much."

Uncle Meyer took a gulp of water and swallowed several pills. His voice was considerably weaker than it had been at Wolfie's the night before, so I had to move in close to hear him.

"Why does that surprise you, Jonah?"

"That they wouldn't be giving a man who was defending his country like that medals?"

"Do you believe doing the right thing gets you a door prize? Haffenden had been trying to get that big ship out to sea, get those troops over to Europe. Instead they ended up blaming him for the damned thing going down!"

Here was an inconsistency. Earlier, Uncle Meyer had quoted Haffenden as saying the *Normandie* had been doomed anyway because of the saturation of U-boats in the North Atlantic. Now he had Haffenden saying the war could have been won more quickly had it not been destroyed. Perhaps Haffenden held both views at different times, but I doubted it. If I was going to do my job right, I would have to return to this before we finished our business.

"Honestly, yes," I said. "I would think a man like him would get medals."

"Let me tell you something." Uncle Meyer wagged his finger at me. "I learned the hard way that it matters how things look. See, Haffenden cared about doing what he had to do to protect his country. He didn't think about appearances. I didn't either, which was a big mistake. You ask your grandfather. Guys like Bronfman, Kennedy, Annenberg, spent a fortune cleaning up their names. I always thought that was bullshit, and I was wrong. Now their families are respectable.

Haffenden, poor guy, didn't factor in how it would look not only if he failed, but even worse, what if he succeeded, Jonah?!"

"If he succeeded, which he did, the good guys won the war, right?"

Uncle Meyer sat up. Perhaps too quickly because he flinched as he turned toward me. I moved from my chair and sat beside him on the edge of his lounger.

"There, that's better," he said. "Now listen. You're a bright boy, you get good marks. You were born way after the war, so you can't remember the day we won. When you think about when America won that war, what do you think of?"

I thought for a moment. I had studied World War II, of course. "I think of that picture . . . there is a sailor who kisses a girl, a nurse, I think."

"You think of that picture, right? When we first started talking about this, do you remember what you said to me, the thing that surprised you about my story?"

"I was surprised I had never heard it before."

"That's right. That's what you said." He gently poked his finger in my chest. "You remember the sailor kissing the girl in the picture, but you never heard about what I did during the war with the navy. Do you think that's an accident?"

"Uh, no."

"Uh, nothing. There's a reason you know one but not the other. I'll give you an assignment, Mr. College. You go to the library and find me one book that talks about the ferret squad, one book, just one, and I'll give you ten grand!"

I laughed. He didn't.

He took another drink of water and rubbed his throat. I scribbled in my pad.

"Uncle Meyer," I said gently, unsure if he was ready to speak again. "I know how things turned out in Sicily—I'm pretty sure that's where Patton slapped the soldier—but I'm not clear of the story behind the story."

"Well, boychick, if it weren't for some of the things Charlie and I did, the old bastard may not have gotten the chance to whack that soldier around."

"So you ended up doing something in Sicily, after all?"

"You bet."

"Is that how you got Charlie out of prison?"

"Are you kidding? Invading Sicily was the easy part."

V.

The Contract

Send men, that they may spy out the land of Canaan, which I give to the children of Israel. Of every tribe of their fathers, you shall send a man, every one of them a prince among them.

—Numbers 13:2

There's a million ways to get things done
There's a million ways to make things work out

—Talking Heads, "What a Day That Was"

Dinner at the 500

It was shortly before sunset. Van Voorst's Buick was parked outside his apartment building on Riverside Drive in Manhattan. As Dasch met with van Voorst at Haffenden's orders, a B-3 operative, Agent #1, approached the Buick holding a metal container the size of a shoebox. He had rehearsed the maneuver he was about to perform a dozen times and figured he could complete it in under five minutes. The wild card was passersby, who might be deflected with the help of fellow agents skulking about while he did his work.

Agent #1 held what was known in American spy circles as the SSTR-1, a transmitter. Along with its power supply, it weighed eleven pounds. If there had been more time, B-3 would have attached the transmitter to the car's engine for power, but that wasn't an option given all the people around.

Having studied this particular Buick model, Agent #1 knew of a gap between the rear axle and the steel body of the car. Agent #2 stood nearby and intercepted a pedestrian to ask her for directions. He didn't really need directions, of course, he just didn't want her spotting the man messing around beneath the Buick. *The George Washington Bridge? Why you go up there two lights and make a right, sir. Sure is a big city when you're from out of town.* And so on.

Agent #1 attached the box to a section of the axle using a patent-pending form of industrial tape intended for use aboard navy warships. He then ran antenna wire around the underside of the car. With the turn of a key—switches had been known to spontaneously flip off over rough terrain—Agent #1 activated the bulky and untested device in its continuous-transmit mode, which had been fashioned in a RCA laboratory in Camden only weeks before.

On December 8, 1941, the day after Pearl Harbor, President Roosevelt outlawed the use of radio transmitters such as experimental ham radios by private citizens. The fear was that private operators could either be corrupted by German agents or inadvertently interfere with military communications. Roosevelt, always flexible when it came to matters of intelligence, was willing to make exceptions to the very laws he had established, especially since his policy had had an unwanted side effect: The same gadget fiends that could have played into the hands of the Nazis were now unable to monitor enemy frequencies. So, when the navy determined that Brahms was likely working his dark magic from the shadows of the Pine Barrens, B-3 dispatched a handful of private-radio enthusiasts to various posts throughout those woods. Their mission was to attempt to identify Brahms's transmissions as well as communicate with navy pilots that were tracking vehicle movements.

The transmitter's signal from van Voorst's car was stronger than the navy pilot who had taken off from Hoboken expected it would be, but that might only mean that the unstable device was tearing through its power early in its adventure, only to decline rapidly at any moment. Van Voorst proceeded at a more rapid clip through New Jersey than he had the last time the navy had tried to track him. Perhaps his swift movements were motivated by new intelligence he had received about departing American convoys. Or, more likely, his movements were about greed. In his recent meeting with Dasch, it became clear that his "importing" buddies were the real deal cash-wise, and van Voorst needed to prove to them that he had the kind of communications resources that could guide small vessels to hidden locations on the coast not readily monitored by the American military. Either way, van Voorst had to report to the ghoul Brahms.

Just as before, van Voorst turned sharply east in the direction of Fort Dix Army Base. The pilot lost visual contact when van Voorst disappeared beneath the trees as he entered the western border of the Pine Barrens. As he skirted Fort Dix, a second spy plane was deployed, this one from the army base, relieving the first one, but also monitoring van Voorst's signal.

In Atlantic City, Haffenden sat in the 500 Café with Mickey Price, who operated a casino away from the law in a large back room. They were finishing dinner in a private room when a Haffenden subordinate came to the table and whispered something in the commander's ear.

"Mickey," Haffenden said, "can we look at my map?"

Mickey flagged down a waiter, who promptly cleared the table and closed the door behind him. Haffenden set down a topographical map of southeastern New Jersey where the Pine Barrens were impossibly thick. He pointed to where U.S. aircraft were currently tracking van Voorst.

"All right, Commander," Mickey said, tapping a section of the map. "Your man is telling you that the German is heading this way. If he goes all the way to the coast, he'll end up here. This is mostly marshland. I've lived around here my whole life and I haven't been over in these parts since Prohibition when I absolutely had to go to quiet places in small motorboats."

"That would be the perfect cover," Haffenden said.

"Maybe, but can Brahms run his thing from a swamp?"

"Solid ground would be preferable given the equipment he probably has. If he's operating by his own boat, I'd think we would have seen him by now, or somebody else would have."

Mickey ran his finger a few inches to the west on the map and stopped, thinking for a moment.

"My bet would be somewhere around here, Commander," Mickey finally said. "It's an area they call Galloway. It's up on what they call the highlands overlooking a bay that leads through the marshland and out into the ocean. It's still in the Pine Barrens along Jimmie Leeds Road here, which isn't far from small towns where Brahms could get food, fuel, and other basics."

"Okay, good. Good," Haffenden said. "I've got a few airplanes tracking him, but that only gets us a general sense of movement. I've also got men over in Pleasantville in plain clothes ready to move, plus some men outside. I'll give the Pleasantville group approximate coordinates, but can you direct me from here?"

"Commander, from what I hear, the Nazis have wiped out whole villages of Jews in Romania, where I'm from. I'd be pleased to go with you and shoot the son of a bitch personally."

It was dark outside because Atlantic City, being right on the coast, was under orders to keep as many lights off as possible. Those orders, however, were not from the federal government, which had no standing whatsoever to enforce such an edict anywhere in the United States, let alone Atlantic City. This order came from Mickey Price. After seeing his way to his Chrysler with a bulky flashlight, Mickey got behind the wheel with Haffenden in the passenger seat. One of Haffenden's aides got in the backseat. A delivery truck holding a handful of heavily armed men followed the Chrysler for the twenty-minute ride over to Galloway. The truck had a retractable antenna on the back, which would have been visible in the up position by day, but not now.

When Mickey got to the intersection of Route 9 and Jimmie Leeds Road, Haffenden asked him to pull over and shut his lights off. One car sped by and Haffenden glanced at it, unimpressed. Another car approached, two cars, actually, slowly. Haffenden asked Mickey to flash his lights three times. The lead car facing them, which carried Haffenden's plainclothes reinforcements, returned the signal and awaited further instructions.

Haffenden got out and went to the truck that had followed him to Galloway. He was helped into the back of the truck, where the dangerous-looking men appeared ready to strike, but against what? He spoke into a microphone to the pilot that had taken off shortly before from Fort Dix.

"Whistler here," Haffenden said.

"Chaser here, roger," the pilot said.

"Do you have visual?" Haffenden asked.

"Negative, too dark, and no coastal lights, but I do have transmitter."

"Status?"

Pilot: "Proceeding east on what I think is Great Creek toward niner."

Haffenden: "How close to our position?"

Pilot: "Stand by."

The pilot checked in with his ham radio urchins; they confirmed that the transmitter was emanating from the same general area being covered by Chaser, the pilot.

Pilot: "You need to proceed north on Route 9. Target is still moving east on Great Creek. If he turns off soon, you'll need to proceed west on Great Creek."

Haffenden: "Roger. We will move north slowly."

Haffenden instructed one of the men in the truck to tell the plainclothes caravan to follow them. The caravan was soon moving north on Route 9.

Haffenden: "Status, Chaser?"

Pilot: "Target slowing on Great Creek. Stand by."

Haffenden: "Roger."

Pilot: "Target now moving south. No road, probably in woods. Over."

Haffenden: "Roger."

Pilot: "Target stationary. Recommend proceed north on Route 9 then west on Great Creek. Good luck, Whistler."

The pilot banked to the north and flew along the coast, then west back to Fort Dix.

B-3 had van Voorst nailed down to about two-tenths of a mile. If Brahms was here, he'd be relatively close to the road.

Haffenden's truck led the caravan quietly onto Great Creek Road, stopping at the approximate area where the pilot, Chaser, said that van Voorst had veered into the woods. They all killed their engines and were instructed not to slam the doors of their vehicles. Haffenden asked Mickey and one of the younger soldiers to remain in the car.

The sky was overcast, and it was impossible to see far under the weak moonlight. Anticipating the weather conditions, the B-3 unit had brought a novel piece of equipment with them. Night-vision devices were rudimentary compared to what they would someday become, but they were helpful. B-3's main tracker carried the device, a bulky infrared telescope. The other men were instructed to follow closely behind one another, holding on in single file if necessary, while the tracker scoped out the forest.

After a few interminable minutes moving through the Pine Barrens, the tracker with Haffenden spotted a squarish man-made shape about fifty yards ahead of them. He turned the scope of the night-vision device in all directions and detected a large metal tower protruding from the roof of the makeshift structure. Two vehicles straddled the shack. One of them was van Voorst's.

"I think we got 'em!" the tracker whispered to Haffenden.

"I can't see a damned thing," Haffenden said.

"About fifty yards ahead. No windows, no light. Big antenna."

Haffenden pulled his men in close. "Okay, boys, this is it. We're going to follow single file to a cabin about fifty yards ahead. Keep your guns drawn. When we get there, turn on your flashlights—I know it's awkward given your guns, but do the best you can—but only so you can see immediately around you. Surround the cabin. Tracker, you frame the door, and then, Gillespie, I want you to ram it down. Gillespie, Potter, Carusi, you go in, scream bloody murder, and fire shots in the air to make them shit themselves, and I'll come in and place them under arrest. Does everyone read?"

Once they were in position, they rammed the door open with a deafening metal clang. Multiple gunshots from M3 grease guns punctured the tiny cabin, which was filled with steel-cased equipment. Van Voorst splayed himself against the far wall of the cabin, his Ichabod Crane neck precariously balancing his little head. His right arm slid down the wall. He was ordered to freeze. Seemingly bewildered, his hand continued to slip, and one of Haffenden's men shot him square in the shoulder. His face registered shock, as if he either hadn't heard the command or was otherwise perplexed as to why an American soldier would shoot a Nazi spy in South Jersey.

There at the controls was a piggish, little man of about

forty with thinning brown hair and wire-rimmed glasses wearing khaki clothes. He looked like the waddling schoolteacher everybody made fun of behind his back, or perhaps to his face. When the pig man turned around in his swivel chair, Haffenden could see the rapid pulse of his jugular.

"So, you're the big monster," Haffenden said.

"He's a runt, isn't he?" one of the men said.

"If I'm such a little runt," the peewee Nazi said, "why did it take you so long to find me?" He evinced a slight piggy smile.

"That's something we hope you'll tell us more about, Mr. Brahms, as we'll be passing your ass around like a pack of smokes," Haffenden said.

Brahms was no longer grinning. Everybody's a tough guy alone and untested in the privacy of his own delusions.

Haffenden emerged from the woods and ordered his men to start their vehicles. When the roadside lit up from the headlamps, Mickey Price saw two soldiers carrying the injured van Voorst from the pines. Haffenden approached Mickey trailed by two soldiers escorting a small, manacled man.

"Mr. Price," Haffenden said, "meet Brahms. You may be seeing a little more of Mr. Price," he added ominously.

Mickey looked over the pudge, and all he could say was *"This?"*

Haffenden waved one of his men over and said to the fettered Nazi, "And now, Mr. Brahms, meet your replacement, Mr. Brahms."

Brahms was not interested in the young American sailor who would replace him at the control panel. It was the little Romanian Jew with the gimlet green eyes that made him shudder.

Mickey got into his Chrysler, drove back to Atlantic City, and did something he never did: He had a drink. *See you soon, Mr. Brahms.*

Husky

Once van Voorst and Brahms were safely in navy custody, and the American naval officer who now sat in Brahms's place was directing the few U-boats that remained to their undersea demise, American ships easily crossed the Atlantic and made their way to the Mediterranean. These safe passages did not embark only from the northeastern United States. Between the late fall of 1942, when Operation Underworld had gotten into full swing, and the end of the war, more than twelve thousand Allied ships in three hundred convoys made it safely to the Mediterranean theater of war via the Norfolk route alone.

In the early hours of July 10, 1943, the Nazis and fascists were paid a visit. When twenty-year-old Vincenzo Ribera heard a deafening rage in the heavens above the Sicilian Gulf of Gela, he thought it was thunder. But no lightning bolt came before or afterward.

The sound belonged to an incomprehensible mixture of the guns of the USS *Boise* and *Savannah* and the landing craft of Patton's Seventh Army. The largest amphibious assault of World War II to date was under way. More than 180,000 men on twenty-five hundred ships from Patton's Seventh Army and Field Marshal Bernard Montgomery's Eighth Army to the east were coming ashore bringing fourteen thousand land vehicles with them. A special contingent of Patton's forces was landing at the same time at Licata, up the coast in a northwesterly direction from Gela.

Young Ribera reflected the Sicilian mind-set. After thousands of years of invasions, his loyalty was to whoever would rape and pillage his island least. This was one reason why Sicilians had developed and exploited a series of underground passages and *qanats*, ancient canals, which they used to hide from and ambush their occupiers. Ribera was not expecting a visit of this scale, but he wasn't shocked that the Allies landed at Gela. His uncle, Calo Vizzi, was a big man in the town of Lercara Friddi, which was two-thirds of the way to Palermo. Ribera's uncle Calo had sent his baby-faced nephew to Gela to "meet some friends."

Ribera hadn't been told much, just that the visitors would be "very serious men" who would mention their former townsman Lucky Luciano. When the serious men came ashore, Ribera was to guide them inland to Axis headquarters. The Nazis had been Ribera's employer for the past six months. He was a spotter.

The Nazis and their Italian partners had long ago riddled the beaches with land mines that would blow up when the Allies landed. This strategy served two purposes. First, the mines would kill or maim their enemies. Second, the explosions would alert the Axis forces that the invasion had begun. This plan did not play out, though, because few of the mines went off.

Charlie Luciano had left Lercara Friddi for America as a young boy. Years later, he did Ribera's uncle Calo a big favor. Shortly after Calo moved to New York from Sicily, he became the target of a manhunt after killing a police officer in Brooklyn. He went to his townsman for aid. Luciano arranged for Calo to be smuggled back to Palermo by way of Canada. The mission was a success, but like everything with Sicilians, good deeds were never done for the soul. Good deeds were like stock certificates because they only had value if the obligations could easily be redeemed.

Vincenzo Ribera was not a gifted spotter, but he didn't have to be. He, and others like him in both directions along the Sicilian coast, played another role besides spotting. The Nazis and Italians had been using the native population to plant land mines on the beaches, a helpful chestnut of information the ferret squad had learned during its preinvasion planning. Few land mines went off when Patton and Montgomery's forces landed because the Sicilian contracting company that planted them was owned by Uncle Calo. After planting them, the laborers dug up the mines at nightfall when their Nazi overlords went to bed. *After* they had been paid in cash by the Third Reich comptroller.

A B-3 officer, Lieutenant Paul Alfieri, who had been briefed by Meyer's Sicilian contacts in New York, made his way hastily to the Axis's Sicilian command center and blew the safe when the fascist commander refused to open it. Patton used the intelligence from the safe to surprise and attack Axis land and sea forces at every opportunity. Mafia-linked Sicilians enthusiastically betrayed their sixty thousand Nazi occupiers. The documents in the safe betrayed Axis ship movements so accurately that Sicilian fishing boats, manned by U.S. sailors, directed Allied warplanes and submarines right to enemy ships to destroy them at a rapid clip.

The Sicilian campaign, known as Operation Husky, lasted

just over four weeks and cleared the Mediterranean for an invasion of the Italian mainland. Mussolini fell in the midst of the Sicilian campaign, and Italy surrendered to the Allies at the Gulf of Salerno on September 9.

The contacts Meyer's boys found for Patton opened up channels in Sicily and on the Italian mainland. In America, the Mafia operated outside the system, but in Sicily, it *was* the system. Shortly after the collapse of Mussolini's government, the Allies released the mafiosi that Il Duce had imprisoned on the Lipari Islands near Messina. The Germans may have exterminated millions of innocent souls in Eastern Europe, but the bastards couldn't penetrate the mysterious *qanats* to shake the Mafia from Sicily.

Mission Mostly Accomplished

ARRANGEMENTS HAD BEEN MADE FOR LUCIANO TO GET A NEWSPAPER a few times a week. He was thrilled with today's headline. He hadn't been this happy since he had become boss. The headline in this morning's *New York Herald* read:

ALLIES INVADE SICILY

Patton's 7th and Montgomery's 8th Armies Hit
Beaches at Gela, Licata, Noto

Operation Husky Is Largest Amphibious Landing of War;
Prelude to Attack on European Mainland for
Final Push Against Hitler, Mussolini

Before the invasion, Patton said, "When we land, we will meet German and Italian soldiers whom it is our honor and privilege to attack and destroy. Civilians who have the stupidity to fight us, we will kill. Those who remain passive will not be harmed." That Patton's bombastic rhetoric was so savagely consummated on the battlefield only broadened the growing feeling that Sicily had definitively turned the tide of the war.

Euphoric over the Sicily victory, Meyer went to B-3's Hotel Astor offices. He tried the door several times. It wouldn't open, so he went downstairs and asked an attendant what time the guests in room 253 would return.

"What is the name of the guest?"

"They were military people," Meyer said cautiously.

"Navy?" the attendant asked.

"Yes."

"They've checked out, sir."

"For the day?"

"No, sir. They took all of their things, files and everything."

"When?"

"A few weeks ago."

"Did they say where they moved?"

"No, sir."

Gravely concerned, Meyer took a cab down to the navy's Church Street offices. There was a new receptionist, young and with the sleepy eyes of a temporary worker. Meyer asked for Commander Haffenden.

"Who?" the receptionist asked.

"Commander Rad Haffenden?"

"Commander?" She was oblivious, as if she had been asked to write a thesis in quantum physics.

"Yes, *Commander*," Meyer said, annoyed.

"I don't think I know him. Let me ask."

Oblivia got up. Not good. Not good at all.

Oblivia came back. "He doesn't work here anymore."

"Where did he go, miss?"

"I don't know."

"Is Captain McPhail here?"

"Who?"

"Captain Oscar McPhail."

"Let me go check."

Vay iz mir. "Wait," Meyer said. "Is Miss Schwenner here?"

"Who?"

Jesus. "Miss Schwenner. She was Commander Haffenden's secretary."

"Let me go check," Oblivia said.

"If she's not there, please check with Captain McPhail."

"Okay."

Meyer knew the answer: Schwenner was gone. And McPhail wouldn't see him.

Yup. That was the verdict. "I'd like you to give Captain McPhail a message for me," Meyer said. "Tell him Meyer Lansky would like to speak with him or Commander Haffenden." Meyer handed her his Manhattan Simplex business card.

"Sure," Oblivia said.

He'd never hear from the navy again.

Meyer had been begging Luciano's patience for months after Sicily, but after a while, having no contact with anybody in the navy proved to be too much. He had a deadly Sicilian pacing his cell at Great Meadow, mad as a hornet when Meyer couldn't instantly exploit the Sicily win. Sure, Luciano was isolated in jail, but he was resourceful. If he got desperate, he could always give up on Meyer and flag down Anastasia for help.

Frank Costello used his juice with the New York City police to find the address of Elizabeth Schwenner in Queens. Meyer's new driver, Phil the Stick, drove his boss to her house. Despite visions of a vast syndicate with infinite tentacles, Meyer wouldn't delegate some things, especially since he couldn't count on his subordinates to have a gentle touch, which was called for here. He knew he had the peculiar gift of being able to play both the shark-eyed crime boss and the harmless accountant.

Meyer knocked on the door of Schwenner's middle-class

row house after the dinner hour. Schwenner's voice came through the thick door. "Who is it?"

"Miss Schwenner, it's Mr. Lansky. Meyer. Do you have a moment?"

Schwenner opened the door cautiously. She was casually dressed and wore no makeup. Under a soft light, Meyer noticed her smooth skin and was befuddled for a moment by her youth. Something about wearing too much makeup made these young girls in the workplace look older and less attractive, he thought. *Kineahora,* she was a kid. *Gentle, Meyer.*

"Mr. Lansky," she said, doe-eyed, betraying a flash of anxiety.

"Good evening, Miss Schwenner," he said, removing his hat. "I apologize for coming to your home. Honestly, I just was very concerned when I couldn't find you or the commander. Don't worry, I don't want to make you uncomfortable and won't ask to come in."

"No, sir, that's not it at all. Um, they moved me to another office." She remained in the doorway. She looked over Meyer's shoulder and saw the hulking man in the idling sedan.

"Oh, he's just my driver. Please don't worry," Meyer said. "Where is Commander Haffenden?"

"Didn't . . . he tell you?"

"Tell me what?"

Miss Schwenner looked over his shoulder toward the dark sedan glinting under a streetlamp. "He was sent to the South Pacific."

"When?"

"Last week. It was so sudden."

"That's where all the heavy fighting is now," he said, as if Miss Schwenner didn't know this.

"I'm sorry," she said. "I don't know what to say."

Meyer thought about saying, *The fucking navy is covering their tracks, the backstabbing rat bastards,* but he saw no dividend in it. He apologized again, donned his hat, thanked her, and left.

Meyer had nothing new up his sleeve, but he did arrange for Miss Schwenner to happen upon $5,000 along with a request for a little information. In the meantime, all he could do was try to placate Luciano with more and more cash from their gambling rackets. So much for Meyer Lansky, Chief Executive Officer of Salomon Brothers. Moses Polakoff spun his wheels in the legal maze until, in the spring of 1945, he received a call from Commander Haffenden's wife, Mary, who told him where he could find her husband.

The Brooklyn Naval Hospital was overflowing with sailors. One of them was Haffenden, who had been seriously injured in the South Pacific. When Meyer got to Haffenden's room late in the afternoon, the big man was snoring loudly. Meyer sat by his bedside. After about a half hour, Haffenden's eyes blinked open and he sat up with a start and choked out what sounded like "God."

"No. Just Meyer."

Haffenden caught his breath. "Meyer. *Meyer?*" he said in a foggy voice.

"I've been worried about you. No one knew anything, Commander. Or at least they wouldn't say anything."

"I was going to contact you when I got back. I just didn't think I'd get back this way. Honestly, I didn't think I'd get back at all."

Haffenden had been among the invading forces at Iwo Jima, where he had been badly injured while under fire for four hours. The shrapnel had torn apart his lower abdomen. He had endured many blood transfusions. After multiple surgeries, he was awarded the Purple Heart.

"That's some adventure," Meyer said, impressed, but sorry for him.

"I felt bad about not telling you I was back sooner, but things were moving sideways on me. I was sworn to secrecy. I thought we'd all get nicked."

Meyer wasn't sure what Haffenden was getting at. "Were you threatened?"

"The whiff of sacrifice is in the air and I'm smelling like a burnt goat. They told me Patton's guys were making noises about . . . some of the guys they had to deal with. Before Husky, and in the early stages of the landing. They called them grease-balls."

"*Some of the guys,* Commander?"

"Sicilians, Meyer. Patton's a prick. It's all about glory with that son of a bitch, public relations. The way I hear it, a few weeks into the invasion he started swearing up a storm. *Dago* this. *Guinea* that. You know the type."

"So, my boys set him up with his leads, he goes through Sicily like a hot knife through butter, and then complains about the people who helped him?"

Haffenden sat up and placed the pillow higher up behind his neck. "You'd think on the face of it people would appreciate what you do, but it doesn't work out that way. Once people win, they start thinking about how it'll get written up. They're 'Boy Scouting' everything, pasteurizing. Everybody forgot the days when we were waking up in a cold sweat. You know how it is. When you've got food poisoning and you're throwing up your guts, you tell God you'll be his servant. The next day when you feel better, God's long gone.

"History's getting rewritten, Meyer. Roosevelt's the only one who could kill all this Lilliputian knife-fighting, and it's not like we can just knock on the door at Hyde Park. Secretary Knox told somebody that the U-boats never even posed a big threat."

"Is that true?"

Haffenden said, disgusted, "Do you know how many we lost at Pearl Harbor to the Japs? About two thousand four hundred, more than a thousand wounded on top of that. You know how many we lost to the Nazis in the Atlantic? We estimated about five thousand in Drumbeat. When all is said and done, we could be talking about tens of thousands. But it's Pearl Harbor that gets all the press."

"I had no idea the U-boats had done more damage than Pearl Harbor. Freedom exacts a helluva vig."

"Nobody'll ever know how bad it got, and I'll tell you why: It was a world-class fuckup, Meyer. We weren't ready," Haffenden raged.

"But we weren't ready for Pearl Harbor either."

"Right, but Pearl was one big fireball. It was a single catastrophe, not a nick, nick, nick with a razor over time, which makes it invisible."

"But now they want it all buried," Meyer said, sick inside.

"Nobody wants to pull at the collar of this sleeping rottweiler."

"Charlie always said he knew he'd get screwed. Do you think there's no way at all the government will play ball on a better deal for him?"

"I wouldn't say no way. It's all about the self-interest of the people involved. You know, Meyer, when you're a sailor, you learn to navigate by the North Star, as journeymen have done from the beginning. My North Star was the defense of this country. Everything else was just stardust. But now the North Star is politics. If they think they can keep it quiet, maybe they'll follow through."

"I see it a little different," Meyer said. "If the government thinks it *can* keep everything quiet, then why would they help Charlie? We're done being polite, Commander."

Suddenly, a nurse that Haffenden had taken a liking to swept into his room, her eyes puffy and bloodshot. Tears were streaming down her cheeks. Meyer got up and asked her what was wrong. She told them.

"Well, Meyer, our jobs just got a little harder," Haffenden said.

Charlie Luciano sprang up in his cell at Great Meadow Prison when he heard the newspaper smack against the cold floor. He shook his head in wonder that he was still in this hell. He read the headline and looked up at the guard, who had been standing on the other side of the bars awaiting the inmate's reaction.

"I'm fucked now."

Silent Partner

Roosevelt had died suddenly in Warm Springs, and dead men—even ones who owed favors to some rough customers who'd helped put them in office—weren't scared of being impeached. Still, living bureaucrats might, so Meyer moved quickly. After collecting sensitive information from Haffenden, and learning from Miss Schwenner about Haffenden's replacement, Meyer sat himself, uninvited, in the guest chair of one Commander Parker at the navy's Church Street offices. Meyer had walked in with Phil the Stick early that morning, pleasantly lying to a receptionist about having an appointment with Parker.

Meyer sighed; to him, everything was about relationships. People were not easily transferred to new tasks based on job descriptions. You couldn't simply convey the nuances of certain things as if they were the recipe for Coca-Cola, which could be mixed anywhere if you had the right ingredients.

Meyer had no illusions about how the authorities saw men like him. Haffenden was special because even though he was wary of racketeers and put pressure on them to deliver, the two wings of the ferret squad had held a lot of stock in each other. Whatever Haffenden may privately have thought of the men in Meyer's world, he knew he needed them and had never expressed resentment for that need. And Meyer knew the mob had been cut a little slack given the times.

If Meyer failed to spring Luciano, he would chafe in prison. If Meyer got richer while Luciano rotted, the Italians would think they had been rooked. That's how these guys thought: The biggest crooks become crooks in the first place with the logic that everybody else is trying to steal from them. Their crimes are just preventative medicine.

It was not lost on the gambler in Meyer that if he doubled down and sprang Luciano from the stony lonesome, Meyer's influence would grow, and it would be in the interest of dangerous men to make certain he remained in good health.

These thoughts were running through Meyer's head as he waited for this Commander Parker while Phil the Stick skulked outside the office.

At nine, Commander Parker came in wearing a white uniform.

"May I help you?" he asked Meyer, who did not stand.

"Have a seat, Commander Parker."

"Who the hell are you?"

"My name is Meyer Lansky. I'm your silent partner in some ventures."

"I don't know what you're talking about." Parker slid behind Haffenden's old desk, as if to put an obstacle between Meyer and himself.

"Where is Commander Haffenden?" Meyer asked, even though he damned well knew the answer, but he wanted to hear the lie firsthand.

"He was reassigned," Parker said.

"Reassigned where?"

"To the South Pacific, I believe. Specifics are classified."

Meyer saw in Parker's face the dead expression of the bureaucrat, somebody who would never rise far, but, if by some chance he did, it would be because he never did anything that tied him to a fuckup. He was—and the joke wasn't lost on Meyer—a ferret-faced character with a worm for a mustache and a lumpy body. Even though Haffenden was also a large man, something about him was kingly. This schmuck-on-wheels held his head atop his neck like a scarecrow. Meyer disliked him right away and was sure the feeling was mutual.

"I wanted to follow up on my earlier discussion with Commander Haffenden and Mr. Gurfein regarding Mr. Luciano," Meyer said.

"What was the nature of that discussion?"

"It involved Mr. Luciano's cooperation with the war effort now that the invasion of Sicily—"

"Mr. Lansky, in order to process that request, you'd need to fill out a special form outlining the program in which you and Mr. Luciano participated."

Yeah, well, Ben Siegel and I will get right on that, asshole. "I don't think that would be a good idea. I would just like to ask you to consider picking up where Commander Haffenden left off and make good on the navy's promise to Mr. Luciano."

"Let me be frank with you, Mr. Lansky. Mr. Luciano is a criminal. He's where he should be. I don't know what flaw in Haffenden drew him to people like you, but I'll tell you right now, I run a tight ship and you and your cronies won't be on it. I've seen no credible reports that anything Haffenden undertook saved any of our convoys or exposed Nazi agents. I heard the stories about the German rallies and the number you and your friends pulled on those so-called spies."

"So-called?"

"Those men on Long Island were as much a threat to America as Shirley Temple. I'm not going to play your game. And I will warn you, Mr. Lansky, in the strongest terms, if you have any notions of . . . how do your people put it? . . . making me disappear."

Meyer put on his hat. He knew that one of his strengths was not the stinging comeback. He was also, contrary to his reputation, capable of rage and vindictiveness. Unlike Siegel, though, he avoided acting on that rage right away.

What Parker had not figured was that Meyer had *expected* he and Luciano would be double-crossed. It wasn't that he hadn't trusted Haffenden; it was that Meyer Lansky had come to not trust America. The gangster of fabled Machiavellian brilliance had gone into the ferret squad, at least in part, hoping he would be helping his adopted country. But, America ganef. The only thing he hadn't known as his navy work wore on was *how* he'd get screwed.

"You talk about a game, Commander," Meyer said. "That's what you said, a 'game.' Games are how I make my living. You started this game. When you change the rules, when you cheat, you lose all your equity unless you straighten out. But I'm offended that you would think I'd ever make you disappear. In fact, I'll do the opposite. You'll be famous. A few days from now the world will know of the great Commander Parker."

A nervous smirk slid across Parker's face. "How is that, Mr. Lansky?"

"I'm meeting my friend Mr. Winchell for dinner tonight. *You're* just the kind of man he likes to write about. A heroic, clever man who did what must be done, found the people who needed to be found—whoever they might be—to help the navy fight the Nazi menace. *Your* recruitment of Mr. Luciano and myself showed a flair for improvisation, Commander. The country was fortunate to have *you* on the job, you might even say . . . lucky."

"I never met Luciano and you know it."

Meyer bore in on Parker, who fixated on the scar next to

Meyer's eye. Parker may have imagined the knife fight long ago where Meyer's attacker had underestimated his prey as he swung for the little man's eye and missed by an eighth of an inch. What had happened to *that* poor bastard? Meyer knew he could scare people with a certain look. Parker swallowed hard, hoping Meyer didn't see his Adam's apple twitch, but he did.

"I make odds, Commander. I don't bet myself, but if I did, I'd play blackjack, and I'll tell you why: You've got the best chance of winning, about seventeen and a half percent. I'll make some odds for you, a courtesy I don't give my patrons. I put your odds at ninety-five percent that Mr. Winchell will get his facts confused. He'll write about our work with the navy to lock down the docks. He'll write about our work on the Reslex matter to get radar onto Navy ships. He'll write about how we fucked up Harry Bridges's little trip to New York. He'll write about how we helped plan the invasion of Sicily. He'll mention every slit throat that the Third Naval District knew about along the way. He'll write about how *you* planned the whole thing. You can always write a letter to the newspaper and ask for a correction. You can also explain to Captain McPhail and Secretary Forrestal how your associates from New York wanted to keep everything quiet, but you thought it best to reward *everyone* who served their country by making their sacrifice public. Maybe Forrestal will present Mr. Luciano, Mr. Siegel, and myself with a medal, too. We'll wear our best pinstripes for the picture."

Parker was seething, a purplish color infecting his gray face. "My sources say that your friend Anastasia set the *Normandie* on fire."

"And you think this helps your case, putz*?"* Meyer turned toward the door.

Finally Parker rose, resembling a marshmallow with a black olive on top. "You people aren't real Americans!" he barked.

Meyer stopped. The thought of turning Bugsy Siegel onto this mutt crossed his mind. No, this was how you got pinched, by doing something for spite, something that didn't pay any interest.

"Really?" Meyer said. "Well, some people have two sides, you know? The side that drinks and the side that says they don't drink. The side that says it's all about honor, and the side that screws the people who made good on their promises. Americans bought my liquor. They play blackjack at my casinos. I'm a gambler, Commander. My bet is when Mr. Winchell runs his story, Americans will appreciate how my boys dealt with the Nazis. You won't turn out as good. Of course, nobody has to know, and I'm done fucking around with you people as long as the Nazis are killing my people by the cattle car. So, do you want another card or will you just stick?"

The Deal

MEYER LANSKY SAT IN A CONFERENCE ROOM IN THE ELLIS ISLAND Ferry Terminal and handed Charlie Luciano $2,500 in traveler's checks and some cash. He also told him that about $30,000 worth of Reslex stock was being held in his sister's name. His sentence has been commuted, but he would be deported to Italy. Meyer showed Luciano a section of Governor Thomas E. Dewey's statement of executive clemency:

> Upon the entry of the United States into the war, Luciano's aid was sought by the Armed Services in inducing others to provide information concerning possible enemy attack. It appears that he cooperated in such effort, although the actual value of the information procured is not clear. His record in prison is wholly satisfactory.

"It took us a while, but we did it," Meyer said. The war had ended a few months ago.

"Yeah, we did," Luciano agreed. "Don't think I wasn't goin' nuts when Roosevelt died and den Haffenden disappeared."

"You're not kidding."

"Dey got me goin' on a ship carryin' flour to Genoa. Ya believe dat?"

"It's best that way, Charlie."

"I figured you'd say dat. I guess yer right. If dey put me on some luzhery liner da whole thing could blow up."

"Right. Knowing you, Charlie, you've got some business ideas."

"Yeah, I got a few."

"Just be careful with . . . you know."

"I know ya disapprove of traffickin', Meyer. We never seen eye to eye on dat. When it comes to cash, nothin' beats it. Not even gamblin'."

"I know, but it's one thing that's nonnegotiable with the authorities."

"Someday it'll be respectable. You study dis stuff. You prolly know some blue-blood families dat got dere start peddlin'."

"The Roosevelts."

"Roosevelts? You shittin' me?"

"Actually it was the Delanos, the president's mother's family. I was reading about them in some old library records."

"You and da libarries! So what was dey pushin'?"

"The president's grandfather Warren Delano went bust in real estate and railroads. But they had gotten used to the lifestyle. You know how it is, how you can't go backward. So he moved his family to Hong Kong, ginned up some old contacts, and supplied the Chinese parlors with opium."

"No shit, he supplied opium dens? Was it legal wit the Chinks in dem days?"

"No. It was all done with bribes to Chinese officials."

"Dat's da way it still is most places. Bribes."

"I know, Charlie, but in Delano's day, nobody saw anything. Now you've got governments—armies even—all set up to chase it down. You've got the church, newspapers reporting what this stuff does to people."

"Always gonna be weak people, Meyer. Dat's what our outfit ran on, always. Booze is a weakness. Broads. Gamblin'. Prohibition's over."

"For booze it is. But look what happened to you on the broads charge. And the stuff you're talking about. I was reading a newspaper a rabbi gave me. Jewish paper. Somebody wrote about heroin addicts at a hospital out in Westchester."

"So?"

"So? *Westchester.* There's money up there, Charlie. The girl they wrote about sounded like Betty Lou Jones, the girl next door with pink ribbons in her pretty blond hair."

"So you're sayin' when Betty Lou Jones gets hooked, da cops pay attention. I get whatcha sayin'."

"I know you do, Charlie. I'll keep you in what we've started in music, Florida, Cuba, other places."

"Dose are long-term, Meyer. Our boys are back in the saddle now that Mussolini's gone. I gotta score quick ta live. I ain't got da time you got with all that legit stuff you like."

"Everybody'll be looking at you, Charlie. Everything will get eyeballed."

Luciano reached out and hugged Meyer. "I know yer just tryin' to protect me. I'll be all right."

You can take the girl out of cheap underwear, but you can't take the cheap underwear out of the girl.

Despite Meyer's wish to have Luciano deported under cover of darkness, it was not to be. A handful of reporters came down to Pier 7 one February morning, where the freighter *Laura Keene* was docked, with designs on interviewing Luciano about the deal that got him sprung. They were surprised to find hundreds of burly longshoremen guarding the pier with baling hooks.

Within the hour, a flurry of calls from New York media came into the offices of Governor Dewey, the New York district attorney, Naval Intelligence, and Dannemora, Great Meadow, and Sing Sing prisons, and immigration authorities. Not surprisingly, word of the media inquiries got back to Frank Costello, who personally came down to Pier 7 to deal with the situation.

The *Laura Keene* departed for Genoa the next morning along with thirty-five hundred tons of flour and Charlie Luciano. Despite fables of a gangland jubilee with kosher delicacies and showgirls, the reality was a sad affair with Costello and a few other men who were there mostly to convince the *Keene*'s Captain Salter to depart New York, pronto. Meyer was not one of them. He predicted the crush of reporters, had said his good-byes, and slipped away to Washington, D.C., with his sons, Buddy and Paul, now sixteen and fourteen, who wanted to visit the museums and monuments.

No Sale

SHORTLY AFTER SUNSET, AS PEACE EMBRACED THE LAND, A CAR IDLED with its lights on in an area of the Pine Barrens known as Ong's Hat. Van Voorst and Brahms stood in the unnatural light and dug deep holes in the whitish earth. After spending some quality time as guests of the clandestine services, the spooks misplaced them. These things happen. When the men were done digging, Bugsy Siegel and Red Levine took their shovels away.

"You killed five thousand American sailors, you worms, and you helped Hitler kill God knows how many Jews and others," Siegel said. "The days of the Hebrew nebbish are over. The *shtarkers* are in charge now, and if you want to know what that means, ask the devil."

With that, Red Levine put his gun in van Voorst's mouth and blew his brains out all over Brahms, who convulsed with terror. "We have civil rights!" Brahms said through chattering teeth.

"There are no civil rights in the Pine Barrens," Siegel said, putting his sawed-off shotgun in Brahms's lippy mouth and savoring the Nazi's terror. He pulled the trigger, but heard only a dry click.

"Shit," Siegel said, inspecting the weapon. Then, satisfied

he had cleared the jam, he shot Brahms in the crotch and kicked the wailing Nazi, still alive, into the grave he had dug for himself. Blue Jaw Magoon and Tick Tock Tannenbaum filled in the dirt while Siegel and Levine fired up De Nobili cigars and flicked the orange fireflies that flew from the ash onto the cool soil.

Frank Costello was pale. He normally had a tan in the late spring, but he had been spending most of his time indoors. He had a lot of things going in business and in politics, and Meyer was back in New York for a few days to keep Costello and his other investors up-to-date on their properties in Florida and Havana and the Flamingo in Vegas. As frustrated as Costello was with some of the things that were happening in New York, he knew he could always count on Meyer for an honest report. Even the Flamingo, which Bugsy Siegel had finally opened, was starting to turn a profit.

Costello and Meyer went for a walk in Central Park, the urbane Calabrian putting his arm around the diminutive Jew as a bodyguard loomed behind them. "You know, Meyer, I think we did the right thing with Charlie. He wanted to come out of the clink on a tear, making up for lost time. There's just no controlling him with the broads, the nightlife, and that dope—the kind of crap that gets the government all angered. Now I can do what I do, you can do what you do, and maybe we'll get a breather from the heat. I'm making a no-dope rule with my men, so you know."

"Smart," Meyer said. "At least if Charlie's going to run that kind of racket, he'll be doing it from Italy. Let their police deal with it."

"I don't know what it is with him," Costello said. "Nobody was pushing harder for the respectable businesses than Charlie way back. But then he . . . what's the word I'm looking for, Meyer?"

"Word meaning what?"

"Word meaning he goes back to his old ways."

"*Revert,*" Meyer said.

"Yeah, *revert.* Kinda like *pervert.* He reverts to when we were kids. Anyhow, I appreciate how you cooked up the deportment, not the commutation with him staying in New York. So I don't fuck up, does Polakoff know?"

"No, Frank. As a lawyer, he couldn't be anywhere near something like this. He's obligated to get the best deal for his client. Moe's position is that the deportment was the best deal we could get for Charlie and that he negotiated it. If he suspects that we *wanted* Charlie deported, he hasn't said anything."

"What did it cost us? The deport?"

"Your friend, Mr. Smith, wanted fifty grand. I talked him up to seventy-five."

"You talked him *up*? You're one lousy Jew."

"So my father told me," Meyer said. "I figured it was good to be extragenerous in case any of that dough moved north."

Costello laughed. "You think Dewey saw a taste?"

"Who gives a shit?"

Costello laughed again. He kept his hand on the back of Meyer's neck as they went home, Costello to the Majestic and Meyer to the Waldorf.

One of the great swindles of the rackets is what the Italians called *omertà,* the code of silence. *Omertà* was a goal, and some people in that life kept quiet when the law came around. What the code ignores is human nature, and the impulse to talk. Sometimes people talk because they think they need to confess. Usually, though, they talk to come off as if they were players in big events. So, when the war was over, people talked whether they knew anything or not.

The thing everybody was buzzing about was Luciano's role in the Allied victory. One story had Luciano storming next to General Patton when he came ashore waving a blazing yellow flag with an *L* to alert the Sicilian countryside that their native son had arrived to liberate them. Reporters interviewed New York dockworkers who were eager to make up stories about their participation. It was idiotic for the navy to believe Operation Underworld could ever remain quiet given that hundreds of people were involved. The campaign had been approved without the slightest hesitation about ethics; the only ethic was stopping Hitler. As President Roosevelt told Ambassador Joseph Davies in 1941 about the partnership with Stalin, "I can't take Communism, nor can you, but to cross this bridge, I would hold hands with the devil."

The one man who had tried hard to hold on to *omertà* was Irish, not Italian. As the months after the war rolled on, though, Commander Haffenden found himself a leper. He retired from the navy, disabled from the wounds he'd suffered at Iwo Jima.

Captain McPhail, who had retired, denied the existence of the ferret squad. A three-column headline in the *New York Post* and story lead read:

LUCIANO DID NOTHING
FOR U.S., SAYS NAVY CHIEF

Luciano, in a move that for many confirmed his involvement, denied having anything to do with the campaign. He was not being modest: He did not want to get crosswise with the American authorities that had with great protest conceded to set him free. Also, since he was to spend the rest of his life in Naples, he did not want to inflame his Italian hosts.

The name Meyer Lansky did not appear in any of the papers.

In between constant hospitalizations for internal bleeding, Haffenden managed to swing a job as the commissioner of marine and aviation for New York City. People whispered around the office that he had consorted with gangsters. One day after coming home to Flushing from work, Haffenden received a letter from the mayor of New York. It accused him of lying to the parole board about Lucky Luciano's role in the war effort. It was delivered by a New York City police officer. He had been shitcanned.

Haffenden reached out to some of his old navy friends for job leads. His telephone calls weren't returned. Eventually, he nailed down a job as a Dictaphone salesman. Recalling that Frank Costello and Meyer had been in the music distribution business, Haffenden contacted them. Nobody would talk on the phone, so Costello invited Haffenden to his office. One of the secretaries there remembered him fondly and told him that Meyer had moved to Florida to manage his investments, which was true. Haffenden remembered Meyer's trips to Florida, but didn't know he had hit the jackpot in the Sunshine State, Las Vegas, and Havana simultaneously.

Haffenden showed up at Manhattan Simplex along with a model Dictaphone. Costello looked sharp and prosperous, smoking in his elegant way, but his croaky voice couldn't hide the Hell's Kitchen knife fight that caused him to speak in his strained voice. Costello thought Haffenden looked terrible; he was grayer and puffier, and he couldn't hide it beneath an expensive suit. Haffenden moved as slow as syrup and breathed heavily when he spoke.

"Whattaya got there, Commander?" Costello asked as they sat in his private office.

"Well, Frank, this was the thing I wanted to talk to you about," Haffenden said proudly, but in a manner that made Costello feel sad. "This is what's called a Dictaphone."

"Looks pretty nifty. What's it do?"

"All the big businesses are using it now, Frank. People are on all kinds of waiting lists for this."

Costello nodded, trying to conceal that he wasn't impressed with the pitch so far. "What's it do, Commander?"

"Here you go, Frank. Hold this part." Haffenden handed Costello a thingamajig that resembled the kind of horn you might see on an animal like a ram. "Now, say something right here."

"Say what?"

"Say, 'Mary had a little lamb.'"

Costello couldn't believe he was about to do it, but he had a sentimental streak. "Mary hadda little lamb." Then he handed the horn back to Haffenden.

"Now, listen to this, Frank, you'll love it." Haffenden fiddled with a knob.

"Mary hadda little lamb," Costello heard his strained voice played back to him, and he didn't like it. "Whoa, Commander, that's me," Costello said, trying not to seem defensive.

"Exactly, Frank. This uses a new science. It used to be a wax process, but now it's a plastic system," Haffenden said, in a mistaken assessment of his market demographic so profound that if Costello had not been devoted to the appearance of respectability, Haffenden would be on the floor bleeding from his throat.

"Wait a minute, Commander," Costello said, losing his

deferential posture. "What are you tryin' to do here, my friend?"

"I'm trying to show you what a spectacular new system we've got here, Frank. I was thinking that since you know a lot about the music business, this is kind of like, I guess, a similar kind of thing. You see what I'm saying?"

"How's it the same?"

Haffenden removed a handkerchief and began wiping his brow. "It records and such."

"Yeah, but one thing's entertainment. Singin' songs, you follow?"

"Right, sure."

"What does that Dicty thing do?" Costello asked.

"It records, Frank. Like you heard your voice."

"You tryin' to sell it to music people? Is that the kinda thing it does?"

"It's not for music, no. It's more for businesspeople."

"Businesspeople? Who wants to hear *them* sing?" Costello asked.

"Nobody wants to hear businesspeople sing," Haffenden said cloudily.

"That's what I'm sayin', Commander. So who buys it?"

"Businesspeople and lawyers, Frank."

"What do they do with it if they don't sing?"

"They keep a record of their voices. Like you dictate a letter to somebody and your secretary types it up. Then you keep a record of what you said."

"No kiddin'? Businessmen want their voices on a record?"

"Absolutely, Frank. So you can talk into this part here and tell somebody what you'd like them to do, then they do it, and you've got a record of it."

Costello sighed. He began to speak a few times, but realized Haffenden was no longer the man he had known and respected so much and might not understand the stegosaurus that had just crapped on the Persian rug under him: THE ENTIRE LIFE MISSION OF GUYS LIKE ME IS TO *NOT* GET OUR VOICES RECORDED! *Yes, Margaret, this is Mr. Costello . . . please make a note here. . . . Be sure we bribe the mayor twenty grand to give us the trash contract, break Johnny Snake Eyes' kneecaps. . . . Tell Vinnie to have Kid Twist tossed from a window at the Half Moon Hotel. . . . Oh, and cancel my dentist appointment.*

Like most people when confronted with a human tragedy playing out in their presence, Costello wondered how such a thing could happen, and whether it could happen to him. Was Haffenden's Greek decline a function of some demon, or was it the effect of the political riptide in which he had gotten himself caught?

"Commander, we got a history, right?" Costello said. "You tell me what you want me to do."

"Well, I usually don't like to be so blunt, but I was hoping you'd want to buy the product."

"How much do these Dictys cost?" Costello asked, impatient now.

Haffenden told him and promised a "special price," which made Costello wonder if he wanted to shoot himself because the whole scene was so depressing, or to shoot Haffenden to put him out of his misery.

"Why don't you gimme five," Costello said.

Haffenden's eyes brightened, and a touch of color returned to his face. "No kidding?"

"You got it, Commander."

And the ordeal was over. Costello peeled off the cash, throwing in a few hundred extra. He instructed Haffenden to arrange for the deliveries with his secretary. He asked to keep the sample Haffenden had brought.

As soon as Haffenden left, Costello told his secretary to have the four machines delivered to other offices on the floor of their office building as a gift.

"Four?" she asked. "I thought there were five."

"Yeah," Costello says. "There's one back in the office. It has my voice on it. I want you to throw it in the incinerator, you follow?"

"I'm not like Meyer," Haffenden told Moses Polakoff when he was told around this time that Congress might investigate what had been code-named Operation Underworld. "I can't tough it out in the shadows."

He was right. Haffenden died on Christmas Eve 1952 at age sixty. He left all $27,000 worth of his assets to Mary, which included his home in Flushing and a 1951, two-door Hudson automobile. He never took Meyer's Reslex stock tip.

The Payout

Miami Beach, 1982

Uncle Meyer was fading in his chair on the terrace, his eyes growing heavier with the burden of a day that was approaching extinction. He made me think of a dried leaf that was curled up on a sidewalk moments before a breeze blew it into dust. I was tired, too, and my hand had cramped from days of writing. The sun was dissolving over America as the day's final bathers retreated from the Atlantic to get ready for dinner.

A fellow retiree on a terrace in a neighboring building waved, and Uncle Meyer waved back. The retiree wore one of those insipid smiles people get when they're in the presence of a celebrity. It was as if they thought when Death scaled the side of their building, they could just look at the hooded ghoul and whisper, "Lansky lives right over there," and Death would haul ass back to Jacksonville or some other hellhole.

"I don't know who these people think I am," he said.

"Paul Newman," I suggested.

Uncle Meyer nodded. "I get that a lot." He winked. "At my last trial, they asked a potential juror if he knew the name Meyer Lansky. The guy said I was the mayor of Miami. We all had a good laugh. Some writer said I was the 'Mafia's Yoda.' What the hell is that, some kind of exercise?"

"You're thinking of *yoga.* Yoda is a character in the *Star Wars* movie."

"What, like a spaceman?" Uncle Meyer was incredulous. "I lived too damned long. At least the government gave me back my voting rights. Found out last week."

"Are you going to vote?" I asked, not thinking through the recent passing of the midterm election.

"Nah. If I vote for one guy and then the other guy wins, the first guy will find something to charge me with. Better I should stay home."

Despite his condition, he wasn't kidding. No, he wasn't a yeshiva boy, but he conveyed what I had begun to learn as a boy when the authorities were stalking my grandfather: When in doubt, the law and the media used certain names and groups as a proxy for orchestrated evil.

I pulled my chair closer to him. "Uncle Meyer, before I leave, can I check a few things with you?"

"Sure, kid."

"When did Charlie Luciano pass away?"

"'Sixty-two. Dropped dead on an airport tarmac in Naples. They even took a picture of him getting loaded into a cheap pine coffin. Still, he died a free man. I sure as hell didn't tell him to fly to Havana and throw parties with Sinatra and his whores right after we got him sprung."

"Is that what he did?"

"That's what he did. Sinatra flew in a planeload of broads from Chicago. Charlie and Sinatra partied like Caligula, girls running around naked by the swimming pool at the Nacional. A reporter caught the whole thing and ran an item on it. Some broad Charlie was *shtupping* hired a publicity man to promote their romance in the society columns. You believe that? Truman went nuts when he read that and told Batista to throw Charlie out. Batista first said no, at my request. Then Truman said he'd stop sending medical supplies to Cuba, so Batista bounced him. Best thing that could have happened. We didn't need that kind of heat."

"Wasn't Batista loyal to Charlie, too?"

Uncle Meyer shrugged. "He was more loyal to the suitcases of cash that your grandfather and I were sending to Geneva every month. It was a good move, getting Charlie deported. The dividends lasted decades. The Mafia returned to Sicily with a vengeance. Frank stayed strong another dozen years. When Anastasia got greedy, his own guys took him out in the same barbershop I met him in that time. The Feds came for me eventually, but having a lightning rod like Charlie gone bought me almost thirty years."

"Jeez. And Ben Siegel—"

"I did everything I could to save Ben," Uncle Meyer mourned. Bugsy Siegel had gone down in an orgy of bullets from a World War II model .30-30 carbine shortly after Luciano was deported. "Given how he was, it was a death by natural causes.

"Ben had a fetish, Jonah. He shot off his mouth, always wanted people to believe he was the big man who made things happen. When we were kids, and we heard some store got knocked over, he'd smirk like he did it, when he didn't. He told people he invented Las Vegas, and after he died, I kept that spiel going because I loved him and because it was good for business. The place that Benny died for was a place worth going broke over. But Ben didn't invent Las Vegas; it was already there. My boys just sold it."

"And you don't think Ben, Charlie, or Albert were behind the *Normandie* fire?"

Uncle Meyer propped himself up. "Jonah, that fire, like I say, it could have been anybody, or it could have been nobody. And it wasn't Ben. It was just one of those things that happen in the tumult of life. When I got some distance on it, I thought of a punk who turned up in a strange dream I had a long time ago. In my dream, the kid had one face that looked innocent and the other that looked guilty as hell. . . . I guess it was somebody without a face at all."

As much as I believed this was plausible, something still bothered me about another aspect of Uncle Meyer's story. I breathed in slowly to screw up enough courage to ask him what needed to be asked.

"Uncle Meyer, there's something gnawing at me, an inconsistency."

Shark eyes from Uncle Meyer. "What's that?"

"That huge ship . . . that terrible fire . . ."

Uncle Meyer's gaze narrowed. "Still with this?"

"When we started talking, you said that Haffenden thought it was a blessing in disguise that the *Normandie* went down because all of those U-boats would have sunk it anyway, killing thousands of troops." I turned to another page in my notes. "But later you said that Haffenden thought the war could have been won faster if the *Normandie* had been finished and sailed on time."

Uncle Meyer turned his gaze from me. "I dunno, maybe he said both. I don't remember so good, you know, with all these drugs they've got me on."

The wiseguy on the stand.

"Don't you think it's amazing that only one man died in that disaster?"

"Meaning what, Jonah?"

"Meaning . . . I don't know, Uncle Meyer, do you really want me getting the *whole* story?"

"Stop with the mush mouth, kid. What are you gettin' at?"

Gettin'. Uncle Meyer had dropped his *g*'s, something he hadn't done during our entire time together. Pure Brooklyn all of a sudden. He began coughing. He motioned for his glass of water, which sat beside his salt-air-ravaged Webster's dictionary. I dutifully brought it to him.

"Do you want to keep going?" I asked.

"Yeah, I wanna keep going. But I wanna know where *you're* going."

"If the Nazis lit up that ship, you'd think they would have done a lot more damage. But if the Nazis knew the *Normandie* would be a sitting duck in the Atlantic, they'd just blow it up at sea where they already had the firepower—"

"You're not listening, Jonah, nobody thought the Nazis did the job on the *Normandie*. That was all bullshit."

"Okay then. But, if the fire was spontaneous, and it did all that damage, wouldn't it have killed a lot more people than one man?"

"What do I look like here, a professor of fires?"

I inched my chair closer to Uncle Meyer. "More than any other man in your world, you were never careless with human life."

He nodded. "I'm glad you understand that."

"What I'm saying is that if somebody very important didn't want that ship going out to sea with all of those young troops, and that very important person also wanted a big propaganda win to show that the Germans were a big threat, he might want the ship to be destroyed at the pier, but he'd have serious reservations about loss of life. He might have had someone very professional do the job to avoid that. Not somebody like Anastasia or Ben Siegel."

Uncle Meyer closed his eyes. His chest was rising and falling with his shallow breath. After a few minutes, one of his eyes opened slightly, as if to see if I was still there.

"Uncle Meyer, are you all right?"

"I'm worried about who takes care of my boy Buddy when

I'm gone," he said in the greatest non sequitur of our journey. The dying *zeyde*, or the prevaricating fox?

I decided he was the fox and kept coming. "People say Roosevelt knew about Pearl Harbor beforehand, Uncle Meyer. I know you don't believe that. But he needed help getting the country riled up to go to war with Germany. He needed a *German* Pearl Harbor, didn't he?"

Uncle Meyer made a swatting motion. "You're meshuga with this," he said, his eyes still closed. "We were just smash-and-grab guys."

"But you were wily enough to get a seat at the table to help America win the war, to get Charlie freed, to get those saboteurs pinched and executed—"

Uncle Meyer coughed again. He blinked hard a few times as if to shuffle his thoughts. "You're a ballbuster, kid. Okay now, what mattered was who people *thought* burned the *Normandie*, and part of my job was to make sure people thought it was the Germans. Remember that anonymous source Winchell quoted saying the FBI suspected the Long Island Nazis of firebombing the *Normandie*?"

"Yes."

"Well, kid, you're looking at his source. You're right: Dasch didn't know bubkes about the *Normandie*. Winchell didn't give a shit either. Pinching those Long Island guys for the fire, puffing them up as master saboteurs, suited Walter's purposes, too. Who knows what kind of arrangement he had with Roosevelt."

Uncle Meyer closed his eyes again, and from where I was sitting, I thought he might be grinning. Despite his feigned disapproval of blowhards who tried to place themselves at the center of major events, his own longevity was rooted in his reflexive capacity to position himself as the indispensable mastermind whether he was or he wasn't; he just did it more strategically and with greater subtlety. One cannot, after all, kill the only man who knows the combination to the vault. But first you have to make people think there *is* a vault.

Uncle Meyer rubbed Bruzzer behind his ears. “Now, that punk, Harry Bridges, really gave me something to work with. All that commie stuff that we got to Winchell wasn’t made up either. Some of our guys in the garment district were wired in with those socialist Jews. For socialists, they were as happy to see a buck as much as the next guy. We found an old pinko to give up Bridges, how he used a fake name when he came to their commie meetings. Hard to stay anonymous, schmuck, when your picture is all over the news talking about what a swell guy Lenin was and how the Nazis were peaceful.

“But Rad Haffenden—boy, did the government ever screw him. The Feds, Jonah, are no different from gangsters: You find some sucker to clip a guy, then you have *him* clipped to keep it quiet.”

Uncle Meyer grimaced. Even if he hadn’t had enough, I had. I’d never know for sure if he had a hand in the demise of the *Normandie;* he would never let me. By depriving me of this resolution, even if he hadn’t laid a glove on that ship, he kept the upper hand to the end.

“Thank you so much for telling me your story,” I said. I kissed him on the forehead and left him holding Bruzzer.

“Jonah,” he said before I walked away.

“Yes?”

“Give me that tablet and the pen.”

Uncle Meyer slid Bruzzer aside, put on his reading glasses, and slowly wrote:

I am a patriot. I recruited Charlie Luciano, Frank Costello, and other Italians who needed to be reminded that America was their country. We all owed America a big debt. Of all the contracts people say I put out on people, the contract to help my country was the only one I ever really ordered.

Uncle Meyer handed back the pad and patted my arm, adding, "No matter what you may think of me, Jonah, there was one thing more than anything else that drove me back then, even more than trying to help the Jews Hitler was killing: I wanted to pay my debt to the country that took me in and gave me my shot. That's all you get here is a shot, not a guaranteed payout like everybody wants nowadays. I tried to enlist in the army and got rejected. I turned my back on my chance to be completely legit so I could do the ferret squad. I couldn't drop my gambling ventures with all the pressure. Then when Kefauver came along, I crapped out. You write down that I wanted to be a good American."

I told Uncle Meyer I would and stepped behind him through the doorway into the living room. For a moment, I considered going back to ask him if he believed that being a *shtarker* was the best way to be a Jew, but wasn't up for the rant that would almost certainly follow. Teddy wasn't here, and I felt funny about skulking through the apartment to find her. I heard Uncle Meyer, who evidently thought I had gone, faintly talking to Bruzzer and remember distinctly what he said.

The crucible of the ferret squad quickly gained meaning and resonance in my mind. I thought back to the Dylan song that had been playing when I had gone for my run, particularly the line "He not busy being born is busy dying." Indeed, while my source had been busy dying, I was just getting started. Part of any birth is learning how the world really is, not how you want it to be, and in some fashion Uncle Meyer's flawed quest to be an American, like my own grandfather's, taught me whom I *didn't* want to be: I didn't want to be like

Commander Haffenden, the victim of a cunning American system I was too naïve to see or too weak to fight—an outsider on the run.

Meyer Lansky and Mickey Price, the myths, haunted the American imagination and shoreline, while Lansky and Price, the men, husks of ghosts, kvetched toward oblivion, their legacies being whatever their wounded children would be able to salvage from their quicksand choices and circumstances.

As Mickey had pushed me toward the Ivy League, Uncle Meyer pushed his son Paul toward military service. Young Paul Lansky's interest in serving his country proved to be more than an adolescent whim. To his father's delight, Paul received an appointment to the United States Military Academy at West Point. He earned a master's in engineering, served as one of the United States' original military advisers in Vietnam, and later was an engineer on the Apollo space program.

While it was Uncle Meyer's tale of the ferret squad that I better understood, it was Commander Haffenden whom I really felt for. He was a bureaucrat who took a risk that was in the country's best interest, but not his own. The navy used him to do its dirty work, but when it was time to consider public relations, they made him walk the plank. It's a strange thing about Americans: We cherish our hooligans, but insist upon being told tall tales about the pristine nature of our achievements.

Uncle Meyer died two weeks after I left his balcony. The news reports were replete with clichés from *The Godfather*, lots of "boss of all the bosses" tripe, references to a vast and hidden fortune, photographs of massacred Bugsy Siegel lying bloody and immortal on his girlfriend's sofa, and of Uncle Meyer's twin masterpieces, Havana and Las Vegas.

I debriefed Tom Simmons in the White House shortly after Uncle Meyer's death. As I beheld Tom's smallness, overlaid with my fresh memory of wizened Uncle Meyer, I thought of *The Wizard of Oz,* a film that frightened me as a child. To me, the scariest parts were neither the flying monkeys nor the witch, but when the little dog, Toto, nipped open the Wizard's lair to reveal the little man behind the curtain. In the end, we are a republic of little men who do our best work from behind curtains, crawling through proverbial *qanats.*

Tom asked me, "So, Jonah, you've collected the data, now step into my world where you put your cojones on the line and tell the president of the United States what he needs to do about terrorists."

Knowing Tom's legendary impatience, not to mention President Reagan's penchant for conclusions over process, I answered, "Everybody gets screwed."

"How so?" I sensed by the way Tom's jaw hung slack for a moment that he hadn't been expecting an answer like this.

"These black operations are effective, Tom. Who knows what would have happened if Meyer would have let Bugsy Siegel loose on Goebbels and Göring? If you're looking to protect the country, there's no better way than releasing the hounds. But if you're looking to come out smelling like a rose, cloak-and-dagger operations won't cut it. During the Second World War, if the press got curious, the White House would smack them down. Hell, Tom, they didn't even report that Roosevelt was crippled. These days, they're rummaging through the White House's trash to see if they can find a tube of hair dye the president threw out."

Tom took my report. "They do that, don't they?"

"Yes, sir, they do. And I'll be damned if I'm clever enough to know a way to keep it secret. Even Dewey got screwed. Rumors that he was bribed to free Luciano dogged him his whole career. Bugsy had it right. He told one of those Nazi spies that Americans don't like war, we like war *movies*. Maybe that was why we didn't do more to save the Jews from the ovens."

Tom and I left things there. At least for nineteen years.

I didn't know what significance my little adventure with Uncle Meyer had until the days following the September 11, 2001, terrorist attacks. In the wake of the endless news coverage, to my surprise Tom Simmons called to invite me to play tennis at one of our old venues, a banker's private estate on Foxhall Road in Washington. By this point, I was no longer a young political novice; I was a successful pollster in early middle-age.

Tom had not aged especially well, his arms and legs having turned spindly, and the once furious blue of his eyes now pale and watery, as if he were struggling with an inner toxin of indefinite provenance. Before Tom and I took the court, he told me that President Reagan, now in the late stages of Alzheimer's disease, had been fascinated by my talks with Uncle Meyer. He had even said that his old talent agent, Lew Wasserman, had dealt with some of Uncle Meyer's and Mickey's boys in the old days, whenever they were.

Tom said that in the wake of escalating attacks on Americans by Muslim extremists, especially Libyans, in the early and mid-1980s, President Reagan had become convinced that dealing with rough customers was a tragic necessity for America's survival. This contributed to his decision to either directly authorize or opaquely wink at a variety of black operations, including the infiltration of the port of Tripoli, the base of Libya's naval operations on the Mediterranean. Some of the infiltrators were pirates the United States had funded to do business with Libya in order to get a toehold in this hostile country. Other spies included a network of Tripoli hotel and restaurant staff that kept tabs on the comings and goings of Libyan naval personnel. The template was lifted directly from the ferret squad's playbook.

On April 5, 1986, a nightclub in West Berlin, Germany, was bombed at the order of the Libyan dictator, Mu'ammar Gadhafi, killing two U.S. servicemen and injuring hundreds. In the aftermath, U.S.-sponsored operatives drugged the drinks and meals of key Libyans and sabotaged their vehicles, acutely limiting their capacity to respond to the impending U.S. retaliation.

In the early-morning hours of April 14, sixty-six U.S. warplanes leaving from aircraft carriers in the Mediterranean and several British bases attacked Tripoli naval installations and other high-value targets. The country's defenses were caught completely off guard and its military was unable to scramble a response. The attack was over in ten minutes. And, yes, the United States did business with some rough men to make this happen, just as we did in World War II.

I listened to Tom's story, shuddering just a little.

"I read in the *Post* that Gadhafi condemned Al Qaeda's attack on the World Trade Center and the other places," I said after a moment.

"I'd like to think his attitude adjustment began on your uncle Meyer's balcony," Tom said.

"So would I. Thanks for telling me, Tom."

Tom's distant blue eyes looked off toward the clouds. "I didn't tell you anything, Jonah."

Tom died of a stroke four months later. Somehow, I wasn't stunned when I heard the news. Tom had always been a guy who could see around corners.

This is Uncle Meyer's story of the ferret squad. Some will say it's just another *bubbameisah,* hype for the mob no less, but I know what I heard, I know what I believe, and I will forever be haunted by the last thing I heard Meyer Lansky say as I departed.

The dying gangster was looking out over the Atlantic holding Bruzzer as the waves rolled in from Europe in a final benediction. "I think the kid'll do a good job, huh, Commander? It's nice, isn't it, the waves? I like to see what comes out in the backwash. Freedom exacts a lotta vigorish, but, hell, America's all about getting something for nothing. But I love it. I love it. You see any Cossacks out there? No? Any Nazi U-boats? Brahms? Dr. Mengele? No? Me either. And we don't have to turn our lights out along the coast before we go to bed. A nice view of a peaceful ocean. *That's* the payout. And if they don't want to know who helped make our lives so sweet, screw 'em, Commander. And God help us."

Acknowledgments

Cynthia Duncan, Thelma (Teddy) and Meyer Lansky's granddaughter, and executor of the Thelma Lansky Trust, provided me with extensive access to the Lansky family's private papers, Meyer's and Teddy's notes, and letters and journals, which I used to write articles for *The New Republic* and *Baltimore Sun*. My appreciation to Meyer and Teddy themselves for their commitment to getting their story told. My thanks also to Julio Blanco for putting up with his share of intrusions.

My wife, Donna, and children, Stuart and Eliza, tolerated the volume of books and documents related to *The Devil Himself* that became part of our home's décor for years. Stuart accompanied me on some of my fact-finding expeditions and assisted me with my historical research.

Ann Murray and John Fox of the National Park Service at President Franklin Delano Roosevelt's home in Hyde Park provided me with intimate access to the property and insight into critical details of FDR's life at Springwood.

My agent, Kris Dahl, at ICM encouraged my obsession with this book's subject matter rather than seeing it as a sign of mental illness, which would have made sense. I also appreciate ICM's Josie Freedman's interest in this project and the editorial input of Laura Neely and Barry Stringfellow. My thanks also to my literary attorney, Bob Stein.

Good listeners included my friends Norman Ornstein, Sally Satel, Richard Ben-Veniste, and Cary Bernstein. Dan Connolly gave me a solid tutorial on the New York legal system. Michael Ledeen helped me locate government documents from the National Archives that dealt with Lansky's and Luciano's wartime assistance. When it comes to gangland history, nobody knows the American back alleys better than Gus Russo and Dan "Luca" Moldea. Lee Rawls and Dr. John Fox of the FBI; retired FBI special agent and organized-crime expert Gary Klein; and Charles Pinck of the OSS Society were immensely helpful, as was Bill Corvo, son of the late Max Corvo, the OSS Italy chief during World War II and a planner of the Sicily and Italian invasions. John Hargett, retired chief document examiner for the U.S. Secret Service, helped me authenticate some of the papers I reviewed in researching this book.

The editor of five of my novels, Sean Desmond, took time out of his busy schedule to give me his always insightful critique. My thanks also to my editor of this book, Peter Joseph, who helped me sharpen the story, and to Tom Dunne, John Murphy, Joe Rinaldi, and Margaret Smith who believed in and supported this project.

My colleague, former navy man Scott Hogenson, who served on nuclear submarines, was a valuable source of insight into submarine warfare and helped clarify for me the mechanics of battle scenarios. Tom Simmons provided helpful editorial guidance and allowed me to use his name as a character in this book. My assistant Malinda Waughtal, as always, helped organize my life so that I could get done the things I needed to.

My deep gratitude to the late William O. McWorkman of

the Twelfth Armored Division, who shared with me his account of being a young soldier who helped to liberate the Dachau death camp in 1945.

Any of the inaccuracies in this book are either my own mistakes or fabrications on my part for storytelling purposes.